The Apache helicopter piloted by Grimaldi streaked overhead

Thunder pealed from above, heralded by machine-gun fire. Suddenly, a swarm of bullets tore into the ground a foot or so from Bolan's position, kicking up geysers of dirt and grass in a horizontal swath before him.

A second pass would likely eviscerate him.

Bolan swung the binoculars toward the tower. He spotted the shooter, whose lips were pulled back in a grin as he rained down fire and death. Bolan aimed his Barrett. The big gun boomed once and wiped the grin off the shooter's face. Permanently.

Even as he reloaded, Bolan saw twin Hellfire missiles leap forth from the Apache and pound into the Gulfstream jet that stood on the runway. Fire enveloped the jet, sending out thick plumes of oily black smoke.

An instant later, a pair of black vans surged from between two buildings. The side doors flew open and at least half a dozen armed men disembarked from the vehicles.

MACK BOLAN ®
The Executioner

#274 Rogue Target
#275 Crossed Borders
#276 Leviathan
#277 Dirty Mission
#278 Triple Reverse
#279 Fire Wind
#280 Fear Rally
#281 Blood Stone
#282 Jungle Conflict
#283 Ring of Retaliation
#284 Devil's Army
#285 Final Strike
#286 Armageddon Exit
#287 Rogue Warrior
#288 Arctic Blast
#289 Vendetta Force
#290 Pursued
#291 Blood Trade
#292 Savage Game
#293 Death Merchants
#294 Scorpion Rising
#295 Hostile Alliance
#296 Nuclear Game
#297 Deadly Pursuit
#298 Final Play
#299 Dangerous Encounter
#300 Warrior's Requiem
#301 Blast Radius
#302 Shadow Search
#303 Sea of Terror
#304 Soviet Specter
#305 Point Position
#306 Mercy Mission
#307 Hard Pursuit
#308 Into the Fire
#309 Flames of Fury
#310 Killing Heat
#311 Night of the Knives

#312 Death Gamble
#313 Lockdown
#314 Lethal Payload
#315 Agent of Peril
#316 Poison Justice
#317 Hour of Judgment
#318 Code of Resistance
#319 Entry Point
#320 Exit Code
#321 Suicide Highway
#322 Time Bomb
#323 Soft Target
#324 Terminal Zone
#325 Edge of Hell
#326 Blood Tide
#327 Serpent's Lair
#328 Triangle of Terror
#329 Hostile Crossing
#330 Dual Action
#331 Assault Force
#332 Slaughter House
#333 Aftershock
#334 Jungle Justice
#335 Blood Vector
#336 Homeland Terror
#337 Tropic Blast
#338 Nuclear Reaction
#339 Deadly Contact
#340 Splinter Cell
#341 Rebel Force
#342 Double Play
#343 Border War
#344 Primal Law
#345 Orange Alert
#346 Vigilante Run
#347 Dragon's Den
#348 Carnage Code
#349 Firestorm

The Don Pendleton's Executioner®

FIRESTORM

A GOLD EAGLE BOOK FROM

WORLDWIDE®

TORONTO • NEW YORK • LONDON
AMSTERDAM • PARIS • SYDNEY • HAMBURG
STOCKHOLM • ATHENS • TOKYO • MILAN
MADRID • WARSAW • BUDAPEST • AUCKLAND

First edition December 2007

ISBN-13: 978-0-373-64349-3
ISBN-10: 0-373-64349-7

Special thanks and acknowledgment to
Tim Tresslar for his contribution to this work.

FIRESTORM

Printed in U.S.A.

We have more machinery of government than is necessary, too many parasites living on the labor of the industrious.

—Thomas Jefferson, 1743–1826

When greedy parasites take advantage of their privileged government positions, they will have to face the people they serve. After that, they will have to answer to me.

—Mack Bolan

THE
MACK BOLAN
LEGEND

Nothing less than a war could have fashioned the destiny of the man called Mack Bolan. Bolan earned the Executioner title in the jungle hell of Vietnam.

But this soldier also wore another name—Sergeant Mercy. He was so tagged because of the compassion he showed to wounded comrades-in-arms and Vietnamese civilians.

Mack Bolan's second tour of duty ended prematurely when he was given emergency leave to return home and bury his family, victims of the Mob. Then he declared a one-man war against the Mafia.

He confronted the Families head-on from coast to coast, and soon a hope of victory began to appear. But Bolan had broken society's every rule. That same society started gunning for this elusive warrior—to no avail.

So Bolan was offered amnesty to work within the system against terrorism. This time, as an employee of Uncle Sam, Bolan became Colonel John Phoenix. With a command center at Stony Man Farm in Virginia, he and his new allies—Able Team and Phoenix Force—waged relentless war on a new adversary: the KGB.

But when his one true love, April Rose, died at the hands of the Soviet terror machine, Bolan severed all ties with Establishment authority.

Now, after a lengthy lone-wolf struggle and much soul-searching, the Executioner has agreed to enter an "arm's-length" alliance with his government once more, reserving the right to pursue personal missions in his Everlasting War.

Prologue

He was sure his heart would explode.

Javier Montesinos thrashed his way through the latticework of vines and branches that covered the jungle floor. Greens and browns rushed at him in a kaleidoscopic flurry. He sucked for air, felt it burn the insides of his overtaxed lungs. Blood thundered in his ears and his arms pumped wildly at his sides as he tried to gain distance from the monster on his trail.

The sound of an engine's growl intermingled with the crash of branches and foliage being ripped from the ground, snapped and crushed beneath something big. Motorcycle engines whined, the insistent buzzing nearly swallowed up by the unseen vehicle's thunder.

Montesinos wanted to stop, wanted to rest, to hide.

He could do none of these things.

He could only run. He needed to escape, to call Maria and let her know what'd gone down. That they were coming for her.

A motorcycle's whine grew louder. The CIA agent tightened his grip on the Uzi he carried, but kept his pace steady. He'd stolen the weapon from one of the camp's guards, snapping the man's neck in return.

He'd covered a couple more yards when something hurtled from the brush. In a blur of black and silver, it shot past him into a large clearing that lay just ahead.

The driver whipped the motorcycle into a J-turn and brought it around 180 degrees. The biker paused, the black shield that covered his face locked on the exhausted agent. He revved the engine, but kept the bike stationary. One hand drifted from the handlebars and slid for a pistol clipped to his belt.

Montesinos jerked to a halt. His chest heaved as he sucked greedily at the exhaust-tainted air. He felt light-headed and the sudden stop caused him to stumble. He caught himself and raised the Uzi. He knew the magazine was nearly empty, depleted by his spraying his pursuers with volleys of gunfire.

The agent heard the rumbling of the big machine as it closed in from behind.

In the instant that he pulled the trigger, the motorcycle blasted forth and bore down on him. The gun chugging out a line of fire, he thrust himself sideways, narrowly escaping the bike's onslaught. When he struck the ground, he ignored the sharp ends of branches that poked into his body. He focused on his target.

Steel-jacketed slugs struck the frame and sparked against the metal, etching a line along the vehicle's side. The bullets punched through the rider's leather boots. An anguished cry exploded from the man on the motorcycle. Frenzied by the sudden onslaught of pain, he twisted the handlebars more than ninety degrees and turned the front wheel into a brake.

Montesinos watched as the bike's rear tire rocketed off the ground until the vehicle toppled over. The force launched the driver from the bike and sent him airborne. When he struck the ground, his shooting hand broke the fall, and the impact snapped bone, eliciting another cry from the wounded man.

Montesinos hauled himself to his feet. His breath still ragged as much from rage as exhaustion, he lumbered across the clearing toward the downed biker, who scrambled to unsheathe the pistol holstered on his hip. The Uzi barked again and a tightly grouped burst pounded through the rider's face shield and into his skull

The Uzi's clip emptied, Montesinos hurled it aside.

The whine of additional motorcycles swelled in his ears. He whipped his head left, spotted three of them crashing from different directions through the trees and brush that ringed the clearing. He knelt next to the dead man and snagged the handgun still holstered on his hip. It was a .50-caliber Desert Eagle.

Crouched behind the motorcycle, he waited for the riders to

close in, rather than chance a long-distance shot through a web of tree limbs and other obstacles.

The nearest reached a point about fifteen yards away. A figure seated on the back of the motorcycle pointed a black object at him. A heartbeat later it began to spit flame. Bullets whizzed out from the forest, buzzing past him like unseen insects.

At about ten yards, the Desert Eagle thundered three times. The driver jerked as a round drilled into his torso. Suddenly flaccid arms detached from the handgrips and the bullet's velocity pushed the driver into the second rider who was scrambling to shove the corpse from his bike and get hold of the handgrips. The second motorcycle launched into a zigzag pattern, apparently to evade any further shots.

Montesinos rose, shoved the Desert Eagle into the waistband of his torn blue jeans and grabbed the handlebar of the fallen motorcycle that lay before him.

But before he could straddle the machine, he saw a big black vehicle lumbering toward him, pushing down small trees, crushing greenery.

He muttered an oath, then let the bike fall to the ground.

You know what's back there, damn it. You know it will kill you! Just go, he thought in a panic.

The mechanical growl filled his ears. As he tried again to mount the motorcycle, he felt something fiery sear the flesh of his calf. He smelled the burned flesh even before he felt the hot lancets of pain coursing up his leg. His lips parted and a sudden scream broke forth, driven as much by shock as pain.

The heat quickly traveled up his leg, even as he dropped his weight onto the motorcycle's seat, leaving a trail of charred flesh in its wake. Adrenaline and terror overwhelmed all rational thought. He knew he needed to get the hell out before it left him nothing but charred flesh and bones.

Like all the others.

Gripping the accelerator, he felt the bike lurch forward underneath him. Thirty or so yards away sat a line of trees. If he could burst through those, lose himself in the surrounding jungle, perhaps he'd make it.

The heat seemed to intensify throughout his body. It traveled beyond his leg and began to burn through his torso and arms. Skin that first became warm heated almost instantly to unbearable temperatures. Within heartbeats, flesh reddened to an angry scarlet, then began to bubble and blister. Montesinos screamed again as the pain overwhelmed him, blinded him. Fingers uncurled and released the handlebar grips and the Colombian began to grab at himself, as though besieged by thousands of unseen insects. In the flurry of activity, he fell from the bike. It shot ahead a few yards before it rolled to a stop and tipped over.

He lay on the ground, curled protectively into a ball. Within moments, paralysis set into the parched flesh of his throat. The skin of his face and lips blistered, grew taut, emitted small curls of smoke. The orbs that had been his eyes sizzled, their remnants oozing from their sockets like tears. His mind, overloaded by pain, had begun to shut itself down, to shield him from the countless lancets of pain that coursed through his body, tearing away at him like parasites. There will be more, he thought. His body shuddered one last time before a blackness swallowed the last bit of consciousness.

MARIA SERRANO, A SUITCASE in either hand, rushed to her car. She popped open the trunk, slipped the bags inside, shut the lid and started back for her apartment. She cast furtive glances as she closed in on the building. Ascending the stairs, she reentered her apartment and moved from room to room, checking to make sure she'd left behind nothing important. She'd packed her calendars, phone books, laptop and a stack of spiral-bound notebooks. She didn't want to leave anything that would provide clues about her true identity or her mission in Colombia.

It had been twenty-four hours since she'd lost contact with Javier and the others from her crew. The longer she waited, the more isolated and worried she felt. A knot of fear formed in her stomach and tightened as she mulled the situation. Javier *never* missed a check-in call. That he suddenly was incommunicado was scary; that she'd been unable to contact her own handler troubled her even more.

What the hell was going on? she wondered.

Serrano was operating under nonofficial cover and, therefore, had to tread lightly as she maneuvered through Colombia. She could visit the U.S. Embassy only infrequently and then only for mundane reasons. She had to studiously avoid anyone even remotely connected with the Company who could implicate her as an intelligence agent.

Her cell phone vibrated on her hip. She grabbed it and put it to her ear.

"Yes?"

"You know the situation?" Serrano immediately recognized the voice as that of her controller, a man she knew only as Fletcher.

"I know enough," she said.

"You need to get out."

"Obviously," she said. "Tell me what's happened."

"Is this a secure line?"

She considered lying for a few seconds but decided against it. Fletcher could hear a lie in her voice in a heartbeat.

"No," she said. "It's not secure."

"Then I have no information."

"Fine. I'm leaving."

"You should. Go to contingency B."

"But I have a flight in three hours."

"Fuck it. You have no flight. Don't risk it. We'll have an executive jet waiting for you when you arrive. Go to contingency B. Miller will come and get you. Go downtown, to the office and leave your gun in the car."

"What?" she asked, startled.

"You heard me. We're going to take you to the airport. But there's been a lot of chatter from FARC about a kidnapping at the airport. The locals are nervous, and they're going to be inspecting every car that comes or goes to the airport. We can't risk them detaining you for any reason."

"What about Miller?"

"He won't be carrying either," Fletcher replied.

Her brow creased with confusion and distrust boiled up from inside. Even on its best day, Colombia was a big slice of hell.

The idea that she was to move around without a gun—to possibly force her way out of the country—was unfathomable. She couldn't even wrap her mind around the idea that her escort also would be unarmed.

"You'll be fine," Fletcher said. "Really. I have two choppers at my disposal. We'll track you from the air, give you an armed escort. If anyone tries to harm you, they'll get vaporized from the sky. They're private contractors, so they have more, um, flexibility when it comes to dealing with these situations."

For reasons she didn't understand, gooseflesh broke out on her arms.

"Do it, Maria," he said. "We're bending the rules by trying to get you out of there. There's no time for debate. Just do this and in a couple of days we'll hook up in Mexico to talk this through."

"Fine," she said. "Give me the details."

SERRANO DROVE HER CAR downtown. When she reached a skyscraper of mirrored glass, one that served as the headquarters for a local bank, she circled the block once to get the lay of the land. When none of the bystanders immediately tripped any alarm bells, she turned onto a ramp that led into a parking garage located beneath the building.

She maneuvered the car down two more levels until she reached the appointed floor. She found a space between two other cars. She put the car into Park but left the engine running.

Turning in her seat, she looked over her left shoulder, then her right to see what was behind her. She saw only more cars and an occasional passerby, but nothing that seemed out of place.

She reached beneath her jacket and drew her 9 mm SIG-Sauer from a hip holster. Holding the gun in her open palm, she examined it. A flurry of questions flashed through her mind as she weighed her options. With the relentless political and drug-related violence constantly rocking the country, she'd never been without the weapon since she'd arrived six months earlier. And, considering what she'd found the previous night, the thought of leaving her weapon behind seemed insane.

Something hammered against the passenger window. Serrano

gasped, but reacted quickly. Her motions a blur, she transferred the gun to her right hand, gripped it and drew down on the interloper at her window. The guy outside gave her a pie-eyed stare that, under other circumstances, might have amused her. At the moment she just felt mortified.

"Hey!" Miller snapped. When he realized that she wasn't going to blow his head off, an angry expression flashed across his pudgy features, replacing the terror that had been there a moment before.

She stowed the weapon and stepped out of the car.

"Lord, woman," he said in anger-tinged whisper, "you damn near blew my head off."

"Sorry," she said.

"Just be careful," he said. He scratched at the exposed skin on the crown of his head and composed himself. From what she knew, Miller wasn't a field agent. Rather, he worked in Colombia's main station as a political analyst where he studied opinion-poll results, newspaper stories and think-tank reports.

As she came around the vehicle, she thumbed a button on her keyfob and the trunk lid popped up. She reached inside the trunk, grabbed her bags by their handles and jerked them free from the compartment.

"Need help?" Miller asked.

She shook her head.

"Suit yourself," he said. He walked away from the car and gestured ahead of himself. "Car's two rows from here," he said. "It's the red Jeep Liberty."

"Fine."

Minutes later, her luggage stored in the rear of the vehicle, they sped from the garage. Miller punched the gas to make a yellow light. Serrano saw the shadows cast by the choppers that flew overhead.

"You were supposed to ditch the gun," Miller groused.

"Go to hell," she snapped. "Last thing I need is some fucking analyst telling me how to conduct myself."

"No skin off my nose," he said. "You want to buck the boss, that's your business."

"Then why are you even talking about it?" Serrano said.

"Just making conversation," he replied.

"Then talk about the weather. Besides, why do you know anything about my orders?"

He grinned. "Because they told me you'd disobey them. The gun part, anyway. Listen, I'm cleared to know the conditions of this transfer, okay? I don't know why you're leaving, why you were here or where you're going. But I do know that you were supposed to ditch the gun."

"You didn't say anything back there about it."

"You almost blew my damn head off!"

"Occupational hazard," she replied.

A stream of cigarette smoke wafted into her eyes, stung them. She waved a hand in front of her face to clear some of the smoke. When that didn't work, she cracked a window to let in some fresh air.

"Damn it!" he yelled. With his left index finger, he jabbed a button to raise the window. "They stay closed. That was an order."

Serrano started to say something but held her tongue. She could tell he was anxious, and agitating him would probably just make him worse.

Serrano stared through the windshield at the sunbaked stretch of road. Within an hour, they left behind the city limits and continued to follow the road to a small military airport that lay several miles outside Bogotá. Heat rose from the road, shimmering like water as it wafted up and eventually disappeared. On either side, they passed a few shacks, but eventually those structures became fewer until they disappeared altogether.

The road sloped downward. Serrano saw a trough at the end of the decline was blotted out by an impenetrable shadow that looked like a puddle of oil, but actually was a trick of the light.

Something on the road glinted, catching Serrano's attention.

She opened her mouth to say something, but Miller stomped the brakes before she uttered a word. Hot rubber squealed beneath the car, but the tires grabbed hold of the road. The car slowed.

Serrano felt herself forced back in her seat by the sudden braking. They hurtled several more yards and the objects in the road became visible. The SUV rolled over the road spikes and the tires were shredded. Farther up the road, a line of vans rolled across their path and blocked them.

"What the hell?" Serrano yelled.

Why weren't the helicopters doing anything? The question raced through her mind. The answer came almost the same instant, and it made her stomach clench.

She looked at Miller, whose eyes were riveted on the road. He stomped the brakes again and the SUV launched into a sidelong slide at the vans. A panel van mushroomed up against the passenger side of the Jeep and the vehicles collided. The force of the crash tossed Serrano side to side. Her teeth clamped down. A side-impact air bag burst from the door panel and kept her head from slamming against the window. In the same instant, the front air bag exploded from the dashboard.

Her ears rang, and powder from the air bag deployment burned her eyes.

Your gun, Maria! her mind screamed. Grab it! Now!

Working her way around the air bag, she slipped her hand inside her jacket. Her fingers scrambled for the SIG-Sauer's butt, found it and jerked the weapon free.

With her thumb, she turned off the safety.

A sidelong glance at Miller showed his limp body hanging forward against the seat belt harness. Blood streamed from his nose, over the curve of his upper lip, down his chin before it dripped onto his white dress shirt. She saw that his chest continued to rise and fall. Thank God, she thought.

She released her seat belt and leaned across the console. Her arms strained to reach the door handle. The whipping of the helicopter's propeller blades grew louder. She opened the door and shoved it hard enough to keep it from swinging closed again. A glance over the seat showed her that the helicopter was landing on the road behind her, its blades kicking up boiling clouds of dust.

She released Miller's seat belt. To get free of the vehicle, she figured she'd have to climb over him, then drag him free of the vehicle. Without knowing what kinds of injuries he'd suffered she couldn't risk pushing him from the car first and making them worse.

Figures decked out in black SWAT-style uniforms ran up on either side of the Jeep, guns held high. They formed a ring around the vehicle. One of them, his submachine gun poised at shoulder level closed in on the wrecked vehicle.

"Hands up," he shouted. Fear swelled inside Serrano, caused her throat to tighten until she swore she'd suffocate. She weighed the situation and realized she was boxed in. Setting the handgun on the dashboard, she raised her hands. The man who'd yelled at her stepped aside and allowed a second man to approach the vehicle. He reached inside, grabbed Miller by the arm and dragged him from the SUV.

"Let's go! Let's go!" the lead gunner shouted. Serrano climbed over the console. Another thug stepped forward, grabbed her by the bicep and dragged her from the vehicle. He ordered her to lay facedown on the ground. She complied and almost immediately regretted it when the heat from the asphalt burned her skin. She squeezed her eyes shut against the sunlight.

Someone from the swarm of black-suited men searched her, but found no weapons.

A shadow fell over her. She opened her eyes, looked up and saw a thick-bodied man stalking toward her.

"Sit up," he said.

She did. She looked him over and saw he had a ruddy complexion and dull green eyes that emitted a thousand-yard stare, as though he was human in form only. A portion of a tattoo—a scorpion's tail—peeked out from beneath his shirt collar. He nodded at one of the men beside her. The man knelt.

A small sting in her left arm caught her attention. She jerked her arm away, but it was too late. The man next to her was back on his feet, a syringe in his grip. Within seconds, she began to feel light-headed. Black spots swirled in her vision and noises began to sound far away. Darkness fell over her.

SEVERAL MILES AWAY, Albert Bly stood at the edge of the clearing and stared at the smoking remains of a body. A satisfied smirk played over his lips. The smell of burned flesh filled his nostrils. He welcomed it, inhaling deeply.

The camouflage fatigues Bly wore hung loosely from his thin body. His black hair was combed straight back from his forehead, exposing a sharp widow's peak. His skin was red, as though blood might burst from his pores at any moment.

From the corner of his eye, he saw the man next to him shake his head vigorously, heard him make a disgusted noise. "My God," Milt Krotnic said, "that smells terrible, like cooked garbage or something."

Bly turned his head and looked at the other man. His lips peeled back into a smile. "It's the smell of money, Krotnic," he said, scolding the other man. "You remember that."

The other man shrugged. "Sure."

Two men brushed past Bly. Surgical masks covered the lower halves of their faces. Their hands were sheathed in rubber gloves that stretched well up their forearms, but stopped short of their elbows. They angled toward the corpse, knelt beside it and stretched it out on a black plastic body bag on the ground. One of the men reached gingerly for one of the dead man's ankles. With a pair of scissors, he began cutting at the fabric of the man's trouser leg and peeled back the fabric. Bly caught a flash of the charred flesh and felt a surge of excitement.

"Hold it," Bly shouted.

As he advanced on the two men, he withdrew a digital camera from his pants pocket. When he reached the body, they rose and moved away to give him ample room to perform his grisly ritual. He aimed the camera at the remains and snapped several pictures, making sure to zoom in on the puckered black flesh that still clung to the bones. When he finished, he lowered the camera a foot or so from his face and, using his thumbnail, manipulated the dial that advanced the pictures. Satisfied with the results, he turned and headed back to Krotnic, who was talking into a two-way radio, while the two medics resumed their work. Bly pocketed the camera.

"Sure," Krotnic said into his radio. "He'll be glad to hear that. You know where to put her? Good, then do it."

The former colonel in the Serb military clipped the radio to his belt and nodded at his boss.

"They found her," he said. "They have her back in Bogotá."

"Good," Bly said.

"She put up a hell of a fight from what I understand," Krotnic said. "We've got a couple of casualties."

"The laptop?"

Krotnic shook his head. "No, she was empty-handed. Couldn't get her to say shit, either."

"A temporary condition," Bly replied.

"Of course."

1

Mack Bolan was seated at the conference table in Stony Man Farm's War Room. The soldier was freshly showered and clad in blue jeans, a flannel shirt and black sneakers. Even within the secure confines of the Farm, America's ultra-secret counterterrorism center, he wore his sound-suppressed Beretta 93-R in a leather shoulder rig. His eyes felt gritty and sore from lack of sleep.

Hal Brognola sat across the table from him, a laptop positioned before him. The director of the Justice Department's Sensitive Operations Group snatched the unlit cigar from his mouth. His forehead creased with concern, he rolled the cigar between his index finger and thumb, studied it while Bolan waited for him to speak. The Executioner set his coffee on the table.

"You look old," Bolan said finally.

Brognola snapped his head up as though he'd suddenly sat on a thumbtack. He glared at Bolan. After a couple of seconds, his dark expression melted and a grin tugged at the corners of his lips. "It's the company I keep," he said.

"Speaking of which, it's five a.m. It's Sunday. You're wearing Saturday's suit and tie. Hell, it may be Friday's clothes for all I know. You need a shave. And probably a shower, though I'm not going to get close enough to find out."

"In other words, why'd I drag your ass of bed at this hour?"

"Something like that."

"Fair enough," Brognola said.

A folder rested on the table at the big Fed's right elbow. He pinned it beneath one of his big hands and thrust it at Bolan. The soldier opened it and began to examine its contents. A picture of a woman was held to the left side of the folder by a paper clip. Blond hair framed an oval-shaped face. Her complexion was dusky, her eyes dark, lips full. "She is?"

"Maria Serrano," Brognola replied. "CIA agent. She holds double majors in forensic accounting and international business. And, from what I understand, she's one hell of an undercover operative."

Bolan nodded and leafed through the papers in the folder, skimming them. It contained a few government memos—from the CIA, National Security Agency and the State Department— as well as documents he recognized as presidential daily briefings and classified executive orders signed by the President detailing the kidnapping and murder of several CIA operatives.

Brognola continued, "Six months ago, the NSA picked up some noise from an American company's operation in Bogotá, Colombia. The various bits of chatter indicated someone in Garrison Industries executive suites was breaking arms embargoes with Iran and China, along with some nonstate groups. Specifically, the company was shipping high-resolution camera components we use in our satellite program. They kept listening but took no immediate action. And, the more they heard, the more concerned they became. Two months ago, they discovered that the company was acting as an intermediary between a Chinese group that produces cylinders and other parts used in centrifuges and a group in Iran."

"For the country's nuclear program," Bolan said. He closed the folder and set it on the tabletop. He'd have plenty of time to look at it later.

"Right," Brognola said. "As far as the satellite components go, the Iranians say they want satellites to track weather and such. Needless to say, we don't believe them. And we don't like the notion of them having aerial-surveillance capabilities. The consensus is that the longer we can keep them blind from space, the better off we are."

"Sure," Bolan said.

While he took a sip of coffee, the door leading into the conference room swung open. Bolan cast a glance in that direction and saw Barbara Price enter. Stony Man's mission controller held several file folders in one arm and a closed laptop in the other.

She flashed Bolan a warm smile, which he returned. The two often spent time together when Bolan was at the Farm. He'd left her room only minutes before the meeting, after he'd received Brognola's page, to get cleaned up and change clothes.

She leaned against the door, holding it open for Aaron "The Bear" Kurtzman, the head of the counterterrorism facility's cyberteam. The computer expert guided his wheelchair into the room and exchanged greetings with the other two men.

On the arm of his wheelchair, he balanced a carafe that Bolan assumed contained coffee. Kurtzman buzzed up to the table, set the carafe on the tabletop and pushed it toward Bolan.

"Top off your cup," Kurtzman said, nodding at Bolan's coffee.

For several seconds, the soldier stared at the carafe. Finally he unscrewed the cap and poured some of the steaming liquid into his cup. The coffee's color looked like dirty motor oil mixed with black shoe polish.

Price moved around the room, distributing folders to everyone. When she finished, Brognola, anxious to continue the briefing, waved her to her seat. In the meantime, the big Fed poured himself some coffee.

"Initially, the NSA wasn't sure what to make of the deals. Garrison's people had a history of being approached by unsavory people. Occasionally, it cut deals, but did so at our behest, as a way for us to gather intelligence on various countries and terrorist groups. But it never passed along any cutting-edge technology or items related to nuclear proliferation."

"Back up," Bolan said. "These guys have sold weapons to our enemies before? And did so with government consent?"

Brognola nodded.

"Most Garrison employees have no idea that this goes on. But, yes, they do exactly that. They have a few agents who essentially work as hard as they can to hook up with the bad guys. Word gets around, usually through some cutouts. Pretty soon, the bad guys come to them. They fork over bribes, ask for stuff they're banned from having. The Garrison people nod their heads, and go along with the gag."

"And feed whatever information they collect back into the intelligence network," Bolan said.

Brognola nodded. "The Garrison agents almost never hand over anything of consequence, at least not on a global scale. The thinking has been that it's better to hand these jerks a couple of RPGs and know they have them than allow them to buy weapons from some freelancer in South Africa, Libya or Iraq. And, historically, the Company—I mean the CIA, not Garrison—always kept close tabs on the weapons. That's why these particular transactions set off alarm bells. But we'll cover that in a minute."

"What's the breakdown on what they sell?" Bolan asked.

"They have a network of soldiers, intelligence people and support personnel they contract out, mostly to our government. We've used their people for operations in Iraq, Afghanistan and Colombia. The majority are top-knotch soldiers, not rogues. They do on-the-ground fighting, security and training so that we don't tie up too many people in overseas operations."

"What about their weapons design and development operations?" Bolan asked. "I assume most of their R&D work also is for the United States."

Price leaned forward on the table. "Mostly," she said. "About seventy-five percent of it is for us and another twenty-four-and-a-half percent is performed for our allies."

The Executioner set his coffee on the table. "Which leaves a half percent unaccounted for. Give me that list."

Brognola sighed. "It's the countries that keep us up at night—North Korea, Iran, Syria. And some bad elements in allied countries like Pakistan and Saudi Arabia have also been known to tap Garrison for equipment."

Price continued, "The intelligence community tried to build in safeguards to minimize any blowback against us or our allies. Sometimes the buyers ended up dead from natural causes." She gestured quotation marks with her fingers to highlight the last two words. "Or thieves stole the weapons. But the thieves actually were on the CIA's payroll. Or we sent in proxies to buy back the weapons. It wasn't a perfect system. It's not unreasonable to assume that some weapons fell into the wrong hands, that someone, somewhere slaughtered innocents with those weapons. But the operation did generate good intelligence for us. I guess the National Security adviser considered any mistakes a fair trade in exchange for the benefits."

"A fair trade, maybe," Bolan said, "but not an equal one."

"Intelligence gathering isn't always neat and clean, Mack," Price stated. "I know that from my own experiences with the NSA. It's as much an art as it is a science. Perhaps more art than science. It's as imperfect as hell. You know that."

Bolan acknowledged her words with a nod.

"And Garrison's been doing this for how long?" Bolan asked.

"About twenty years," Brognola said.

"And we've known about it how long?"

"About twenty years," the big Fed stated.

Bolan searched his old friend's face and waited for the punch line.

"I'll bite," Bolan replied. "So it's twenty years later and suddenly we learn that someone within the organization has gone rogue, and we have an emergency. Are we just concerned about the satellite parts and the tubes?"

Brognola shook his head. "It seems that some of these creeps have begun moving up the Garrison food chain. They're getting their items more quickly. They get to meet with select members of the senior management team. We're worried that the Iranian and Chinese transactions are only the tip of the iceberg. So was the CIA, which is why they sent a team of agents down there to investigate.

"And it gets even more complex. Garrison doesn't just play these cloak-and-dagger games out of a sense of patriotism. They're sort of enmeshed in the intelligence community."

"Enmeshed with or part of the intelligence community?" Bolan asked.

"Give the boy a cigar," Kurtzman said.

"The whole damn operation was planned and sanctioned by the National Security Council," Brognola said. "Using money from a slush fund, the council bought a small research-and-development firm a couple of decades ago and grew it into what it is today. Unfortunately, it seems to be taking on a life of its own, which has everyone from the White House on down worried."

The big Fed set down his cigar long enough to take a swig of coffee. His face puckered in distaste, and he shot Kurtzman a dirty look. The computer genius just shrugged and studied at the contents of his coffee mug.

Brognola continued, "Most of Garrison's money comes from black budgets. Or it uses its proceeds to pay for operations. Traditionally, most of what it made, it sold back to us or other allied governments. So the few politicians who knew about it, ignored it. The thinking behind it is that it allows us to have more control over the weapons we make and buy and it's a source that, at least ostensibly, has our best interests at heart."

"Plus it helps folks sidestep congressional scrutiny when budget time comes," Bolan said.

Brognola gave the soldier a weary smile. "We've both seen too much of Washington, haven't we? Fortunately, most of what they sell to the bad guys is crap. And they sell them precious little of that."

He lifted his coffee cup about three-quarters of the way toward his mouth, paused and set it back on the table. Instead, he pulled out a roll of antacid pills and popped a couple into his mouth.

"This wasn't part of a sting operation," the man from Justice stated. "We already ran all the necessary traps to make sure that that wasn't the case. No one knew anything about these particular deals."

"And you believe that?" Bolan asked.

Brognola shrugged. "My gut says they're telling the truth. What we're looking at here, in my opinion, is an operation that's gone out of control. We can debate all day whether it was a good idea to begin with. But the reality is that it's out of control and we need to pull the plug on the whole damn thing, fast."

"Explain," Bolan said.

Brognola tapped a key on his laptop. An image appeared on a wall screen. The image depicted a limousine, the door held open and a young Asian man in a dark business suit stepping from the vehicle. A pair of hardmen flanked him. Bolan could tell from the angle of the photo that it had been shot from above.

Brognola let the soldier study the image for several seconds. With another keystroke, a close-up shot of the man in the middle filled the screen. A whitish scar ran from below the man's shirt collar and up the left side of his neck, disappearing beneath his hairline. His black hair was long and pulled back into a tight ponytail.

"Name's Chiun," Brognola said. "He's triad. He's a boss in Ciudad del Este, Paraguay. There are several Chinese gangs operating down there, but his group is the biggest. Runs all the usual stuff—prostitutes, protection, counterfeiting, drugs. Launders money for Hezbollah. Does the same thing in Hong Kong and Malaysia."

Bolan sipped his coffee. Ignoring the awful taste in his mouth, he studied the photo and committed it to memory.

"He's a real piece of work," Brognola said, "but he's smart and ambitious. He started out as an enforcer for the gang, now he runs it. Spilled lots of blood along the way to get to where he is. Other gangsters, illegal immigrants, police officers—doesn't matter to him. Everyone's just a speed bump while he races to the top. When he was an enforcer, that wild streak served him well. Sure, it pissed off a hell of a lot of people back in China, but it also got him where he wanted to go. At least for the moment."

"How does he fit in with all of this?" Bolan asked.

Price took over, "He's in tight with Chinese intelligence. Rumor has it that his ties with the government helped him get where he is. Three days before he took over his gang, the government stepped in and snapped up most of the leaders."

"Giving him a clear path," Bolan said.

"Exactly," Price stated. "And he seems all-too willing to repay them for the help. A couple of our intelligence reports indicate that he and his people pull off work for the Chinese all the time. We know of several dissidents killed by his thugs. The victims had no ties to him, but had made enemies in the government." She snapped her fingers. "Suddenly they end up shot on a street corner or stabbed in alley by one of his people. Chiun's gang also has smuggled weapons for the Chinese and carried out some small-scale industrial espionage on their behalf, primarily through his own network.

Brognola flashed another picture on the screen. This one showed another Asian man, his gray hair combed back from his forehead. He had a wide face with thick lips turned down in a deep scowl. Bolan saw that the decorated collar of a military tunic encircled the man's thick neck.

"Colonel Chi Pu Deng," Price said. "He came up through the People's Liberation Army, but has focused exclusively on espionage for at least fifteen years. According to some very good sources—one of them a friend of Hal's who operates in Hong Kong—Deng and his surrogates have maintained regular contact with Chiun and his gang for years. There's more information on him in the packet I gave you." Price indicated a folder that sat on the table in front of Bolan. "But the consensus of people paid to know these things is that Deng is the middleman. He pays Chiun for weapons and information and takes those things back to his government."

"What else do we know about him?" Bolan asked. "If he's working that close to a gang, he must be skimming money off the top. Or getting some other benefit."

Price shook her head.

"Surprisingly enough," she said, "he's clean, at least from China's perspective. Consensus is that he's a patriot and incorruptible. That's earned him more than a few enemies within his own government, as you can imagine."

"Sure," Bolan said.

"To take it a step further," Brognola chimed in, "we think that's one of the reasons he sticks so close to Chiun. There are more than a few guys on the take who'd just as soon see this Boy Scout taken out of the mix. But no one has the guts to do it, because they know he's Chiun's meal ticket. Or one of them, at least. And he'd be damned mad if someone took the colonel out."

"Are they that close?" Bolan asked.

"Their only bond is money," Price replied. "Apparently Chiun thinks Deng is a sentimental idiot. Deng thinks Chiun's greedy and unpatriotic. But neither of them wants to pull the brakes on the gravy train. That's why they tolerate each other. It's an uneasy alliance, to put it mildly."

"And up here is Albert Bly," Brognola announced.

Bolan turned and saw a photo of a Caucasian man clad in a tuxedo. He was shaking hands with another similarly clad man whom Bolan recognized as a U.S. congressman. Bly balanced a champagne glass in his other hand as the two mugged for the camera.

"This is from the *New York Times* society page," Brognola said. "Up until about two years ago, Bly was a very public face for Garrison. He was all over the news shows. Had audiences with congressmen from both parties. Then the company hit some rocky financial times. The board of directors named him chairman, kicked him upstairs and he disappeared from the public eye, seemingly overnight. We think there's more to it. We're still digging around to see what we can find out, but there are a couple of theories."

"Like?"

"His corporate jet has filed a lot of flight plans to the Dominican Republic and Thailand, if that tells you anything," Kurtzman said.

"It tells me plenty," Bolan said. The soldier knew that both countries had booming sex tourism trades, an industry he'd confronted more than once. "Seems a guy in his position was courting disaster by going to those places."

"No doubt," Brognola said. "And, if either Chiun or Deng know this, it'd be an effective lever to force him to cooperate."

"If they had to push him that hard," Bolan replied. "Money alone can be a hell of a motivator."

"It could be any combination of things," Brognola agreed.

"So what's the request?" Bolan asked.

"We need someone to find Serrano," Brognola said. "We have to know what she learned, what her team learned. It had to be big for Bly to risk snatching and killing those agents."

"*If* he was the one who took those agents," Bolan said. "Do we know that yet?"

"There's a chance that someone else did it, but I'd be surprised. This was a very coordinated snatch-and-grab operation. It's not something Chiun would've pulled," Price stated.

"Why is this our gig?" Bolan asked. "I mean why won't the CIA go in and pull her out?"

"Two reasons," Brognola said. "First, all these operatives are nonofficial cover. That means that our government can't officially acknowledge any relationship between them and the agents. We aren't worried so much about the kidnappers themselves, since they're probably nonstate actors. But, what we can do is send in a Justice Department agent to look for an American kidnapped in another country. And there's another reason, which more specifically has to do with you."

"And that would be?"

"The President doesn't like how this went down, and neither do I. Bly has a lot of contacts in the intelligence world. Not just in the United States, but intelligence agencies in Britain, France, Saudi Arabia, Jordan. Name it. He knows people. We want to handle it because we operate outside normal channels. You'll have a handful of vetted contacts when you hit the ground, but all the interfacing with other government agencies will happen through us."

"Did you just say 'interface'?" Bolan asked.

"Will you take the job?" Brognola asked, ignoring the gibe.

"Of course," the Executioner said.

"Grab your gear then," Brognola said. "Jack's already warming up the plane."

2

What the hell was happening? Were they going to kill her? What did they know? The thoughts raced through Maria Serrano's mind as she regained consciousness and found herself seated in a wooden chair, hands bound behind her back.

Think, she told herself. Don't panic. Use your brains. Use your training, not your emotions. She took a deep breath and looked around the room. She was positioned in the center of the cramped cell. A naked bulb hung from the ceiling and beamed down meager white light that the dark brick walls seemed to absorb. She still wore the blouse and pants she'd had on when she had been captured. Her shoes, belt and watch were gone. She had no way of knowing how long she'd been unconscious.

Her mind still was fuzzy from whatever drug they'd used on her. But she could vaguely recall being brought here by a pair of hulking men, one of whom spoke in heavily accented English.

On the other side of the door a bolt slammed back, then the door swung inward without a sound. A tall man filled the doorway and stared down at her.

Even with his face partially obscured by shadow, she recognized Albert Bly in an instant. He walked slowly to her, reaching into his pocket. Her muscles tensed involuntarily until his hand came back into view holding a white card laminated in plastic. He studied it for several seconds.

"Gina Lopez," he said.

"Yes. That's right," Serrano said.

"What brings you to Bogotá, Gina?"

"Business," she said.

"Business? Of what sort?"

"I'm not at liberty—"

"Of what sort, Gina?" The volume of his voice didn't change, but she detected a hint of menace, cold, quiet, unspoken. A seething rage that was, at once invisible but seemed to fill the whole room.

"What business?" he repeated.

"I'm an auditor."

He waited for more.

"I work for the government. The U.S. government."

"Of course you do."

Her mouth went dry, her throat tightened. Something in his tone left her feeling suddenly exposed, as though he knew everything about her, about her classified status. She swallowed hard.

"I work for the Government Accountability Office," she said. "We investigate things for Congress. I'm not a criminal investigator. This was a fact-finding mission."

"And what facts did you find?" Bly asked.

"Who are you?" she asked, feigning confusion.

"I think you know," he said.

"Why are you holding me here?"

He didn't respond.

She knew that playing the indignant bureaucrat wouldn't move Bly, but it fit in with her cover.

"I mean it," she said. "I'm an employee of the U.S. government. If this is some half-assed kidnapping plot, you might as well let me go. You won't get a dime from me. We—"

Bly's hand snaked out in a blur. His flattened palm struck her right cheek. The force jerked her head hard to the left. Flecks of spittle flew from between her parted lips. A moment later hot needles of pain jabbed her skin where she'd been struck.

Her muscles tensed and she strained at her bonds. Maria Serrano, a Central Intelligence Agency agent, didn't put up with that shit. The rare man stupid enough to strike out at her found himself on his knees, sucking for air. Or begging for his life.

Gina Lopez, on the other hand—

She forced a tear from her right eye, trying to put together the right combination of fear and confusion, minus the righteous rage that smoldered inside her. "Why'd you do that?" she asked, her voice small.

"I'm a reasonable man. I'm not stupid," Bly said.

She ground her teeth and nodded vigorously. A gesture of appeasement, not understanding. The coppery taste of blood seeped between her teeth and onto her tongue. As the physical shock of the blow wore off, she realized she'd bitten the edge of her tongue. He'd drawn blood. Bad mistake!

Bly's face remained inscrutable. Pale blue eyes remained riveted on her. If smacking a woman made him feel bad or got him off, she realized, he gave no outward sign.

"Please continue," he said.

"We're here to investigate Garrison Industries," she continued. "It's part of a larger study."

Bly leaned forward. His hand reached toward her face, this time slowly, deliberately as though to brush a stray lock of hair from her vision. Reflexively, she began to jerk back. Before she completed the move, his palm hammered against the damaged cheek. She yelped in pain and surprise.

She spit a gob of blood and saliva to the floor. She turned to face him, staring at him through the veil formed by her mussed hair. She found his face emotionless, unreadable, like the rattlesnakes she'd seen as a child growing up in New Mexico.

"Will you—will you please stop hitting me?" she asked.

"Ms. Serrano," he said, "we both know you're with the CIA. Let's please cut the shit. In case you haven't figured this out yet, I have no compunctions against inflicting pain if things don't go my way. It doesn't have to be like this. But it certainly will, if you don't cooperate."

He leaned forward and she tensed again, braced herself for another blow. Instead, he took a handful of photos from his jacket pocket. One by one, as though dealing cards, he set each on her thighs until she had five of them on her legs, a row of three on top, a row of two on the bottom.

She looked at the first, gasped and looked away. Nausea

overtook her and she found herself gulping for air to quell the urge to vomit. Even with her eyes averted, the image stayed with her, seared in her mind. A crumpled skeleton, flesh burned black, marbled with streaks of red, clung to blackened bones. Except for a few wisps, the hair had been burned away, along with the facial features.

"You came here with a group," Bly said, his voice steady. "There were six of you, I believe. Well, now there's only one. You can see what happened to the others." Then he told her about the weapon and how she could escape the fate of the rest of her team.

She started to feel light-headed, and her mind wanted to race away from her. "I don't know—"

"What I'm talking about? Really? Let me explain it, then. You and your comrades have slowly infiltrated my company. It took a couple of years, but you did it, and I find myself suitably impressed. But once I realized that you were here, well, I couldn't allow that. I had to deal with you. I would have assassinated you, clean and simple, of course. However, at about the same time as my security people identified you, a laptop went missing."

Serrano shifted in her chair. "Please, I don't know what you're talking about."

"My chief financial officer, Rick Perkins, lost his laptop. Actually, it was stolen and replaced with another. Unfortunately for me, that laptop carried all sorts of information about what we've been doing here. I believe either you know who took it, or you took it yourself. I want it back."

He leaned forward until his face was just inches from hers. "Otherwise, you may very well end up like these other people. Your friends. You do recognize them, don't you?"

"No," she said. She tried to wrap her mind around the idea that these charred corpses were other members of her CIA operation. The notion made her feel sick.

"You seem upset," Bly said.

"Well," she said, "look at them. They were burned to death. Their skin looks like crepe paper. They must have suffered horribly."

"They did," Bly said, grinning.

"What? You actually saw this happen? Why didn't you stop it?"

His head flew back and he laughed hard. "Stop it?" His voice sounded incredulous. "Why would I do that?"

She stared at him for a long moment, and saw that his delight wasn't a put on. An icy sensation raced up her spine, and she suppressed a shudder. The bastard really was enjoying his little horror show. Rage and grief roiled inside her. A cold dread filled her spine as she realized that her team was gone. No one knew she was missing, except for her handler.

"Where's the laptop?" he repeated.

"What are you talking about?" she asked.

He sighed and slipped his hand under his jacket. He brought out a Glock handgun and pressed the muzzle to her head. "You have one last chance," he said. "Guess I won't use Firestorm on you."

Tell him, her mind screamed. Tell him whatever he wants to know! She licked her lips and shook her head. "I don't know."

"Goodbye," he said.

A scream welled up in her throat as she waited for the inevitable. He pushed the muzzle harder against her temple and pulled the trigger. The gun emitted a sharp metallic click when the hammer struck an empty chamber.

Empty. The gun was empty.

Damn him.

Her lips parted and she released a rush of trapped air from her lungs. Tension drained from her body. Her mind struggled to understand that she still lived.

The mirthless smile returned, and he appraised her for several seconds with what seemed to be a clinical detachment. Without averting his gaze, he slipped the pistol back into its holster.

"Next time," he said. "I'll kill you. Maybe."

He spun on a heel and moments later he was gone.

3

"We got her," said the voice on the phone.

"Okay," Mike Stephens said. "What's that mean for me?"

"Watch your bank balance. We'll make this all worth your while."

"How much?"

"Quarter million. Just like we discussed."

Stephens leaned back into the chair, propped his feet up on the coffee table. "I've been thinking about it," he said. "What I did, it was dangerous, you know."

"Don't—"

"Seriously, I'm thinking you owe me more. Like one million."

"Take your money and shut up."

"Bullshit," Stephens said. "We both know this would've cost you a hell of a lot more if you'd hired someone else."

"Leave it alone."

"The hell I will," Stephens said. He was on his feet now, stalking through the apartment, his cheeks scarlet with rage. "You wanted her. I gave her to you. Now I want some real money. What's the problem?"

"Take your cash and shut up," the other man said. "Now's a hell of a time for you to try to change the terms."

"Change the terms? Yeah, I'll change the terms. I can make a couple of phone calls and let people know what you're up to. That'd put a little crimp in your plans."

"If you were smart, you'd shut the hell up, take your money and disappear into your haze of booze and hookers. Or else."

A cold sensation traveled down Stephens's spine. Don't back down now, he told himself. Don't let this piece of Euro-trash push you around. You push back hard enough and he'll give you what you want.

"Or else? What does that mean?"

"It means Maria Serrano is on her way out. And you keep popping off, something might happen to that little whore you're keeping at your apartment."

Stephens felt his pulse quicken, but when he spoke his voice was flat and cold. "Don't go there," he said.

The other man laughed.

"Spare me," he said. "If you're smart, you'll just shut up and walk away. Take your lady on a trip or something. Disappear. 'Cause maybe you can take me. *Maybe*. But you can't take the people backing me."

"You mean, Bly?"

"For starters. But he's got friends. Ones who'd be only too happy to burn you down, if it meant fewer headaches for them. You can't handle all that heat. By the way, what's your girl's name?"

"Go to hell!" Stephen shouted.

"I can make her disappear. You'll never see the body. You'll never see that baby she's carrying. And I'll have a good time doing it. It will be just like the war."

Stephens clenched his jaw and he held his tongue.

"We understand each other?" Milt Krotnic asked.

"Yes."

"Good. Now, why don't you take that money and buy your lady something pretty."

The phone went dead and Stephens stared at it for several seconds. He tossed it on the couch and sank onto the cushion next to it. Squeezing his eyes closed, he dropped his head into his hands. His mind reeled from the enormity of what he'd done. He'd betrayed his country, and he'd done it for no reason other than greed. He'd caused a half-dozen people to die.

This wasn't how it was supposed to work, he thought. The way Krotnic had laid it all out to him had been different. The lying creep had assured him it'd be bloodless. Stephens would pass along the names of his teammates to the Serb who, in turn, would pass them along to Bly. The executive then would quietly ring up his contacts in Washington and tell them he'd identified their agents and that Langley should recall them. They'd go home, alive, and no one would be the wiser for his role in the whole thing.

And he'd walk away with some cash in a bank account in Zurich. Plenty enough cash for him to leave the cloak-and dagger crap and make a real life for himself. Now he had blood on his hands.

His stomach suddenly tightened and he launched himself from the couch, sprinted for the bathroom. Crouched before the toilet, his guts heaved violently and he emptied their contents into the bowl.

He thought of Eva, locks of lustrous black hair set against smooth brown skin. A chill raced down his spine as he remembered that she'd gone shopping. She'd be out in the open, vulnerable to Krotnic.

Stephens got to his feet and staggered to the sink. Setting his hands on either side of it, he leaned his weight on his arms to support himself as he leaned in close and studied his face in the mirror.

You gotta do something, he told himself. Get cleaned up, get out there and handle this.

A BALL OF NERVOUS ENERGY, Krotnic paced the room while he spoke to Bly on the speakerphone.

"He's going to turn on us," Krotnic said.

"Stephens? Well, do something about it, then," Bly said.

"Sure," Krotnic replied. "You got some guys I can use?"

"Of course."

"Send them my way. I need maybe ten."

"He's not that good," Bly said.

Krotnic laughed. "Hell no, he's not. I just want to play it safe. He lives in an apartment building. I think we should do a little housecleaning, if you get my drift."

"Are you crazy? That will draw all kinds of attention!"

"I've got it under control," Krotnic said. "We drop a little cocaine in there, buy a couple of witnesses, maybe a local cop and it's done. They'll write it off as a drug-related killing. The locals won't press too hard."

"Where do I send them?" Bly asked.

Krotnic told him. "And send Doyle, too."

"Why him?"

"Because he won't fall apart if he has to kill someone."

"None of my people will," Bly replied, his irritation audible.

"I'm talking about a pregnant woman," Krotnic said. "He won't freak out about killing a pregnant woman. If his people won't do it, then he'll do it himself."

Krotnic heard Bly sigh heavily on the other end. "Yes," Bly said. "I suppose he would. I assume all this is necessary?"

Krotnic grinned to himself. "You going soft?"

"Ask me that again," Bly said, "and you'll learn what a stupid question that is."

Krotnic felt his mouth go dry like a well-wrung sponge. "Sure," he said. "Forget I asked."

"Like hell," the other man replied. "Give me two hours and you'll have your people."

BROGNOLA PUNCHED HIS FIST into his open palm as he stood in Barbara Price's office. He always worried when he sent his people on missions, always considered his decisions to send them into certain battles. The searing pain in his stomach and the onslaught of worst-case scenarios that raced through his mind told him this time was no different. The priorities in the field continued to shift as new intelligence flowed into the Farm. He glanced over at Price, who was seated at her desk. He knew she was combing through the various intelligence reports so she could prioritize and present them to him during a briefing that loomed a couple of hours away.

When the secure phone rang, it startled him. The big Fed hurried to it, snagged the receiver, raised it to his ear.

"Brognola," he said.

"I need you to make a call," Bolan said.

"What are the particulars?"

"I need Leo Turrin to run some traps for me," the Executioner said.

"Sure, I'll contact him. What's the message?"

"The intelligence I have on Chiun is too spotty," Bolan said. "I'm wondering if any of Leo's less-savory friends might have some light they can shed on Chiun and his organization."

"I'll make the call," Brognola said. "Tell me what to ask."

Bolan recited his questions while the big Fed jotted them down on a canary yellow legal pad. When Bolan finished Brognola said, "I've got other news."

"Go."

"Police found the team's controller, Clark, a couple of hours ago. Dead. He was in some apartment in Bogotá. It wasn't his obviously. The CIA and FBI have already scrubbed the place down to the walls."

"How long had he been dead?"

"Not sure," Brognola said. "The body sat in the heat for a while and was pretty badly decomposed when they found it. Actually it was the smell that tipped them off. The neighbors complained about the stench. The custodian went into the apartment to check on the smell and found the guy sprawled out on the living-room floor with a dozen bullet holes in his torso. We're assuming that the shooter used a sound suppressor. The place i pretty upscale. If the shooting had been audible, someone would have called the cops."

"Great," Bolan said. "I guess I'll scratch him off my list o people to talk to."

"Yeah. Have faith, though. Barb's been working her contact in Washington and she's come up with some interesting information about Mr. Clark."

"Yeah?"

"Now that the proverbial shit has hit the fan, suddenly everyone understands what's been happening for the past couple of months with the Garrison investigation. Bly apparently knew it was happening for a while at least. We're still trying to figure out how he knew, but he knew. Unfortunately for us, he was smart about it. He offered up a couple of sources to the team, and

Clark took the bait. They were offering him all kinds of information, some of it too good to be true."

"Which means it was," Bolan stated. "He was an experienced field guy. How'd he fall for that?"

"Hard to say," Brognola replied. "It's possible that he was too taken with the information to analyze it and determine whether it actually made sense given what we know. Or that it had enough of an air of credibility about it to make it worth pursuing."

"That'd make sense," Bolan said, "considering that the guy at the top was the one feeding the information to him."

"Sure, it could've had just enough truth in it to make the lie seem plausible. I mean Bly was pulling the strings on most of what came out, so he could direct traffic and lead the CIA where he wanted it to go."

"Do we know who was feeding the controller his information?"

"I've got a contact," Brognola said. "There's a guy on the ground there, name's Bill Wallace. He's a ballistics expert and a gunsmith and a former commando. The U.S. sent him to Colombia a couple of years ago to consult with their military. The assignment stuck and he's still there. Whenever we—meaning Langley, Justice or the Pentagon—send someone into the country covertly, whether for a drug investigation or some other clandestine op, he provides the weapons and equipment. Saves us the headache of smuggling guns through airports. I know him. We go back a long way. The guy's absolutely incorruptible."

"Did he arm Serrano's team?"

"Can't say for sure," Brognola replied. "But, it's likely he did, and he'll tell us what we want to know. I'll let him know you're coming."

BOLAN GUIDED THE CAR into a curved driveway that led to an iron gate. He parked and waited for a guard to appear. Jack Grimaldi undid his seat belt and opened his windbreaker, giving him better access to his handgun.

A minute later, Bolan sensed someone coming. He looked into the rearview mirror and saw three guards approaching the car from the rear. Two of the men stopped a few yards behind the vehicle and stood on either side of it, their FN submachine guns cradled in plain view.

A third man came up alongside the car and stopped just behind Bolan's shoulder. The position made it easier for him to get the drop on the Executioner, should he make a play for a weapon. The guard, a scarecrow-thin man with a bushy black mustache, his eyes shaded by a billed cap, rested his hand on his sidearm.

"Quick," Grimaldi said, mock urgency in his voice, "hide the joint."

"Comedy," Bolan said. "Just what we need."

The Executioner rolled down his window. A blast of hot air tinged with oppressive humidity blasted his face.

"Can I help you?" the guard asked.

"Matt Cooper," Bolan said. "I'm supposed to meet Mr. Wallace."

"ID?"

Bolan dug out the leather carrying case that contained his wallet from the cup holder built into the car's console. He handed it, already flipped open, to the guard. The man studied it, nodded and handed it back. They repeated the process with Grimaldi. Then the guard reached up and keyed the microphone clipped to his shoulder and ordered the gate open.

Once inside the compound, Bolan navigated the car along the curved driveway. He noticed most of the land around the house was stripped of trees and most shrubs, for security purposes, he assumed.

The rooftop became visible before the rest of the house did. He turned another corner, followed the driveway as it dipped and finally rolled up in front of the big hacienda-style house.

Wallace stood in the driveway and watched them roll in. Except for the Glock that rested on his hip, he otherwise looked like a father waiting to take his kids to soccer practice. He wore a polo shirt, khakis and brown loafers. His wide face seemed to swallow up a pair of glasses with small, round lenses that were perched on his nose.

Bolan parked the vehicle. He and Grimaldi exited it.

Wallace ambled toward them. He shook hands first with Grimaldi and then with Bolan, who found his handshake firm and confident.

"Sorry about the theatrics," Wallace said. A soft Southern accent colored his voice. He made a sweeping wave that took in his house and a pair of Mercedes SUVs parked nearby. "People see all this and they want to help themselves to it. They can have it. But it's my family I worry about. Place is filthy with kidnappers."

"Understood," Bolan said.

"Come inside," Wallace said.

They followed Wallace through the house, ascended a circular staircase that led to the second floor and adjourned to Wallace's luxurious study.

Several bottles of water and a carafe of coffee stood with some cups at the center of a small conference table ringed with chairs.

"Help yourselves to a drink," Wallace said. "Cop a squat. Do whatever you want. Any friend of Hal's is a friend of mine."

Wallace seated himself at the conference table. He took a bottle of water, twisted off the cap and gulped some. Grimaldi took a seat at the table while Bolan continued to stand.

"Did Hal tell you why we're here?" Bolan asked.

"He told me enough," Wallace replied. "I work with the Feds on pretty big projects, so my clearances run pretty high. Not bragging. Just letting you know that I have access to things other nongovernment folks can't touch. Hal said that a CIA ops team that was looking into Garrison went missing. Said you'd come down here to find them."

"You familiar with the team?" Bolan asked.

"I provided them with some surveillance equipment," Wallace said. "And a secure phone, along with a few pistols and submachine guns. They were under nonofficial cover, so they couldn't go through any of the traditional channels. They couldn't go near the embassy or meet with anyone from the local CIA station. It'd raise too many eyebrows."

"Meeting with you wouldn't?" the Executioner asked.

Wallace nodded. "Hell, yeah. But they didn't meet with me. I have a couple of freelance operatives I run around here. I used one of them to pass things along."

"Which means they met at least some of the team."

"Wrong," Wallace said, a hint of irritation in his voice. "I've done this a few times, remember? My guy was brand-new to the area, an unknown quantity to everyone but me. I had him leave the stuff at a dead drop, get the hell out of there before the recipients arrived. He never met anyone face-to-face. I monitored the drop by camera until someone picked up the gear."

"Was it someone from the team?"

"Of course," Wallace said. "I would've sounded the alarms in Washington if it'd happened some other way."

Bolan nodded. "Have you heard anything from them since?"

"Not personally," Wallace said. "But I am hearing other stuff. Funky stuff."

"Like?"

"I've got a couple of buddies with MI-6. Occasionally, I do a little work for them. They have a couple of guys on the ground here in Colombia, including a guy named Richardson. Ethan Richardson. He does a lot of the same work I do here. He's just not quite as choosy about his clientele. It's all just business to him, whether it's Hezbollah or the Chinese. That's his reputation and he likes it."

With loud gulps, Wallace guzzled down more water.

"A few hours ago, someone contacted him. An American. The guy was looking for weapons. It was a stupid move on his part, too. He wanted a couple of handguns and an Uzi. This place is lousy with that kind of stuff. But he called the Brit who was more than happy to sell him the guns. And then he immediately called me and passed along the information."

"For a price," Grimaldi said.

A weary smile spread across Wallace's features. "Friend, nothing comes free in Colombia. Anyway, Richardson assumed that I'd want more information on this American even before we spoke. Once he sold him the weapons, he put a tail on him so we know where he's going. He also gave me a picture."

He punched a key on his laptop, turned it around so Bolan and Grimaldi could see it. Bolan saw a pair of photos positioned next to each other on the screen. In one, the soldier observed the grainy image of a man wearing a baseball cap. The second depicted a close-up shot of the man's face. It was a Caucasian with a flat, wide nose and thick black eyebrows and dull brown eyes.

"Michael Stephens," Wallace said.

"What do we know about him?" Bolan asked.

"Drifter, of sorts. He used to be with U.S. Army intelligence. According to his file, he was sharp. But he couldn't stand to take orders from anyone. He took a swing at his sergeant over something petty, like a bad evaluation. The guy repaid him with a busted nose and a dishonorable discharge. He blew a twelve-year career over something stupid. He scrounges around for information, occasionally comes across something that he can sell to us, the Colombians, the rebels, whoever might buy it. Most of what he learns is penny ante stuff, including things compiled from foreign newspapers that he rewrites into intelligence reports. I buy it anyway, just to keep some goodwill with him. Occasionally he comes across something I can use or pass along to someone else. But we have to watch him. He's a backstabber."

"You have an address?"

"Yeah," Wallace said. "And that info's on the house."

"So who's he arming himself against?" Bolan asked.

"Hard to say," Wallace replied. "Maybe you guys."

"Not too many people know we're here," Grimaldi said.

"Then maybe something else scared him," Wallace offered. "Maybe his erstwhile employers parted company with him. Or he just pissed somebody off. From what I know about this little turd, there's no shortage of people who'd happily snap a cap on his ass for free. Hell, a couple might even pay for the privilege."

"Which means that someone else is going to be heading out there to talk with him," Grimaldi said.

Wallace nodded again. "Probably. By the way, Hal gave me a shopping list. I have your gear packed in a helicopter and ready to take you wherever you want to go."

A smile ghosted the Executioner's lips. "Thanks," he said.

"WHAT IS GOING ON?" Eva asked. Her voice was marked by fear. "Why are you doing this?"

Stephens shot her a withering look. "Shut up and pack," he

said through clenched teeth. "You've asked me three times, and it's the same damn answer every time. So do as I say."

Anger flared in her eyes, and her lips tightened into a thin line. Crossing her arms over her chest, she stared after him for a few minutes while he packed. Stephens could see at least part of this from the corner of his eye, but ignored her, knowing she'd give up quickly.

After several tense seconds, Eva spun on her heel and headed for the bedroom to pack.

Once she was gone, Stephens pulled his shirttails from the waistband of his pants and let them drape around his waist. He reached inside his nearby briefcase, rooted around inside it for a moment until he found his newly acquired Glock still sheathed in a nylon holster. Lifting his shirttails, he clipped the weapon to his waistband and let his shirt drape over the weapon's butt. He'd already stowed the second pistol in an ankle holster before Eva had returned home. He didn't want her to see the weapons. He knew she'd panic and bombard him with questions he didn't want to answer. Maybe he'd tell her more when they got to the United States. Maybe not. But he'd make that decision later. Right now, getting the hell off the bull's-eye was the main priority. And, if she had any gratitude, she'd shut her mouth and let him handle the situation. He was, after all, doing all this for her and the baby, which was all she needed to know.

He checked his watch and muttered a curse.

"Eva," he shouted, "get moving! We've got to go."

"Why do we have to go?" she shouted from the bedroom.

"Shut up. Pack. No questions!" he shouted.

The phone on his belt trilled. He cursed again and answered it. "Yeah?" he said.

"Hello, Mike," Krotnic said.

"What the hell do you want?"

"Do you like the guns you bought? Do you think they'll keep you safe?"

Unconsciously, Stephens's hand dropped to the Glock moored to his hip. "What do you want?"

"I asked you a question," Krotnic said.

"Why don't you come up here and I'll answer it."

"Sorry," Krotnic said. "I can't make it. But I sent some friends over for a visit. I hope you're a good shot. There are a lot of them."

The phone went dead.

4

Doyle pulled open the van's rear doors to reveal five men seated in the back. The gunners, all togged in street clothes, stared at him, awaiting their orders. He stepped away from the door and gestured for them to disembark.

"Look alive, ladies," he said. "Got no time for you to be back there, darning your socks, for pity's sake."

Silently, the men filed out of the vehicle. Doyle swept his gaze over the whole crew.

Each carried a duffel bag strapped over his shoulder. All the bags contained an identical weapon, a Ruger MP-9, and extra clips. They also carried Beretta 92 pistols fitted with sound suppressors. Every last one of them hailed from a military background, and they were veterans of some of the world's worst killing fields. This particular group consisted of three South Africans, an Israeli and a Russian, each formerly from the special forces of his respective country.

When it came to technical proficiency, each was a top-notch fighter, unafraid to mix it up with anyone. However, they all had little discipline and even less desire to develop what they did have. They were fighting for money, not cause or country. Doyle knew that made them inherently weaker than traditional soldiers.

A second van rolled in behind them, bits of gravel popping as it approached. The driver guided the vehicle left and parked it next to the first van. A second group of mercenaries joined the first. Doyle had split them into two teams. One would hit the building from the outside. The second would scour the inside for their targets.

"We need to take out the bastard," Doyle said. "He's starting to make noises, ones we don't like. Sounds like he's starting to have pangs of a conscience."

A couple of the gunners shot Doyle a knowing smile. He ignored them.

"We find his change of heart unacceptable," the Irishman said. "Another important point. Your target has a housemate, a young woman who's carrying his child. We want no witnesses, period. Zero. Variation from that plan is unacceptable. She takes a bullet. If anyone's too squeamish to drop the hammer on her, speak now or forever shut up. The last thing I need is for one of you nancy boys to choke when you get that stupid wench in your gunsights. Clear?"

He fell silent and slowly dragged his eyes over the motley assortment of hired guns lined up before him, made sure his expression telegraphed heavy doses of disdain for each of them. He wanted them to know that, while they got paid handsomely for their work, he had no personal regard for them. More important, he didn't fear them or care what happened to them, as long as the mission succeeded.

"You also need to go from apartment to apartment," he said. "Take out anyone unlucky enough to be home tonight. Do we all understand?"

A couple of them nodded, while others fixed their thousand-yard stares somewhere over his shoulder, like they'd heard enough.

"No questions? Fine, then get your damn asses in that building and raise some hell."

THE EXECUTIONER WAS a block away from his destination when he spotted several hardmen entering the apartment building through the front door. The sight of them set off his combat senses. The warrior brought the com-link to his lips and pressed the talk button.

"Jack?"

"Go, Sarge," Grimaldi replied.

"I've got five guys entering Stephens's building."

"Weapons visible?"

"No. I'm acting on instinct."

"Good enough for me," Grimaldi said.

Bolan signed off. He trekked toward the building until he reached the fire-escape ladder, jumping up to grab the bottom rung in his powerful grip. Once his other hand got hold of it, he pulled himself up the ladder, hand over hand, until his foot could gain purchase on the lowest rung. Bolan reached the top of the ladder and pushed through a square opening that led onto the first landing. Taking the steps two at a time, he reached the next level.

Slipping off his jacket, he wrapped it around his fist and lashed out at a windowpane. The glass disintegrated and fell inside the apartment on the other side. Bolan was through the window in seconds. He tossed aside the jacket and fisted the Beretta 93-R as he crossed the sparsely furnished apartment. No lights were on and it appeared to be empty.

Before he reached the door, he spotted shadows as they edged past the door. He halted in midstride and listened. The shuffle of feet registered with him, but he heard no one speaking.

He brought the com-link to his lips.

"Jack?" Bolan asked.

"Go," Grimaldi replied.

"I've got a team on the second floor."

"Clear," Grimaldi said. "The second team just entered the building. I'm coming in from behind them. My guess is they're either going to knock off any witnesses or they're the B-team in case Stephens actually gets away."

"Fat chance of that happening," the soldier said. "Not under his own power, at least."

Bolan signed off. In the next instant, from out in the corridor, he heard the crash of a door being kicked in. He grabbed and twisted the doorknob and yanked open the door.

He found three of the gunners stationed outside Stephens's apartment. He assumed that the other two were already inside. A heavyset thug with his hair cut into a blue Mohawk stood between Bolan and Stephens's suite. The other two gunners had taken up positions on either side of the door, apparently waiting for the command to enter.

They'd never get it. Not if Bolan could help it.

The gunner with the mohawk whipped around. His MP-9 came up with him. His lips were creased into a grin, and Bolan guessed that he was expecting one of the other residents, a helpless bystander. The Executioner was neither. The grin melted away, and the guy's arm twitched as he started to bring the MP-9 to bear.

Bolan fired and three subsonic rounds drilled into the guy's nose. His body suddenly fell limp, as though his skeleton had turned to dust. He crumpled to the floor. Bolan barreled forth, the Beretta seeking its next target.

The two men at the door spun toward him in unison. Bolan tapped the Beretta's trigger twice and two swarms of bullets drilled into the torso of the man closest to him. The force pushed the man into the wall behind him, his gun falling from his grip.

Tracking fire erupted from the third killer's MP-9 and cut a swath toward the big American. The soldier brought the Beretta to bear on his opponent. A 3-round volley erupted from the handgun's barrel and lanced into the man's throat, the hollow-point rounds nearly decapitating him.

Bolan changed out magazines and headed for the apartment. The sound of gunfire crackled from inside the suite. He came around the door, his weapon held at shoulder level, and looked for a target. Running a quick check of the living room and kitchen, the first two rooms inside the apartment, the soldier double-timed it toward a hallway that ran off the opposite wall. He peered around the corner, spotting one of the gunners crumpled in the corner. A collage of a half dozen or so red blooms that indicated bullet wounds were stitched across his chest. Empty hands, palms pointed upward, hung at his sides and his head lolled to one side, mouth agape.

The second shooter, his body wrapped around the doorjamb, squeezed off several shots into the bedroom. He whipped back into the hallway, using the walls for cover. The instant he did, he spotted Bolan, who'd already bracketed him in the Beretta's sights. Another trigger pull by the Executioner, and the man suddenly found himself retired from the gun-slinging game.

His limbs rubbery, he dropped to the floor, his body falling across the doorway he'd been shooting through moments ago.

The corpse's sudden drop-in elicited a scream from someone inside the room. Bolan took a couple of steps down the hall but pulled up short. Small shafts of light, mottled by flocks of dust motes, filtered through a couple dozen holes punched through the plasterboard during the gunfight.

"Michael Stephens," Bolan shouted. "This is Matt Cooper. U.S. Justice Department. Throw out your guns. Step out here with your hands in the air. Eva, do the same."

Gunfire chattered from the floor below Bolan, and he knew Grimaldi likely was taking fire. His grip tightened on the Beretta. He wanted to go downstairs and help his friend, but he couldn't risk Stephens escaping. Without the backup team outside the building, Stephens could slip through his bedroom window and take off, either with or without his girlfriend.

"Come on," Bolan shouted again. "I want to talk. I have some questions for you."

"Screw you," the woman yelled. "You just want to kill us."

"If I wanted you dead," Bolan replied, "I never had to lift a finger. I could've just let these guys take you out. Both of you."

Ears still ringing from the gunfire, Bolan tried to hear whether they were speaking to each other, but the surrounding noise made it too hard.

"I'm coming out," the woman shouted.

"Okay," Bolan yelled.

"Don't hurt me."

"Sure." Standing off to the side of the door, Bolan trained his pistol on it, felt his body tense slightly as a slow-moving shadow poked through it and began to grow and climb up the wall opposite the door. The woman came into view, her hands held above her shoulders. She took a sideways glance and saw Bolan aiming his weapon at her. Her eyes grew wide.

Bolan motioned with his hand for her to come closer.

"It's okay," he said.

She started toward him. After her third shuffling step, another shape filled the doorway and Bolan turned his attention to it. Stephens came into view, his weapon hunting for a target. The soldier changed the Beretta selector switch, and the weapon coughed out a single shot that whistled past Eva and slammed into the man's hip. The impact spun Stephens and caused his shooting hand to flail. His finger squeezed the trigger, and the weapon pumped a round into the ceiling.

The soldier surged forward, his pistol held high. He shoved the woman aside and inserted himself between her and Stephens. The other man, his attention temporarily focused on his injury, saw Bolan bolt for him and raised his pistol. The soldier's hand stabbed out and he grabbed Stephens's wrists, shoving his hand skyward. He stabbed the Beretta's still-hot muzzle against Stephens's neck, and he responded with a yelp.

"Drop it," Bolan shouted. His face was only inches from Stephens's.

The pistol fell to the floor with a dull thud.

The Beretta still trained on his opponent, Bolan gathered up the fallen weapon and shoved it into the waistband of his blue jeans.

From behind him, the woman screamed, "You bastard! What the hell are you doing to him?"

She took a step toward Bolan, who turned his head slightly to look at her. She halted. Anger flared in her eyes and she lowered her fist, which had been raised over her head like a hammer. She looked at Bolan, then at her boyfriend, then back at him.

Bolan, his heart still pounding from the confrontation, said, "Get me a sheet."

She gave him a confused look.

"A sheet," he repeated. "His hip needs to be bandaged."

The tautness of her lips signaled that she still was angry, but she disappeared into the bedroom. Bolan hoped she was going to retrieve the sheet and not another weapon. He hated to let her out of his sight, but it couldn't be helped.

Stephens remained propped against the wall. His face looked pale; it glistened with sweat. His breathing was ragged. He pressed a bloodied hand to his injured hip and glowered at the Executioner.

"Who the hell are you?" he asked.

"Not a friend," Bolan said.

"No shit."

"You're going to tell me things," Bolan said.

Stephens swore at him.

Bolan wagged the Beretta's muzzle at the floor. "Lay down," he said. "I want to have a look at that hip." Stephens gave him an uncertain look. After a few seconds, though, he sighed and eased himself to the ground. Bolan gripped one bicep to help him to the floor.

"You were talking to Clark."

"Who?"

Instinct told the Executioner that Stephens was trying to be cute with him, but Bolan kept his cool.

"Clark," the Executioner repeated. He gently rolled the guy onto his uninjured side. The movement elicited a sharp intake of breath from the man.

"Hey," he snapped.

Bolan ignored him and studied the wound. He found a single entrance wound, but no exit. He guessed that the slug had struck the pelvic bone and came to rest.

Eva returned with the sheet.

"Tear it into strips," the soldier said.

She nodded and began to do it. Bolan heard more gunfire downstairs, followed by the slamming of a heavy door. "Jack," he said into his throat mike. "Sitrep."

His request was greeted with silence.

GRIMALDI HAD COME AROUND the corner of the building that housed Stephens's apartment. He'd spotted a member of the death squad positioned outside the door. The hard-eyed shooter, dressed in jeans and a black T-shirt, had one hand and part of his forearm stuffed inside the duffel bag that hung from his shoulder. Grimaldi guessed that the bag held a weapon of some sort that the guy wanted to keep out of sight.

The pilot closed in on the thug. He judged the distance between them to be about fifteen feet, short enough for an easy shot, too far to easily launch into a physical attack, even for someone of Grimaldi's speed and skill.

The man caught sight of him and tracked his progress as he came closer.

Grimaldi forced himself to don a vacant smile. Unsurprisingly, it went unreturned. He continued to close in on the building's entrance. He brushed past the sentry, muttered excuse me in Spanish and rested his palm on the doorknob.

He felt a hand grab his shoulder. Fingers dug into his shoulder muscles, and he winced with pain. A force spun him and he let it happen. He found himself facing the guard.

The man opened his mouth to say something.

Grimaldi's knee rocketed up, and he buried it in the man's groin. The face of his opponent suddenly reddened. The man exhaled sharply and sank to his knees. Grimaldi reached down, grabbed a fistful of the sentry's shirt and hauled him back to his feet. His other fist fired out in a punch that rocked the guy's head back. The pilot drew back his bloodied fist for a second strike, but the guard went limp.

Grimaldi cast his gaze around the street but saw no one. Reaching around, he opened the door and dragged the unconscious gunner inside the building. He untangled the duffel bag's straps from the man's inert form and slung it over his own shoulder. He shoved the man into a corner, got to his feet and checked the bag's contents. Inside he found a Ruger MP-9 and several clips, as well as a pair of flash-stun grenades.

Gunshots rang out upstairs. The Stony Man pilot spun in the direction of the noise, his newly acquired weapon in his grip. Striker was in trouble, he thought. He reached for his throat mike to contact the Executioner, but stopped when he heard something behind him. He whirled and spotted another of the shooters stepping from an apartment. The man caught sight of Grimaldi in the same instant and brought up his submachine gun to unleash death in the pilot's direction.

The American fighter bent slightly at the knees and triggered the Ruger. Autofire ripped from the barrel and lanced past his opponent's left flank, chewing into a wall behind the man. Grimaldi swept the stuttering weapon right and scythed the man down.

Another shooter popped out from the apartment and unloaded his weapon at Grimaldi. The pilot dived to the floor and thrust himself into a roll, wanting some distance between himself and the shooter. Bullets smacked into the walls behind him, chewing up plasterboard and shattering glass. Just as Grimaldi brought up the Ruger, he caught a third gunner from the corner of his eye. The guy cut loose with his Ruger, and a relentless swarm of bullets buzzed around the pilot. Grimaldi responded in kind, his weapon laying out a murderous barrage that cut down his two opponents.

Reloading as he sprinted across the lobby, Grimaldi ducked into the apartment vacated a few seconds ago by the three shooters. A haze of gun smoke hung in the air. The sharp odor mingled with the smell of cooked onions and garlic. A threadbare couch stood alongside one wall. Between it and the opposite wall stood an easy chair and in front of that was a television turned up to blaring levels.

Grimaldi's heart sank.

The back of the chair had been rent by bullets. It was a mess of shredded fabric, stuffing and wood. A look at the floor revealed several clusters of shell casings, indicating that several shooters had let loose with their weapons at once.

He rounded the chair and found a figure, his torso lined with bullet holes, slumped forward in the chair, head turned sideways, eyes open. The man's brown skin was etched with deep lines, his hair gray and thin.

A quick scan of the room revealed a pair of hearing aids set aside on a nearby table.

Grimaldi clenched his jaw to contain his rage. He surmised that, for what it was worth, the man had never heard the bastards sneak up on him. His death likely had been as sudden as it was brutal.

Small consolation.

The pilot quickly searched the quarters, but found it empty of other people.

Bolan's voice came through his earphone. "Jack. Sitrep."

Before Grimaldi could respond, footsteps sounded in the lobby, followed by the slamming of the front door. He rushed out of the apartment. But, by the time he reached the lobby, he found it empty, other than the corpses of the other three gunners. At least they had the sentry, he thought. A quick interrogation ought to give them a lead or two to follow up on.

He advanced on the man and quickly saw that a pool of blood surrounded him. He moved in closer and saw that a burst of gunfire had savaged the man's torso. Grimaldi couldn't be sure whether the man had accidentally taken fire during the gun battle or whether someone had shot him after the fact. Regardless, that was one more lead gone. He muttered some choice expletives and headed upstairs to search for Bolan.

Bolan's voice sounded again, this time with a hint of urgency. "Jack. Sitrep."

"Okay," the pilot replied.

THE VAN ROCKETED AWAY from the apartment building. Inside, Doyle wrung the steering wheel in his hands like a wet towel and worried about how he'd explain this disaster to his boss.

He cast a glance at the man in the passenger's seat, watched him fumble for a cigarette, and turned back to watch the road. The guy obviously was shaken by whatever had happened in that building, which only heightened Doyle's own anxiety. The team's lone survivor, Max James, was a hard bastard who'd fought dozens of brutal battles in countless shit holes in Africa. If he was scared—

Doyle didn't want to think about it. He needed more information before he went too far in his worrying.

"What the hell happened back there?" Doyle demanded, his voice carrying an edge of rage. "How the hell did ten soldiers storm that building and only one survive? How does that happen against a punk like Stephens?"

James whipped his head toward Doyle. Judging from his slitted eyes and his labored breathing, his anxiety had turned in a heartbeat to anger.

"It wasn't one guy," he shot back. "And it sure as fuck wasn't Stephens who did this to us. From what I heard on our radios, that dumb bastard holed up inside his bedroom with his woman. It was these two other pricks. One of them, I didn't see. But I sure as hell heard our people yelling when he was upstairs slaughtering them."

Doyle nodded. "And the other?"

"Some lanky SOB. Doesn't look like much, but he's fast as hell."

"Not fast enough to catch you," Doyle said. "As you were scampering out the damn door."

"You want to go back?" the man asked. "I'll have another go at them. I ain't going to do it by myself, though. Let's go. I'm sure they'd love to see what you've got."

"Go to hell," Doyle said. He knew it wasn't much of a reply, but it was all he could muster at the moment. Two guys? Who the hell were they? And what did their arrival mean? Was someone coming for Maria Serrano? If so, whom? Sure, it could be the CIA. They had the talent and the resolve to avenge one of their own. But, if that was the case Doyle knew this was going to make life difficult for all of them. He stomped the accelerator and the van lurched forward. He needed to contact Bly and bring him up to speed on what had just gone down. Then they needed to eliminate these two bastards before they stirred up more trouble.

"SO WHAT WAS YOUR PRICE?" Bolan asked.

"What the hell are you talking about?" Stephens shot back.

"To betray your country," Bolan replied. "What was your price?"

Bolan had bandaged the guy's wound, but left him lying on his side to keep the pressure off his hip. Stephens had lost a lot of blood, and his skin looked pale and slicked with sweat. Eva knelt next to the former intelligence officer, one of his hands clasped in both of hers. She glared at Bolan.

"Leave him alone," she snapped. "Can't you see he's hurt?"

Bolan ignored her. He guessed that she had no idea what her man was into, or at least to what depth. And Bolan had neither the patience nor the desire to explain it to her.

"Who was paying your bills, Stephens?"

"I don't know," Stephens said.

"Like hell," the soldier said.

"I have no damn idea who was footing the bills. I got hooked up by the Serbian guy. Name's Milt Krotnic. He was a Serbian colonel. He was part of some secret outfit over there. Used to disappear people for the government."

"A war criminal," Bolan said.

"He had money."

"Fine, a war criminal with cash."

Grimaldi who was leaning against the wall, snorted out a derisive laugh. "At least you've got your priorities straight," he said.

"The U.S. Army screwed me," Stephens said. "I've got no reason to be loyal to it or to anyone else. Understand? My only priority is me. Got it? Me. You holier than thou jerks have no idea how it is."

A bemused smile creased Grimaldi's lips, but he stayed quiet.

"Where was Krotnic getting the cash to pay you?" Bolan asked, though he guessed he already knew the ultimate source.

"I don't know," he said. "I just took my money and did what he asked."

"Which was?"

"Get information from Clark or take information to Clark."

"You were the go-between."

"Yeah, and it was a good gig, too."

"So what happened?" Bolan asked.

"I asked for more money," he replied. "It pissed them off. Krotnic told me that he'd come after us. That's why I went out and bought the guns."

Eva broke in. "You knew this was going to happen? That they'd try to kill us? Why didn't you tell me?"

"I told you to pack your stuff," Stephens said. "That was all you needed to know."

The woman began to say something, but Bolan gestured for her to be quiet. "Sort this out later," he said.

He turned back to Stephens. "Where's Serrano?"

"The CIA woman? I have no idea," Stephens said.

Bolan's gut told him that the guy was telling the truth. "What about Krotnic?" the Executioner asked. "Where do we find him?"

"Don't know. Whenever he wanted to communicate with me, he'd call me. I didn't call him. I just took whatever he gave me and passed it along."

Bolan swallowed his frustration. "We're going to get you out of here," he said. "Have a real doctor look at your hip."

"Thanks."

"Spare me the gratitude. After that, we're turning you over to the Feds so they can question you more. I didn't forget what you did. Six people are dead, in part because of you. You're going out of here with your life, but not your freedom. It's a hell of a lot more than you deserve."

5

Bolan and Grimaldi climbed the stairs that led to Maria Serrano's apartment.

The woman lived in a three-story brick apartment building several blocks from Garrison's headquarters. The stairwell was stifling hot, and Bolan felt moisture collect between his collar and the back of his neck. The soldier wore a T-shirt and had covered that with a short-sleeved button-up shirt to hide the Beretta 93-R in its shoulder holster.

When Bolan reached the landing, he followed a corridor that was hotter than the stairwell until he reached the third door on the left. Jennifer Simmons, a local CIA official at the U.S. Embassy had provided him keys to the apartment. Agents already had swept the place, but Bolan wanted to see where Serrano lived and give it his own once-over. He had to see if they had missed anything the first time through. He unsealed the door and entered, followed by Grimaldi.

The apartment was sparsely furnished and uncluttered by personal effects like photos or other items that might give an insight into Serrano's personality. However, as Bolan looked at tabletops, shelves and other flat surfaces, he saw the fine sheen of dust on them had been broken by disk- or rectangular-shaped spaces, an indicator that items that once had stood there had since been removed. The couch cushions had been slit with neat, nearly uniform cuts and the stuffing pulled from them.

Bolan moved to Serrano's desk, which was situated in a corner, out of the line of sight of the window. He began opening the drawers and made a quick check of their contents, but found them nearly empty except for generic items like pads of sticky notes, pens or an occasional book.

"They took everything," Grimaldi said. "It's like she never was here."

The Executioner moved to a window. With two fingers he hooked the edge of a curtain, drew it back and peered outside. The window faced a street that ran past the front of the building. Bolan stared across the street and saw a spacious park with a fountain in the center that looked reasonably new, though no water sprouted from the top.

"We should check her bedroom," Bolan said.

They searched the bedroom and found that all the clothes had been taken, too. The mattress had been cut open and searched in a fashion similar to the couch and chair cushions. Bolan spotted a pair of worn running shoes, tossed in a corner. Next to them stood a small selection of iron dumbbells, some resistance bands for strength training and a yoga mat.

"Fitness buff," Grimaldi said.

They returned to the kitchen. Bolan looked behind the stove, finding nothing of interest. In the meantime Grimaldi pushed aside the refrigerator, dropped to his hands and knees and began to search around its base. He pulled a penlight from his shirt pocket and searched underneath the appliance. He did likewise with the stove.

"Hey!" the pilot suddenly said.

Bolan halted his search of an overhead cabinet and turned to his friend. Holding up a piece of paper, Grimaldi climbed to his feet and crossed over to a table. He set the dirty scrap of paper on the table, smoothed it out and studied it for a moment.

"I think this is what we call a clue," Grimaldi said. "Not much of one. But it looks like a secure document of some kind. See the gray lettering and the weird background on the paper? That's to prevent people from photocopying it. So it could be a check. Or a money order or something similar."

Bolan nodded. "Let's drop Bear a line and see what kinds of purchases she made."

BOLAN PUSHED OPEN THE DOOR and a small bell that hung over it announced his arrival. He stepped inside the herb shop and looked it over. It was clean and well-lit, unremarkable in every aspect.

The Asian man positioned behind the counter seemed equally unremarkable at first. His black hair was cut at a respectable length. He was togged in khakis and a polo shirt. It wasn't until the man turned to look at Bolan that he saw the man was missing his right arm. An empty sleeve hung from his shoulder.

"*Hola,*" the man said.

"Hi," Bolan replied.

"You speak English? I never know until someone says hello," the guy replied.

"Sure," Bolan said. "Mind if I look around?"

"Help yourself."

Bolan walked past the front counter. Movement from behind it caught his attention. He looked again and saw two small girls playing jacks. He guessed their ages to be about two and five years old. The smallest one looked at Bolan, which prompted the older girl to turn in his direction to see what she was staring at.

"Hello," Bolan said.

"Hello," the older girl said. The little one just stared.

The soldier continued through the store. He slipped between two rows of shelves and pretended to be searching for something. He grabbed a clear glass jar of mushrooms from a shelf, held it at eye level and stared at it. At the same time, he monitored the shopkeeper's reflection in a nearby window.

According to intelligence supplied by Kurtzman, the shop owner, a man named Xhiung Cho, was a former triad accountant who'd gotten caught with his fingers in the till. Bolan wanted to ask the man some questions, but the presence of the little girls complicated matters. The man didn't have a history of violence, but Bolan couldn't be sure things wouldn't turn rough if the guy panicked. He didn't want anything to happen with the girls in the shop.

The scrap of paper, it'd turned out, had been a piece of a money order Serrano had written. That had prompted further digging by Kurtzman who eventually discovered that she'd dropped several thousand dollars in money orders and wire transfers to the herb store.

Under other circumstances, Bolan would have left and caught Cho at another time to mitigate any danger to the kids. But time wasn't a luxury he had. He had to make his play immediately. If he approached the man right, maybe Cho would keep his cool.

Bolan headed up the aisle toward the front of the store. The doorknob rattled and the door swung inward. At the same time the bell rang. Bolan ducked behind the shelves and waited to size up the situation.

The Executioner peered around the side of one of the shelves at the new visitors. The three Asian men strutted to the counter. One, dressed in an expensive-looking suit, stopped a foot or so from it and cocked his fists onto his hips. A second man, who stood well over six feet tall, crossed his arms over his chest and stared down at the shopkeeper. A third man, head shaved, a winged dragon tattooed on his temple, brought up the rear. He shut the front door, locked it and drew the shades.

"Hello, Xhiung," the man in the suit said.

"Tang," the owner replied, his voice strained.

"Been a while."

"Yeah."

"You know why we're here?"

"No."

Bolan heard the unmistakable snap of someone getting smacked across the face.

"My kids are here, Tang!"

"Where is he?"

"Where's who?"

"The guy who just came in here. Where'd he go?"

"He's in here someplace," Cho said. Bolan heard the slapping sound again.

"You're a bad liar," Tang said.

"I'm not lying. He's still here! Did you see him leave? You want him, then go find him."

Bolan grabbed the Beretta and, his body in a crouch, moved

to the rear of the store. He hid behind the end panel of a row of shelves. He listened hard for any signs of an approach. The sole of a shoe scuffed to his right and prompted him to turn his head that way. He saw a bulky shadow protruding from the aisle. It whispered its way across the floor to a wall across from him. The warrior tensed, but he stayed rooted, waiting for the man to reveal himself.

When he heard the rustle of fabric rubbing together, and the sound of erratic breathing, he knew someone was almost upon him.

He uncoiled from the ground but didn't straighten to his full height. Rounding the corner, he caught the big man in mid-stride. Surprise registered in the other man's eyes. He halted, starting to raise his handgun. Before his shooting hand made it to forty-five degrees, a single round from the Beretta hammered into the flesh under the man's chin and rocked him off his feet. His bulk slammed backward into a shelf lined with large glass jars, which gave way under his weight. Bottles plummeted to the floor, shattered, littered the carpet with shards of glass and powder.

Bolan surged away from the fallen thug. Already he heard noises from the front. The guy in the suit alternately shouted a name and cursed. Cho was yelling, too.

The Executioner started for the little girls. He wanted to put himself between them and the triad thugs. Three steps later, his combat senses kicked into overdrive, begged for his attention.

In response, he dropped into a crouch. Thunder clapped. A blast roared seemingly out of nowhere, shattering glass and shredding plastic. White-hot needles of pain struck several places at once, jabbing into his cheek and throat.

The Executioner ignored it. He saw the shooter pop back into view, a shotgun locked on him. Bolan thrust himself sideways and squeezed the Beretta's trigger. Once. Twice. The man's nose exploded in a spray of blood while a hole opened up on his forehead. He crumpled to the floor.

Bolan heard the cries of the frightened children, and he continued on. He reached the rear wall, glided along its length, the Beretta poised before him. He found the two girls a few feet from where he'd earlier seen them playing. This time, though, they huddled in a corner, arms wrapped around each other. Stepping between the counters, the warrior stepped in front of the girls. They shrank from him, wailing louder. Bolan thumbed his handgun into triburst mode, even as he scanned the room for threats.

A heartbeat later, the man in the suit came into view, a micro Uzi clutched in his hands.

The man spotted Bolan at almost the same instant.

The Beretta chugged out three rounds, the slugs stitching a red line from the gunner's waist to his shoulder. His knees buckled under the punishing burst, and he slammed to the ground.

The Uzi spit flame and hot lead intended for Bolan. However, the injured man's wounds were bad enough to throw off his aim, and the bullets chewed into a wall several feet to the soldier's right, and well away from the children.

With the three men down, Bolan headed to the front of the store. As he came upon the cash register, he found Cho, a pistol clutched in his hand, stealing toward the back of the store. Bolan drew down on the man.

"Cho," the Executioner shouted.

The guy halted, tensed, as though he might make a move.

"Stay still, Cho," Bolan said.

"Fuck you. I want my kids."

"They're okay."

"No shit," the guy responded. "I can hear them crying. I want to see them."

"Drop the gun," Bolan said.

"Like I said, fuck you."

"We both know I have the drop on you," Bolan said. "Why make this difficult? Just drop the gun. Step away from it. I came here to talk with you, not to kill you."

"Talk? No, thanks. I've seen how you talk."

"Drop the gun," Bolan repeated. "You get only one chance and I just gave it to you."

The shop owner hesitated for a couple of seconds. His shoulders sagged, and he cursed just loud enough that Bolan could hear him. Finally, he bent slowly at the knees until he could se

the gun on the ground without dropping it. He rose to his full
height, hands held high.

"What now?" he asked.

"Now I ask you some questions," the Executioner said.

6

"We need to get the hell out of here," Cho said. Tremors passed through his voice as he spoke.

"I'll remove you and your family," Bolan said. "Don't worry."

Cho licked his lips as his eyes drifted to the bloodstained fabric of Bolan's shirt. "Define 'remove,'" he said.

"Get you and the kids to safety," the Executioner said. "Get you some form of witness protection, either in the United States or through another country. Tell me what we need to know, and I'll make sure you get security."

Bolan almost could see the tension drain from the other man's body. They stood across from each other in a storeroom located off the back of the shop. Bolan leaned against a wall, his arms crossed over his chest. The former triad accountant had positioned himself between Bolan and his children, who sat on the floor, playing. Occasionally one or the other shot a furtive glance Bolan's way, and he replied with a smile or a wink.

White cardboard boxes, most still sealed, lined two of the walls. Bolan noticed that someone—presumably Cho—had positioned the boxes so that the identical side faced out. None was stacked more than four high. Plastic bottles labeled with Chinese characters filled one shelf, none more than two deep.

The concrete floor was painted battleship gray but shone like glass. No horizontal surface carried dust. Apparently, Cho liked things well ordered, and his current situation was anything but.

"I want to go now," the man said. "He knows where to find

me. He knows where to find my children. Now that I killed Jimmy Chu, I'm fucked. You realize that? Fucked. He's Chiun's cousin or something. I probably should've let him shoot you."

"Listen—"

"No, you listen!" Cho shouted. He stressed each word with a jab of his index finger.

"Shut up," Bolan said. His voice had grown quiet, but the ice that had crept into it registered with the other man and he fell silent. "We have FBI and State Department guys out there toting MP-5 submachine guns while they go over the scene. With one phone call, I'll have a helicopter come here and take you and your family wherever you want to go. But you have to work with me. Understand? Tell me what I need to know, and I'll be gone."

Cho opened his mouth to protest. Bolan silenced him with a gesture. Cho gave him a go-to-hell look, but kept his mouth shut.

"I don't like the triads," Bolan said. "I don't like triad accountants any better than I like triad gunners. You're all part of the same big damn cancer, as far as I'm concerned. But I want your kids safe. I'll do everything in my power to make it happen. You want to throw that away? Explain it to them."

Cho studied him for a moment before his gaze fell to the floor. He shook his head vigorously. "Fuck," he muttered.

"A woman, name's Gina Lopez, came in here. Why?"

"Got a description?"

Bolan knew it was a stall tactic but gave him one anyway.

"Oh yeah, her. Beautiful. She came in here, asking all kinds of questions," Cho finally said.

"What kind?" Bolan asked.

"Kind that get you killed."

"Specify."

"Kept asking questions about Garrison Industries. The defense people."

"She ask about Albert Bly?"

"Yeah."

"Chiun?"

A pause. "Yeah."

"What'd she ask?"

"Wanted to know the scuttlebutt in Chiun's organization in regards to Garrison."

"And you told her…?" Bolan asked.

"That I didn't know."

"Try again," Bolan asked.

"Seriously. I told her I didn't know anything. She laid her pretty smile on me. Nodded a lot. Then she laid a couple of stacks of hundred-dollar bills on me. U.S. dollars. I told her I didn't want the money. She called bullshit on me, and she was right. I needed the cash." He waved an arm in the direction of the kids. "I have mouths to feed."

Bolan gave him a cold glare. "Spare me the struggling single-dad routine. You've got one million dollars stuffed in black bank accounts in Zurich and the Cayman Islands."

Cho smiled. "Just who the hell are you, guy?"

"Someone who doesn't answer questions."

"Fair enough."

"And you told her?"

"That I didn't know who was buying those weapons."

Bolan crossed his arms over his chest. "Damn it, Cho."

Cho raised his hands, palms facing forward, in a placating gesture. "Really," he said. "I had no idea at the time. But I knew who could answer the question."

"Give."

"Marc Haley."

Bolan searched his memory. "Means nothing to me," he admitted.

"Used to be in U.S. intelligence. Don't ask me which agency. I have no damn idea. Guy's a closed book. For all I know, Marc Haley isn't his real name. He just showed up one day and knew everything about everyone. Freaked a lot of us out."

"You send her to Haley?"

Cho snorted a small laugh. "Send her to Haley? You don't send someone to Haley. You want to see Haley, you put out the word. Then he finds you."

"So you put out the word. Is that right?"

The accountant nodded.

"Put it out to who?" the soldier asked.

"Arthur Doyle. He owns a titty bar nearby. He spends most of the day with his big ass planted on a bar stool, and swills beer. When he gets ambitious, he screws a stripper or two. Occasionally, he uses the girls to set a honey trap for the local diplomats, catch them in a compromising position, get some film and recruit them as spies. Not for any certain country, of course. Doyle and his boss, Haley, they're free agents."

"But Doyle's the conduit," Bolan asked.

"He's the conduit. He knows where and how to find Haley."

"How does Chiun fit into this?" Bolan asked.

The other man shrugged. "Could be anything. Chiun has lots of secrets."

"How about secrets involving Garrison Industries?"

Cho licked his lips, swallowed hard. "I don't know anything about that."

"Which is why you suddenly need a change of underwear."

"Seriously. I'm telling the truth."

"Like when you said you're a poor Dad, just trying to make ends meet," Bolan said.

"What? So now you're an expert on me? Screw you."

"Don't play with me," Bolan said. "I'm trying to find the woman, and I'll burn down anyone who gets in my way. Anyone."

Cho gave him a pleading look, which Bolan met with an impassive stare. He knew Cho was trying to play on his sympathies, especially for the kids. The soldier had lost patience with the games.

After a few seconds, Bolan said, "Give me answers, Cho. I can be your best friend or your worst enemy. Make the right choice."

"You're a hard-ass. You know that? Okay. They've got something in the works, Chiun and Garrison, but I have no idea what. Don't give me that look. I'm serious. It's not like Chiun and I are buddies." With his remaining hand, he grabbed the cuff of his empty sleeve, lifted it, then let it fall. "In case you didn't notice, we're not on good terms. It's a miracle I'm still breathing."

"Happy miracle at that," Bolan said.

The guy shot Bolan a dirty look.

"Look," Bolan said, "you may be a step above Chiun, but quit jerking me. Someone's life is at stake and my patience is gone."

"You want to find Haley and Bly? Track down Arthur Doyle. He's the guy in front. No one sees those two unless they get through Doyle."

The Executioner nodded, happy to find himself on familiar turf. Going through people was what he did best.

THE ANTICIPATION NEARLY DROVE him mad. Seated aboard the Gulfstream jet, the doctor drummed his fingers on the armrest of his chair as he contemplated his day's work.

When he'd received Bly's call, he'd been in the middle of some business in Brazil. But Bly had convinced him to finish up and hop a private jet to Colombia. He shut his eyes, leaned against the headrest, grinning as he considered his just-concluded business.

The federal police there had captured a member of MS-13, the street gang, and found his apartment packed with guns and drugs. They'd spent three days grilling the man, hoping to find his supplier, but he'd withstood the tough tactics.

That's when he'd gotten a call. A friend of a friend had put the Brazilian authorities in touch with him. It'd been easy work, easy money.

A damn good time.

He sighed, smiled. Amazing what a person could do with pliers, a car battery and some alligator clips. And the electric saws. He couldn't forget those.

The call from the former CIA man had been a surprise, not a welcome one.

"I need you to work on something," Bly had said. "How soon can you be here?"

The doctor had told him.

"Not good enough! I'll send a plane."

"I thought you didn't work with me anymore," he replied. "You know the stuff I did in Lebanon. I thought you were angry about that."

"Water under the bridge."

"But your two agents—"

"Forget it."

"I didn't mean to kill them," he said. "I just got, um, excited."

"Forget it," Bly had replied, "before I decide not to."

Even now, Bly's words—no, not the words, the undercurrent of barely contained rage in his tone—caused a thrill of fear to race through the doctor's gut. Bly never forgot anything.

"I'm not so sure," he said.

"Say no, and you're not turning down a job, you're begging to be killed. One phone call and they find your head in a freezer next Christmas. You're the best, but I've got a list of five other sadistic freaks I can call. You're just the most expedient option."

That pissed him off.

"I'm not a freak. I'm a doctor. A surgeon."

"Were," Bly had said. "Were a surgeon. Now you're just a sadistic freak who cuts up people. You torture people. I'm sending a plane for you. You either ride it back here, do a little interrogation work, and walk away with full pockets. Or—"

"I'll come," he said.

THE CLICK OF THE LOCK jarred her awake.

Serrano, curled up on the floor, opened her eyes slightly and stared at the door as it swung open. Her muscles tensed and fear knotted her gut. She decided to feign sleep, until she could identify her latest visitor.

Bly stood in the doorway. His wide shoulders and chest filled the frame. He appraised her with the same dead-eyed stare he always did. She opened her eyes fully and sat upright while he studied her with what appeared to be a scientific detachment.

"The laptop," he said.

"Fuck off," she said.

His eyes emotionless, he studied her for several more seconds before retreating back into the hallway. Damn, she thought. What now?

The answer came moments later when a guard—a muscular man with lightning bolts tattooed on his forearms—stepped into the room. In his hands, he gripped what Serrano recognized as a fire hose nozzle. The thick hose trailed down from it, snaked down to the floor and disappeared in the hallway.

"Go," Bly said.

His face stoic, the man pulled the lever on the fire hose. A shaft of frigid water fired from it, smacked her like a mule kick to the stomach. Her breath exploded from her mouth as the force pushed her onto her back. Acting on instinct, she rolled over and crawled to a corner. The guard was on her. A punishing column of water continued to pound into her, pinning her against a wall.

Something encircled her wrist, squeezing hard. Her lips parted to yell. Water blasted into her mouth, and she swallowed reflexively to clear it. Gagging, she whipped her head side to side, tried to catch her breath.

She glimpsed Bly next to her. Pain shot through her scalp as he took a handful of her hair, yanked back her head and kept it nearly immobilized. Water continued to strike her full in the face, covering her nose, forcing her to hold her breath until she swore her lungs would burst. She popped open her mouth to breathe but found herself gagging again. Bly and the guard kept at this for an interminable amount of time, before the treatment stopped.

Bly threw her toward the floor. Hands still cuffed, she struck the concrete with her shoulder, grinding her teeth together to quell the pain.

As she lay there, panting, he stood over her, studying her as one would a rock or another inanimate object.

"The laptop," he said.

Her mind reeled. Tell him! A voice screamed inside her head. Fucking tell him! No one's coming to get you. No one will ever know you caved.

She looked at him, swallowed hard, struggling to catch her breath.

"Fuck you," she said between breaths.

The corner of his mouth twitched. Lips peeled back into a smile.

"Fine," he said, his voice even. "I have a friend coming to see you. He's going to hurt you, and then you'll tell us what we want."

Spinning around, he exited the room. The guard followed. As

he left, he cast a look her way and grinned. "Dead meat," he said, closing the door behind him.

SOME TIME LATER—a minute or an hour, she wasn't sure—recessed lights in the ceiling blazed to life, filling the room with a glare like that of truck headlights. Grinding heavy metal music set at ear-splitting levels blared through unseen speakers. Guitars screeched. Drums pounded. Drenched clothes clung to her body, growing colder as the temperature in the room dropped. Shivers seized her body. Blood thundered in her ears, one pressed against the floor, the other covered with the palm of her right hand. She lay there, exhausted, but unable to pass out.

7

The SUV raced through the streets of Bogotá. Bolan, one hand resting on the steering wheel, guided the car to their destination. With his other hand, he dialed a number into his encrypted cell phone and waited as the call worked its way through a series of cutout numbers. Grimaldi sat in the front passenger seat, checking the action on a .40-caliber Glock handgun.

"Striker?" Barbara Price asked.

"What did you get for me?" Bolan asked.

"Hello yourself," Price replied. Bolan heard a trace of a smile in her voice, and knew she was ribbing him for his brusque manner. "We ran a quick dossier on Arthur Doyle. It's incomplete, but it's something."

"I'll take it," Bolan said.

"He's former IRA. By former, I mean he got booted out. Apparently, he was working as a double agent for the British. He ratted out half a dozen IRA officials, and another dozen foot soldiers. British SAS took out all the low-level guys and three of the big fish that Doyle fingered. After a while, the upper echelon got suspicious. They realized that Doyle was the mouthy one, and they planned to take him out. He fled Belfast before it could happen."

"Did it for queen and country, I'm sure," Bolan said.

"Try twenty thousand pounds," Price replied. "He turned on the British more than once, too. Truth be told, it's a miracle that he's not dead. But, apparently, he's managed to stay a step ahead of anyone who carries a grudge against him. My guess is having friends like Bly and Haley helps."

"Luck of the Irish," Bolan said.

"That too."

The Executioner saw that he was rolling up to an intersection. He tapped the brake pedal several times and the vehicle slowed to a crawl. Cutting the wheel right, he turned onto a street lined with small shops and prodded the gas as the vehicle rolled out of the turn.

"Anyway, Bear tapped into the state police's records and intelligence system. Guess Doyle spends most of his time at the club. He maintains an apartment a few blocks away. He rents the floors above and below him, too, presumably for security reasons. But he also has a sleeping area at the club. He usually travels with a contingent of private security, mercenaries mostly. And he's as paranoid as hell."

"With good reason," Bolan said.

"Of course. But that means that any strangers who get within thirty feet of him will find themselves up to their neck in trouble."

"Jeepers," Bolan said.

"I'm serious," Price said. "Doyle's no pushover. He's not the type to go peacefully. The intelligence we have indicates that after he fled Ireland, he spent about five years fighting dirty wars in South America. He's a small-arms expert and always keeps a gun close at hand. He made his bones in the IRA doing assassinations before he started climbing the ladder."

"Point taken," the soldier replied.

"Just don't underestimate him," Price replied. "That's all I'm saying, Striker."

Bolan knew the lady had a point. And he knew her worries went beyond his safety. Like the others at the Farm, both the warriors and the support staff, she'd seen some damn fine soldiers fall in the field. And no one, regardless of his or her experience and professionalism, ever truly forgot them. The way Bolan saw it, to do so would have been a betrayal of the highest order. And, overconfidence was poison for a soldier, no matter how skilled.

"I'll stay sharp," Bolan said. "Especially since Jack's my only backup."

"Hey," the pilot protested.
"Do that," Price said.
"Striker out."

8

Arthur Doyle towered over the bar. He clutched his beer—the day's first—anxious to suck it down. The first always went down quickly; the other dozen or so, he savored. The Irish brew, brown and thick, rolled down his throat, and created a warm spot in his gut.

The big man slammed the empty mug onto the bar, then gestured at the bartender for a refill. In the meantime, out of habit, he stared at the mirror that ran the length of the bar and checked out his surroundings. A pair of women, their figures lithe, twirled around poles. Men gathered around the elevated dancing platforms.

When the next beer arrived, he hefted it and dropped onto the bar stool. A fine state of affairs this is, he thought. Can't even enjoy a beer without watching my fucking back the whole time. A veil of depression fell over him, and he tried to drown it by guzzling half the pint.

He set the beer on the bar and dragged a thick forearm dotted with freckles over his lips to sop away the remnants. The hair on the back of his neck stood up. He swigged more beer and scanned the room behind him. He spotted the young man, tall and lanky, his face pinched with anger, as he navigated the crowd. Sure, his height made him stand out. But what really separated him from other patrons was the purpose he moved with. He cut a straight line through the assembled drunks, shouldering more than one of them out of his path and ignoring their protests as he continued forward.

Doyle felt a familiar flutter of excitement in his stomach as the man closed in on him. He could tell when someone was looking for a fight, especially with him. He'd be only too happy to oblige the SOB.

He swiveled on the bar stool, exposing his left side. The beer mug remained in his grip. Out of sight, his right hand drifted under the tails of his floral print shirt. He rested his palm on the butt of a Browning Hi-Power kept there, and waited.

A couple of his thugs started for the man. Doyle gestured for them to halt. A Chinese woman—an acquisition from one of Chiun's snakeheads—stopped dancing on her platform, covered her mouth with her hand as she saw the confrontation unfold.

The Colombian man stepped from the crowd and halted less than five yards from the big Irishman. The young man's chest heaved, though Doyle guessed more from anger than exertion. His arm hung straight at his side. A machete, the edge nicked, the metal's gleam extinguished by years of hard use, protruded from his fist.

Doyle grinned. "Help you, lad?"

"I'm looking for you!" the young man bellowed.

"And aren't I lucky for it?" Another drink. "Spit it out, boy. What do you want with old Artie Doyle?"

"My sister," the young man said, "you brought her in here. Fed her poison and caused her to sin."

Doyle flicked his gaze around the room, then settled it back on the Colombian. He gave him an easy smile. "Lots of sin here, my friend."

The man took a step forward. A couple of Doyle's guards started for the man, but Doyle waved them off again.

"You turned her into filth," the man said. "Destroyed her."

Doyle tipped back the mug, drained it. As he lowered it, he stared over the rim at the man. "Your lady got a name?"

The man spit out the name. Doyle searched through the light fog enshrouding his brain. He quickly realized he couldn't remember the woman, or even whether it'd been his club she'd worked at. There'd been so damn many of the little harlots….

To hell with it. It was a slow day, he thought.

He flashed the guy a lecherous grin.

"Sure," he said. "I remember. Nice little piece of ass, that one."

He set the mug on the bar, then waited for the other man to make his move.

BOLAN DRIFTED THROUGH THE crowd and advanced upon the bar. An untouched bottle of beer sweated in his hand.

He saw the young man standing before Doyle and caught the glint of lights reflecting off the machete's blade.

He keyed his throat mike.

"Jack," he said, "you see what I see?"

"You mean Doyle's barber?"

"Right."

"Got him. Seems like a complication."

"Fair assessment."

"Good guy or a bad guy?"

"Hard to tell," Bolan replied. "Can't hear a damn word the guy's saying."

"If he hates Doyle, he can't be all bad."

"Just watch him. Judging by the way he's dressed and his weapon, he's not one of Doyle's men. So he stays safe until we have reason to think otherwise."

"In the meantime?"

"Follow my lead. It's about to go bad."

BOLAN HAD COME TO THE club ready for war.

A Desert Eagle rode on his left hip, holstered butt-first in a cross-draw position. The Beretta was snug inside a shoulder holster under his right arm. In an unzipped canvas bag that hung from his right shoulder, he carried an MP-5. As he neared Doyle, his hand dipped inside the bag and he fisted the small submachine gun.

Bolan came within twenty feet of the big Irishman. A thicket of thugs, waitresses and bar patrons had formed a ring around Doyle. The soldier shouldered his way into the wall of people, trying to close in on the unfolding conflict to get a better look.

"Jack," he said into his throat mike.

"Go."

"Too many people. If someone starts shooting—"

"Let me thin the herd."

Bolan waited several seconds.

A rapid patter suddenly sounded from the opposite side of the club. A heartbeat later, the music went dead. In the sudden silence, the gunfire became more pronounced, followed by screams from panicked patrons. Bolan saw Grimaldi, his Uzi spitting fire as he wove his way between tables.

The hail of bullets shredded the glass of an aquarium built into the wall. A cascade of water, glass and piranhas spilled onto the floor.

Patrons, their thirst for conflict satiated, surged away from the bar and headed for the fire exits at the rear of the building.

A couple of Doyle's thugs, guns drawn, headed toward the disturbance. Others stayed with their boss, ready to save him if he was too drunk to outshoot or outfight the Colombian.

"Incoming," Bolan said into his throat mike.

He turned his attention back to Doyle and saw the man bringing up a Browning Hi-Power. The Colombian, now faced with a pistol, threw his machete at Doyle and launched into a sprint away from the big Irishman. The machete's tip buried itself a couple of inches in a square wooden support column that stretched from floor to ceiling.

Bolan saw Doyle flinch, but the man reacted like a pro. He swung the Browning toward the fleeing local man and drew a bead on him.

Bolan brought up the MP-5, prepared to shout a warning at him.

Two men fell across the soldier's vision. Moving side by side, pistols raised, they were ready to take the warrior out. He whirled toward them, the MP-5 blazing. The fusillade of bullets from Bolan's SMG cut the men down.

The sudden flash of gunfire to his right caused Doyle to spin in the Executioner's direction. The soldier's MP-5 was swinging toward Doyle.

In an instant, Doyle sized up the situation and made his move. Flame lashed out from the Browning's muzzle several times, as the Irishman dived from his bar stool. Whether because of surprise or alcohol, Doyle's shots whizzed inches past Bolan. Doyle hit the ground hard and rolled.

A ragged line of thugs were closing in on Bolan. He locked eyes with the man closest to him and folded at the knees just as the man squeezed off a burst from a small gun. Bolan's MP-5 spewed a line of slugs that stitched the man from right hip to left pectoral. Even as the man folded to the ground, a second gunner fell across the warrior's line of sight. He hesitated for a heart-beat as he watched his comrade fall to the ground. While he took in the view, Bolan already had locked in on him. The small machine gun chugged out more rounds and scythed the gunner to the ground.

Doyle, up and on his feet again, grabbed big handfuls of the third guy's jacket. With a powerful twist of his torso, he heaved the man in Bolan's direction. The man stumbled, tried to simul-taneously recover his balance and draw a bead on the Executioner.

In the same instant, Doyle was on the move, knocking over chairs and tables as he went, leaving an obstacle course of upturned furniture.

A relentless burst from the Executioner's MP-5 pierced the off-balance thug's torso. Eyes wide and jaw slack, he was dead by the time he hit the ground.

The MP-5 spent, Bolan dropped it and drew the Desert Eagle and the Beretta. A yellow rectangle popped into view and cut through the darkness. Bolan instantly recognized it as a door opening to the outside. An instant later, a big silhouette filled the doorway, then disappeared just as quickly. From his six, a strobe of orange-yellow muzzle-flashes and the accompanying rattle of a submachine gun ripped his attention from the fleeing man, if only for a second. The gunfire partially illuminated Grimaldi as his weapon loosed an unforgiving onslaught of autofire that cut a horizontal arc through a knot of Doyle's fighters. Bolan saw the pilot race past the dead thugs and head his way.

Bolan broke into a run and headed for the back door. Shat-tered glass cracked beneath his boots. The ring of gunfire con-tinued to sound in his ears. His gaze darted around as he watched for an ambush. From what he could see, only he and Grimaldi remained upright.

The pilot had fallen into step behind him. "Doyle?" Grimaldi asked.

"Went out the back," Bolan replied.

"Got a plan?"

"Find him, capture him. Kill him if we have to."

"No problem," the pilot said.

When they reached the door, Grimaldi set a hand on the release bar.

"I'll go," Bolan said.

The pilot nodded. He raised the Uzi and opened the door. Bolan dropped into a crouch and darted through the door, just in time to see Doyle fling a car door open. The soldier raised the Beretta and squeezed off a quick triburst that hammered through the vehicle's rear windshield.

Doyle spun. His hand came up, clutching a pistol. He squeezed off several quick shots that whistled past Bolan's head, forcing him to break off his approach. Grimaldi unloaded with the Uzi and the slugs hammered into the concrete and threw chips into the air.

Bolan was positioned about forty-five degrees to Doyle's right, and he had the bastard dead in his sights.

"Drop it, Doyle," the Executioner shouted. "You can't hit both of us."

The Irishman swung the gun toward Bolan, but halted when he realized Bolan had the drop on him. He glanced back at Grimaldi who also was positioned to take him down with the stroke of a trigger. His face turned bright red and his nostrils flared like those of an angry bull.

Bolan let a couple of tense seconds pass. Doyle was pissed, but he was outgunned. Judging by the barely concealed rage on his face, he already knew it.

Doyle dropped the weapon and raised his hands.

9

Bly slipped his laptop into a leather carrying case, lifted the bag and looped the strap over his right shoulder. He carried the bag across the room and placed it next to his other luggage, which waited next to the door leading into his temporary quarters. Marc Haley, seated in an armchair, watched the other man prepare to leave.

"Maybe I should go, too," Haley said.

"No," Bly said. "You're staying here to deal with this problem. You and your people need to take out this man who's been tearing through our various operations."

Haley licked his lips. "He may not come here."

"He will," Bly replied without looking at the other man. "If they've got Doyle, then this man's coming here. Doyle probably hasn't given me up yet, but he will. When he does, I want to be gone."

"What about Serrano?"

Bly shrugged. "Give her to the doctor. See what he can learn, if anything. At this point, the U.S. government is gunning for me, which means I have no choice but to leave. If we can find the laptop, fine. But it's become a secondary concern to me."

With his cell phone, Bly called for someone to take his bags out to the private jet waiting on the tarmac, alongside two others. When he finished the call, he snapped the phone closed and returned it to his belt.

"If recovering the agent is this man's primary job, then perhaps leaving her here will buy me some time," Bly said.

"Time for what?"

"To get the hell out of here," Bly said.

"If he survives," Haley offered. "He'd have to get through a lot of guys to get to her. He can't do it."

Bly turned to the other man and nodded in agreement. "Regardless, I want to be long gone. If he wants to find me, he'll have to start at ground zero. Fortunately, no one knows where I'm going at this point. Or almost no one. You know, of course, because you checked my flight plan."

The gun seemed to appear in Bly's hand out of nowhere. Haley saw it, but it took a moment before what was about to happen sunk into his brain. When it did, his mouth opened to protest. The pistol cracked once and a bullet crashed into Haley's forehead and exploded out the back of his skull, splattering its contents on the wall behind him.

Bly holstered the gun and drew his jacket back over it. He made a mental note to have someone clean and reload the weapon during the flight. He gave Haley one last look. The man's head had lolled to one side, and Bly noted the indentation that interrupted the curve of the back of Haley's skull. He hadn't wanted to kill Haley, not at this stage at least. He was a useful tool. But Bly knew that the man bought and sold information like some people traded stocks and bonds. And, if this man who'd been burning his way through Bly's operations got to Haley—he wouldn't, but just in case he did—Bly didn't want him offering any information in exchange for his life. So it was best to eliminate him as a variable and move on to the next phase of operations.

HIS ARMS CROSSED OVER his chest, Bolan leaned against a wall in the interrogation room at the police station. At a wooden table, its surface scarred by countless gouges and scratches, sat Arthur Doyle. The big Irishman stared at Bolan as he leaned back in his chair and stroked his beard with his thumb and index finger. If being in the custody of a man who'd just killed ten of his thugs bothered Doyle, he gave no outward sign.

"Did you drag me in here just to look at me?" Doyle asked. "Really, I could've mailed you a picture and saved us all a lot of trouble. And a lot of blood."

Smiling, he leveled the chair. He leaned forward, trapped a pack of cigarettes on the tabletop underneath one of his hands and dragged it to him.

"Really, lad, if you want to frighten me, you'd better try harder. If the roles were reversed, I'd have you shitting your britches right now. You need to learn how to play the game."

"No game," Bolan said.

"We're all playing a game here, boyo. And don't you think otherwise or you're a damned fool."

"I want answers. Either give them or I'll give you the same retirement package I gave your people back at the Pirhana."

"Be rather hard, considering that you've left your piece in a locker outside our lovely accommodations here."

"I don't need that. Not to take you out. We both know that," the Executioner said.

Something flickered in Doyle's eyes. Bolan guessed that it was a realization that he was dealing with someone unlike anyone he'd ever met before. Doyle opened his mouth to reply, but a loud buzz filled the room and cut him off. A moment later the door opened and Jennifer Simmons entered, a folder clutched to her left breast. Bolan had met her previously at the embassy. She was medium height, pretty with red hair and a trim figure. Bolan had gotten a bad vibe from her, a certain underlying coldness that troubled him.

Doyle gave her an appreciative glance as she entered the room.

"Well, hello, darlin'. You my lawyer by chance? You one of Carlos's girls? Carlos couldn't come down here himself and put an end to all this nonsense? Lazy bastard. I get half the service, he gets all the money."

"Shut up," Simmons said.

This seemed to amuse Doyle. His bushy eyebrows arched in surprise. A laugh burst from his mouth, and he slammed an open palm down on the desk.

"Well, now, aren't you the tough one?" he asked.

"You'll find out how much so."

"Really? And what have you got planned for me. Zap my balls with electrodes? Pull my nails off with pliers? Do your worst, you silly bitch. You can torture me, you can cut off my fingers one by one. I've been burned, cut, shot. Hell, I've gotten to where I rather like it."

Simmons looked down at the Irishman and shook her head sadly.

"I guess the psychological workup we did was right."

"And how's that?" Doyle said.

She fanned open the folder and began leafing through several pages of its contents. Without looking up at him, she said, "Apparently, you like the rough stuff. You're suicidal, but you don't have the guts to kill yourself. You have a definite issue with authority. You especially hate men. And you think women are just toys for your personal gratification."

He grinned.

"Not surprising," she said. "Probably because your daddy was a whore-chasing drunk."

Doyle's face turned scarlet. He popped up from the chair so fast that it fell with a loud clatter. Bolan tensed, ready to tear into the man if he became violent.

"You little slut!" Doyle screamed. His index finger stabbed in her direction as he spoke. "You don't know what the hell you're talking about! You keep talking like that, and I'll strangle the life out of you, you little bitch!"

Bolan came off the wall. His hands hung loose at his sides. He'd had enough of this blustery loser, and was ready to drop him.

Before he could make a move, Simmons, with an almost casual gesture, tossed a folder onto the tabletop hard enough that its contents came free and spread out over the surface. Bolan saw several photographs. Each depicted a child or teenager of various genders. And in at least two of the shots, he saw a pretty Colombian woman with the children, all of them smiling.

Doyle froze. He gawked at the pictures spread out before him. His hands folded up into fists, the knuckles red, the skin around them pale, save for brownish freckles that dotted the backs of his hands.

He looked up, his expression a mixture of confusion and rage.

"Recognize them?" Simmons asked.

"How did you get these?" Doyle asked.

"Camera."

"Bitch, you know what I mean!"

Though it hadn't been laid out for him, Bolan instinctively knew what was happening. Simmons was applying a lever, one that Bolan never would have touched. He felt his stomach turn in disgust, but he held his tongue.

"Nice kids," Simmons said. "If you take one step toward me, if you say something I don't like or believe, even if it's true, something bad could happen to them."

"God damn you!"

Doyle grabbed one edge of the table and flung it aside. Simmons took a step back. The Irishman lunged at her, his right fist raised over his head.

Bolan was on him in a heartbeat. His fist rocketed forward and collided with Doyle's jaw. The surprise impact knocked the IRA man off course, causing him to stumble into the upended table. His legs became entangled with those of the overturned table. He lost his balance and plummeted to the floor.

Bolan dropped to one knee next to Doyle. He buried his fist in the man's eye socket. Doyle's skull hit the floor with a resounding thud.

Before he could recover, Bolan grabbed an arm, rolled him onto his belly and bound his hands with plastic cuffs. Doyle strained against the bonds, writhed around on the floor, cursed them. Simmons crossed the room, scooping up a couple of the snapshots along the way. When she reached Doyle, she dropped them where he could see them.

"Where's Haley?" Simmons asked.

Suddenly Doyle's body went limp, save for his chest heaving as he tried to catch his breath. He rested his head on the right side. Blood that had dripped from his nose and lips pooled on the floor in front of his face.

"Where is he?" she asked once more.

He told her what he knew.

"WHAT THE HELL WAS THAT?" Bolan snapped.

"What?" Simmons asked sharply. She had righted the table

and was kneeling next to it, gathering up the fallen photos and papers that littered the floor.

"The kids," Bolan replied. "You threatened them to get at him."

She shrugged but didn't look up at him. "So?"

She slipped the photos and papers back into a file folder that she was sliding into a large white envelope.

"That's not how it's done," Bolan said.

With narrowed eyes, she looked up at him, brushing a stray lock of hair from her vision. "Really? And just how is it done? Before I came in, I listened to you on the intercom. You threatened to kill him. How's what I did any different?"

"He's a killer," Bolan said. "A terrorist. But his children are just that. Leave them alone."

She got to her feet. Setting the envelope on the table, she crossed her arms over her chest and stared defiantly at him.

"Look," she said, "they've got an agent out there—one carrying classified information—being held prisoner. I've got Washington breathing down my neck to get her back. The South American station chief already authorized me to take, and I quote, 'all means necessary to effect the rescue of Maria Serrano.' If that means killing his illegitimate kids to accomplish that, then fine. I've got the stomach for it. It's the only soft spot I found in his profile."

"I could've made him talk," the soldier replied. "He just needed the proper motivation."

"That being?"

"His life."

She threw up her hands and rolled her eyes. "I told you," she said, "He is suicidal. He doesn't care if he dies. Read the dossier. He doesn't care whether he lives or dies. Why don't you get that?"

"He's a hired gun. His only loyalty is to whoever's paying him. That kind always talks. Always," Bolan said.

She gave him a pitying look. "You can't work that way anymore. Not now. You play like they do. Doing anything else is naive. So if I have to bend the rules—"

"Bend the rules," Bolan said. "Break laws. I'm not talking about that. I'm talking about doing what's right. Your cure's worse than the sickness. I won't allow any more of this crap."

The woman parted her lips to say something, but as best as Bolan could tell, she thought better of it and stayed silent. Gathering her things, she spun on a heel and left the room.

BOLAN HAD COMMANDEERED the ambassador's office and a secure phone so he could call Stony Man Farm for an update. Thanks to the Farm's massive data-mining capabilities, Kurtzman had compiled a dossier on the soldier's next target. Bolan paced the floor and listened to the computer expert's briefing.

"Haley's an information merchant," Kurtzman said. "He runs a private intelligence-gathering operation out of Bogotá, and his network of sources is fairly impressive. So is his customer list, which includes Mossad and the intelligence operations of most major countries. But it looks like he does have a burn notice here from the CIA. Apparently, he sold them some crap at some point in his career. He used to work for the State Department's spook operation as an analyst. Then he became the Latin American desk officer shortly after that. State loved him. He was running the fast track for sure."

"Sounds like there's a 'but' coming," Bolan said.

"Right. Several years ago, his boss caught him freelancing. He was passing along sensitive information to a couple of drug dealers, who, unbeknownst to him, also were selling weapons to the Taliban. They drummed him out in the proverbial heartbeat. He went underground for a while, then turned up at some defense-policy think tank in the U.K."

Bolan heard the frenetic clicking on the other end of the line as Kurtzman worked his keyboard. From half a world away, Bolan could envision the man at work, his excitement growing as he found more information about their target.

"Well, well," he muttered.

"What?"

"Looks like the think tank got its money from an obscure foundation in Maryland. I'll e-mail the information to you. But what's really interesting is when you cross-match the foundation's donor list with a roster of directors of the think tank. Guess who pops up?"

"Albert Bly."

"Damn it, you stole my punch line. Yeah, Bly. Along with a couple of senators, a retired deputy FBI director and another Garrison executive or two. And I just got another report. We've been combing through Bly's travel records, along with Chiun's various travels. Haley made several trips to Hong Kong and Beijing. And apparently they overlap with the others. Not a perfect match, but still interesting."

Bolan stood before one of the floor-to-ceiling bookshelves that lined the office. He studied a line of leather-bound books, noticing that the spines remained smooth, as though the books had never been cracked open. "What else do you have on Haley?"

"Very little, unfortunately. His bank account looks normal. We're searching through Treasury's database for any offshore funds he may have. Same goes for Bly. On that front, my guess is we've hardly scratched the surface. These guys likely have their money tied up in offshore black accounts, ones not easily accessed by snoops like me. The deeper we go, the more paper we find. It may be a couple more hours before we can sort through everything."

"No worries. My guess is it's more than enough evidence to tie them together. At least for my purposes," Bolan said.

"Yeah, it's not like you're taking them to trial or anything."

"Not even close."

10

"You think you can do this without killing me?" Bolan asked.

"Honestly?" Grimaldi replied, his voice clear in the headphones.

"Never mind," Bolan replied.

Crouched in a ravine, the big American focused his attention on the hardsite that lay outside Bogotá. According to Kurtzman, the facility was once a military airbase. Aided by binoculars, the soldier sized it up. The entire complex encompassed about thirty acres.

Though allegedly abandoned for at least five years, it teemed with life. Guards armed with assault rifles whizzed about the grounds on all-terrain vehicles. A pair of Stryker vehicles lumbered over the roads that snaked through the compound. Satellite dishes and antennas bristled from a multistory building that Bolan recognized as the air-traffic control tower. Three single-story, sand-colored buildings stood opposite the terminal. He pegged one as the motor pool and guessed that the others served as barracks or offices, though he couldn't be sure.

Two Gulfstream executive jets stood ready on the tarmac, one in front of the other. The air around the first jet's engines shimmered with waves of heat.

According to Doyle, the base was where Serrano was probably being held. Technically, Bly occupied the complex full-time and populated it with a dozen or so technicians and analysts. He also kept a few guards on hand.

The Executioner heard the distant sound of a helicopter's rotor blades. Through the binoculars, he saw one guard whip his head in the direction of the approaching aircraft. He swatted his partner on the arm to get his attention. The guy nodded, spit out his cigarette and brought a two-way radio to his mouth.

The guard, his assault rifle at the ready, dropped into a crouch, ready to fire.

Thunder pealed from above, heralded by machine-gun fire.

Suddenly, a swarm of bullets tore into the ground a foot or so from Bolan's position, kicking up geysers of dirt and grass in a horizontal swath before him.

A second pass likely would eviscerate him.

He swung the Barrett toward the tower. Through the scope, he spotted the shooter, his lips pulled back in a grin as he rained down fire and death. Bolan aimed his Barrett. The big gun boomed once and wiped the grin off the shooter's face. Permanently.

The Executioner slung the Barrett over his shoulder and took up the Mark 6 rifle. The Apache helicopter piloted by Grimaldi streaked overhead.

Bolan felt the downwash push on him like an invisible hand. Even as it passed, he climbed out of the ravine and surged toward the complex.

Three all-terrain vehicles shot out from between the cluster of buildings and raced toward Bolan, flames shooting out from their gun barrels.

The Apache's .30-caliber machine guns flamed to life. The cannons delivered a blistering barrage that scythed through the gunners who'd been careless enough to cluster together. A couple of shooters had leaped free from the slaughter, and continued to pelt the Apache with small-arms fire as it zoomed by.

Bolan moved within a dozen or so yards of the shooters. He dropped to one knee and drew a bead on them. The Mark 6 chugged out a relentless onslaught of fire and fury that struck down the gunners.

Even as the big American reloaded, he saw twin Hellfire missiles leap from the Apache and pound into one of the Gulfstream jets that stood on the runway. The rounds cracked the fuselage and columns of flame burst from the craft's interior. Moments later, the flames and heat reached the fuel tanks and a second explosion ripped through the craft with an ear-shattering roar. Fire enveloped the jet, sending out thick plumes of oily black smoke.

An instant later, a pair of black vans surged from between two buildings. The side doors flew open and at least a half dozen men disembarked from the vehicles.

11

Bolan reached the main building. He dropped into a crouch and surveyed its exterior. Steel doors and barred windows cut off access to the outside world. Waist-high concrete barriers rose from the ground and made a direct approach toward the doors impossible. Bolan knew this was to prevent attackers from ramming their vehicle through the front door.

His assault rifle at his shoulder, the soldier uncoiled from the ground and surged toward the building. A heartbeat later, he heard glass shatter from above. A stolen glance told him that an assault rifle poked out of the building, and was being maneuvered to get a good shot at him. Autofire erupted from the weapon. The punishing blasts of gunfire chewed it into the concrete pad where the big American stood. Bolan raised the muzzle of his own rifle, squeezed off a couple of quick bursts that hammered into the building's exterior, but missed the shooter by several feet. At the same time, the front doors slid into recessed spaces within the walls. Gunmen, their bodies wrapped around the door frames, came partially into view.

Without slowing, the soldier turned at the waist and fired his grenade launcher. A high-explosive round hissed forth and cleaved through the yawning doorway. An explosion thundered from within the building, thick black smoke pouring from the interior.

In the meantime, autofire from above continued to lash at Bolan. He darted left a few paces, sprinted at a forty-five-degree angle to the right, then repeated the pattern once more before his movements brought him to the closest cover, a large white panel van. When he reached cover, the warrior crouched and thumbed another HE round into the grenade launcher.

Thick waves of gunfire pounded the vehicle. Slugs pierced its metallic skin and drilled through windows and shredded the tires. The vehicle dropped onto the wheel rims and teetered slightly to the right.

Bolan keyed his headset. "Jack!"

"Go."

"I'm pinned down over here. I need some air support."

"On it."

Seconds later, the soldier heard the thumping of chopper blades, the growl of the war bird's engines as Grimaldi guided the aircraft toward him. The chopper hovered over Bolan and jagged tongues of flame leaped from the muzzles of the chopper's machine guns. With the first few bursts, the hammering of bullets against the van seemed to stop. Ignoring the downward pressure from the rotor wash, Bolan edged along the van until he reached the rear. He chanced a look around the vehicle and saw the relentless fusillade of bullets hammering into the building's exterior.

Several moments later, the guns went silent. The windows that had served as perches for the killers looked as though they'd been torn apart by the jaws of a great white shark. Pockmarks left by the bullets peppered whatever hadn't been pulverized by the on-slaught of concentrated fire.

"I think they're all dead," Grimaldi said.

"Safe bet," Bolan replied.

"I'll give you some cover while you make a break for the building."

"Roger that."

Bolan surged out from behind the van. Legs pumping furiously, he advanced on the building, the M4 held at waist level. One of Bly's handmen stepped out from behind a concrete support column, his submachine gun stuttering a searing line of tracking fire that cut its way toward Bolan.

The Executioner cut loose with the M-4, sweeping it in a tight arc. The fusillade slammed into Bolan's attacker and cut a jagged line across his torso. From the corner of his eye, Bolan caught a second fighter pop up from behind the cover of a concrete planter.

The Executioner loosed a fast burst that drove the man back behind cover. Before the soldier could try another shot, the Apache's automatic weapons chattered again and rained down a firestorm of bullets that quickly disintegrated the guy's cover. The thug darted from his position and almost immediately found himself enveloped in a fatal swarm of lead.

When Bolan entered the building, he found himself in a big room about half the size of a high-school gymnasium. A television, its screen shattered by gunfire, sparked. Tiles had been ripped loose, exposing large patches of the concrete floor underneath, a weird mosaic of white and gray camouflage. A big desk, like those found in the lobbies of office towers, stood in the middle of the room. Bolan approached it, mindful to step over the clusters of spent brass and the chunks of plaster that covered the floor.

From somewhere near the desk, he heard what he thought was someone groaning. He brought the assault rifle to his shoulder and headed for the desk. As he moved, he noted blood splotches on the floor. Most were smooth, though a couple had been broken by a footprint. The blood trail wound around the circumference of the desk, disappearing from view.

Bolan glanced over the desk at a bank of elevators that stood directly behind the security desk, each separated by a floor-to-ceiling mirror. In one of the mirrors, he spotted the man, crouched below the desk. His sweat-drenched hair was matted against his head, and his mouth hung open as though he were panting. His shooting hand rested on his knee, the muzzle of his weapon pointed at the aperture leading inside the security area.

Bolan took a couple of steps forward. "Drop the gun," he said. "Toss it out onto the floor."

"Go to hell!" the guy yelled.

"Your funeral," Bolan said. "I'll light up a cigarette, sit here and watch you bleed to death. Beats the hell out of TV."

The guy swore at him again.

"Your call, tough guy. I'm not the one bleeding to death. I can bandage you up, maybe increase your chances of leaving alive."

After several seconds, the guy swore again, this time with less gusto. He tossed his handgun over the lip of the desk.

"Good choice," Bolan said.

The soldier slung the M-4 and drew the Beretta. When he reached the wounded man, he saw him lying on his side, both hands in view. The warrior knelt next to him, took a compress from a compartment on his combat suit and held it up so the man could see it.

"Give me that," the guard said.

Bolan shook his head. "Where's the woman?"

"Bandage me up and I'll tell you."

"You've got it backward. Is she in this building?"

"Sublevel three. My key card is in my shirt pocket."

"Room?"

The man told him.

Bolan applied the compress to the wounded man's shoulder. In less than a minute, he'd secured it with medical tape. He did likewise with a bullet wound to the man's stomach. The guard winced, inhaled sharply, but said nothing. He lay there and watched Bolan work, but his eyes became increasingly less focused and occasionally closed for several seconds before they'd snap back open.

"The woman," Bolan asked, "is she okay?"

"Hard to tell," the man said, his words slurred. "The boss brought someone in to talk to her. Hear he's a real freak. Who knows what happened to her?"

The man laid his head back on the floor. Within seconds, he'd slipped into unconsciousness. Taking his key card, Bolan headed for the elevators.

SERRANO WATCHED AS A big European everyone called Krotnic unlocked the final cuff and slipped the shackles from her wrists. She rubbed at the red rings that marked her skin where the cuffs had been. The big man backed away from her and tossed the cuffs to the side. He stood somewhere behind her and seized her arm while another man, wearing a leather apron, set a suitcase on the floor.

She took a moment to size up the newcomer. He stood maybe an inch or two taller than her. His mouse brown hair was combed back from his forehead and lacquered against his skull was some kind of hair gel. He had what seemed to be a lipless mouth.

His dime-sized eyes traveled over her, and she swore she could feel his gaze brush over her skin, an unwanted, ice-cold caress. He stepped within a few feet of her, but seemed reluctant to get too close. He slipped his glasses from his face and rubbed one of the lenses clean with a fabric of his shirt.

He walked over to the suitcase, then knelt beside it. The first lock opened with a click, followed by the second. The lid of the big case came up. For several moments, he studied the contents, humming under his breath as he did. Serrano felt a hollow pit of fear open in her stomach as she watched him. What the hell was he up to?

Finally, he brought out a towel so white that it seemed to gleam under the artificial light. He laid it on the floor, unfolded it and smoothed out the wrinkles with an open palm. Swerving back toward the case, his hands stabbed back inside and came out clutching a pair of pliers. He laid them on the towel. He returned again to the case and came out with a small acetylene torch. When Serrano saw it, her knees turned rubbery, her head suddenly felt light. When his hands came back into view, he clutched a small surgical saw, its metal frame gleaming.

He arranged the tools slowly, deliberately, on the towel. At the same time, he spoke. His voice had an authoritative tone, as though he were delivering a lecture to a group of medical students.

"I can tell you're a fighter," he said. "And I've always found that fascinating. It's really little more than the human equivalent of the alpha dog. Everything they encounter, they must dominate. There's no reason, no selectivity. They simply have a single reaction hardwired into their brain for every situation they encounter, a reaction that they repeat ad infinitum, regardless of previous consequences. Or the odds of it working in their current situation."

His hand reached out, his fingers encircling the handle on the surgical saw. He held it aloft, poised before him, and seemed to study it. Stealing a glance in her direction, he broke into a grin.

Was her terror that obvious? she wondered.

"Those who use this approach, they use it to cover for something else," he continued. "Poor self-esteem. Feelings of inadequacy. What they don't know is—"

A phone trilled from behind Serrano. The man stopped in mid-sentence, his irritation palpable. Serrano felt the iron grip on her left arm ease as Krotnic's hand drew away.

"Leave it," the guy in apron snapped. "I'm working."

"Fuck you," Krotnic said.

The phone beeped. Her other arm was released. Black motion blurred to her right, spurring her to sharply inhale. A handgun's hammer clicked in her ear. It took a moment before she realized that weapon was being aimed at the man with the saw, not her.

The little man froze.

"Yeah?" Krotnic said. He listened for a couple of seconds and took a step forward, seemingly ignoring her. She saw his face turn into a mask of rage. "Shit! Where are they? Send green team. What? All of them?"

He pushed her aside and looked at the man in the apron. "Someone's hitting us," he said. "We must go up and help."

"But we need to interrogate her."

"Later. Grab a gun and let's go."

"I haven't got a gun. I don't use them."

The bigger man glowered. "You're going to now."

"I. Don't. Use. Them."

"Fine. Stay here, you fucking freak. I'll remember this," Krotnic shouted.

The man in the apron stared after the other man for a couple of heartbeats. Then, with a shrug, he turned and started back toward Serrano. She saw a syringe protruding from between the first two fingers of his hand. The ball of his thumb rested on the top of the plunger.

"It's better this way," he said. "Trust me."

Serrano knew she needed to act fast and without hesitation, but wondered whether she could muster the strength from her battered, exhausted body. She'd get one shot. Two, if she was lucky. Considering her run the past twenty-four hours, she had little faith in good fortune at this point.

He moved within a couple of feet. She shrank back, allowed herself to drop to one knee. This put her line of sight at just about belt-buckle level.

"One little shot, and you won't be able to move," he said. His voice was soft, as though soothing a frightened child. "That always makes these sessions…easier."

She waited until he was on her and her hand fired out, her knuckles sinking into the softness of his groin.

A sharp intake of air from above alerted her that she'd hit the right spot. He froze, then dropped a hand over his crotch protectively. He stabbed wildly at her with the syringe. The needle caught the fabric of her shirtsleeve, penetrated it, but whispered past the skin of her bicep. He yanked it free and drew back his hand for another try. Face contorted with pain, he stumbled closer even as she shot up to her full height. She snapped her head forward. Their foreheads collided and a bright flash of white exploded behind her eyes.

His body suddenly sagged, and he collapsed to the floor.

She kicked the syringe, and it skidded over the concrete and into a corner.

She rubbed her forehead and stared down at him. Get the hell out of here! her mind screamed. What the hell are you waiting for? Her eyes traveled over him, pausing at his fingers, which were unnaturally long, his nails manicured. What horrors, what pain had he inflicted on others with them? If she let him live, what would he do to someone else? A tide of rage rose within her and drowned out the panicked voice that clamored for her to ignore him and escape. Moving to his suitcase, she grabbed a scalpel and returned to him. Seconds later the weapon jutted from a ragged, sucking wound. Blood, warm and sticky, covered her hand. She wiped it on his apron, then rose to her feet.

The sound of footfalls in the outside corridor reached her. She whirled and saw that two small blocks of shadow interrupted the line of white light that ran along the bottom of the door. Someone was out there.

THE ELEVATOR DOORS SLID APART, and Bolan found himself face-to-face with a guard wearing a Hawaiian shirt and toting an Uzi. The man swung the machine pistol in Bolan's direction. The warrior took a step forward and triggered the Beretta. The handgun sighed once and a Parabellum round drilled a small hole into the man's forehead. Bolan came through the door, the Beretta clasped in both hands, and stepped over the twitching corpse, his weapon searching for the next target.

His combat senses screamed for him to turn left. He whipped around just in time to spot a gangly man, who resembled a praying mantis, trying to draw down on him from behind the cover of a large concrete support column. Three shots from the Beretta drilled into the circular support column and pocked its once-smooth surface. The shots forced the man to ground. In the meantime, the big American snagged a flash-bang grenade from his web gear. He yanked out the pin with his teeth and tossed the weapon at the other man.

The explosion echoed through the chamber.

Bolan started for the other man. Disoriented, he'd stumbled out from behind the column. The Executioner tapped out a pair of bursts that ripped into the man's chest, causing rosy geysers of blood to spring up. His body crumpled to the floor.

Bolan wheeled around and headed for the corridor. Occasionally, he heard a muffled thump that shook the walls and broke loose bits of mortar, sent them showering to the ground.

"Striker to Ace," Bolan said into his throat mike.

"Go."

"I've got a lock on our friend," he said. "Going to roust her now."

"Roger that. I guess you'll be needing a lift."

"If it's not too much trouble."

"Least I can do, seeing as how I just destroyed the motor pool and all."

"I've been trying to make a beeline to her," Bolan said. "That means I haven't had time to clear out all the opposition before I get there."

"Meaning your rear flank's exposed," Grimaldi said.

"Yeah. Can't be helped, though. Last thing we need is to go

through all of this, then have Bly or one of his people decide to kill her."

"Right. If you get pinned down, let me know. I can come in behind these bastards and we'll take them out in the cross fire."

"Exactly. I'll be in touch. Striker out."

Bolan had moved a short distance down the corridor. Up ahead he saw that the passage ended and split off into two other directions, forming a T. Recalling the injured man's directions, he continued down the hallway. He spotted a big man several yards ahead, gun drawn and headed for Serrano's cell.

The warrior made his move.

KROTNIC SEETHED WITH RAGE as he went to get the woman.

Though he'd been angry at the little freak Bly had imported, now he was ready to kill Bly himself. If the bastard didn't owe him money—

Minutes ago, he'd received an urgent call from Bly via two-way radio. The dumb bastard had ordered him to go back, retrieve Serrano and take her to the underground monorail station so he could move her out. The rail system had been installed to safely ferry government officials and visiting dignitaries to the tarmac. With kidnappings and assassinations by FARC rebels a regular occurrence, Haley and Bly regularly used it to come and go, minimizing their exposure to surveillance satellites or rifle scopes.

The Serb reached the cell and unlocked it. He steeled himself to see something awful. He wasn't at all squeamish, having raped and tortured people himself. But he wasn't sure how much damage the little sadist had done to the woman, and Krotnic wondered whether she'd be in any shape for an unexpected departure.

Before he could open the door, thunder rolled from above and the lights winked out. The emergency lights recessed into the floorboards winked on. Shit, he thought, they hit the fucking power plant. Whoever was up there was doing a number on this place.

He opened the door.

His eyes came to rest on the woman, crouched on the floor, her gaze leveled at him. She held a scalpel out in front of her, like a sword, and seemed coiled and ready to strike. The Glock leveled before him, he drew down on her. He stole a glance at the freak, who lay on his stomach, arms sprawled out. Blood had pooled around his head.

"You must come with me," he said.

"Go to hell," she said.

He saw something in her eyes, recognizing it immediately. The torture had driven her to her limits, left her thinking she had nothing left to lose. He guessed that she was exhausted, physically and emotionally. Crushed spiritually. She probably thought it was better to go for broke. End it here and now.

Truth be told, he thought, she was right. But she also had little to gain, other than a merciful death if he shot her to stop her charge. But he needn't shoot her. He could handle a woman. He holstered the pistol and balled his fists.

"Come, then," he said.

A shadowy figure suddenly snaked out of the darkness and descended upon him, a black mass of strength and speed. Something as hard as iron encircled his neck and squeezed so hard he swore his head would separate from his spine. His hands scrambled and grabbed at the forearm. At the same time he realized with cold horror that he couldn't breathe. Digging powerful legs into the floor, he tried to push back against his attacker. He hoped to push hard enough to knock the person off balance so he could land on top and show his attacker a real fight.

The bastard didn't budge. Block spots began to swim before Krotnic's eyes, and his thoughts seemed to slow. Suddenly a white-hot bolt of pain lanced into his rib cage, a perfect foil to the cold sensation of suffocation. From somewhere distant he heard something crack, felt the pain in his chest only grow hotter. He tried to scream but emitted only a gurgle.

ONCE BOLAN TWISTED THE knife and broke a rib, he drove it deeper into the other man's chest until he was sure the point found his prey's heart. The man gurgled and his head lolled to one side. Blood frothed at his lips and his body went limp.

Bolan released his grip and the man dropped.

He looked at the woman and, despite the bruises and the

hollow-eyed stare, he recognized her as Maria Serrano. She still held the blade and remained in a crouch. Bolan had no doubt that, at the slightest provocation, she'd lunge at him.

He held up his hands in a gesture of surrender. When he did, rivulets of the other man's blood trailed down his left forearm.

"Ms. Serrano? I'm an American. I'm here to get you out of here."

She stared at Bolan for what seemed like forever. Doubtless, the abuse had left her shell-shocked, guarded. And he guessed that it'd only get worse for her as the shock wore off.

Without a word, she fell in behind him.

12

Two hours later, Bolan was seated in the living room of a safe-house, located several blocks from the American Embassy. Blankets pinned to the walls hung over the windows. Threadbare carpet covered the floors. Cigarette burn marks marred the couch Bolan rested on and the coffee table positioned before him.

He'd fieldstripped, cleaned and reassembled his weapons. They rested on an oilcloth spread out over the table and next to a secure satellite phone. Though he couldn't see them, the soldier knew a small contingent of Delta Force commandos, all armed but dressed in civilian clothes, were positioned outside.

Serrano had demanded that she be brought to a safehouse, rather than the embassy. Bolan had agreed. The way he saw it, the woman's former captors probably wanted to either kill or capture her again. Considering Bly's CIA connections, the Executioner figured it best to avoid the embassy, which likely was crawling with spooks.

When Grimaldi and Bolan had reached the house, they'd taken turns watching the woman while the other showered and ate.

The satellite phone rang once. Bolan answered it.

"Yeah."

"Cooper, is that you?" It was Jennifer Simmons.

"Yeah."

"Where the hell are you? Where's Serrano?"

"Not at the embassy."

"No kidding. Tell me where you are."

"No."

"Excuse me?"

"No."

"What the hell do you mean, no? What gives you the right to parachute in here and do whatever the hell you please?" Simmons asked.

"Presidential authority."

The woman made an exasperated sound. "Dumb son of a bitch."

"I'll call if I need something," Bolan said.

She started to say something, and he hung up the phone.

Someone whistled from behind him. He turned, saw Grimaldi leaning against the door frame, a can of soda clutched in his hand.

The pilot wore an ear-to-ear grin. "That your girlfriend at the embassy?" he asked.

Bolan nodded. "She wants me."

"You silver-tongued devil." Grimaldi stepped into the room. Serrano, barefoot but clad in jeans and a flannel shirt that seemed several sizes too big, followed close behind. She hugged herself as she found her way to an armchair. Her hair was still wet. She looked at Grimaldi, then Bolan.

Bolan flashed her a tight smile. "You okay?"

"Medic says I'm dehydrated, and I feel like one big bruise. But, otherwise, I'll be fine."

"How about your head? Those guys played pretty rough with you," Bolan said quietly.

Her expression hardened. Anger flashed in her eyes. "You mean am I going to fly into hysterics? You think that's how I operate?"

Bolan shook his head. "I don't know how you operate," he said. "But, from the looks of the guy in the apron, you handled yourself just fine. I just wanted to ask how you're doing."

"Would you ask me that if I was a man?"

"He would," Grimaldi said.

She turned her head toward the pilot and stared at him for several seconds, as though trying to gauge his sincerity. She turned back to the Executioner and her defiant expression softened just a bit.

"I'm fine," she said. "Even if I was the falling-apart type, I don't have the luxury."

"Understood," Bolan said.

The woman gave him a small nod.

"Why the rough play by Bly and his thugs?" the warrior asked.

"They wanted something," she replied. "Something they thought I had."

"Which was?"

She chewed on her lower lip for a moment. "What's your security clearance, Agent Cooper?"

"High enough to debrief you, if that's what you're getting at," Bolan replied.

"It is. Look, don't think I'm not grateful for what you did. I am. But I know nothing about you or—" she gestured at Grimaldi with a nod "—him. For all I know you guys are just two more rogue operatives, working an agenda. My orders were to share my information with Jennifer Simmons. And I don't see her here."

"She won't be coming."

"Why?"

Bolan sighed. "You saw my credentials," he said. "And his."

She nodded.

"It's got to be enough," the soldier said. "We don't have time for you to run through all the channels. Am I right?"

She scrutinized Bolan's face for a long time.

"Okay," she finally said. "Here's what I know. Bly is up to something. If you're here, I assume you've already gathered that much. The question is, what? Well, for starters, he's up to his neck in Chinese mafia."

"Chiun," Bolan said.

"Yes, Chiun. And you know that Garrison has ties to Chiun that predate Bly?"

"Among others," Bolan said. "We know that elements within the company were in bed with Chiun, along with other organized crime figures, dictators and terrorists. It was an intelligence-gathering operation. Garrison kept tabs on the bad guys by mixing with them. How am I doing so far?"

"Fine," she said. "And, yes, I wanted to hear what you know. I usually operate undercover. I'm not used to dumping my guts to everyone I meet."

"The woman of my dreams," Grimaldi said.

She shot him a perturbed look, then turned back to Bolan. "It goes a hell of a lot deeper than that," she said.

"How deep?" the big American asked.

"Scary deep," she said. "As in handing over defense secrets to the Chinese. Deliberately. And I'm not talking about a coordinated disinformation campaign OK'd by the National Intelligence Director. This is treason. Pure and simple."

She paused again, and Bolan instinctively anticipated the question that raced through her mind.

"If we're going to stop it, we need to know all of it," he said.

She nodded. "Garrison has access to mounds of weapons-related technical data. Traditionally, the company always kept a wall between the high-tech and the low-tech stuff. Part of our charter was to help develop off-the-books security technology for the United States. Anything we sold to private industry was done with the executive branch approval. It helped fund our operations."

The anger seemed to have drained from her face, replaced by a cool impenetrability. The quiet, but steady tapping of her left foot betrayed the concern and fear that Bolan imagined roiled inside her.

"Bly approved a project to develop a new weapon that appeared to fail monumentally. The problem was that he believed in the project. The company sank billions into R&D for Firestorm. Since the company was publicly traded, he couldn't hide the losses, at least not completely. The shareholders and the financial press beat him like the proverbial red-haired stepchild. But he secretly managed to complete the project." She went on to explain what she knew about Firestorm and told them about the horrendous notes.

After he digested that intel, Bolan said, "I assume that he kept the why of the losses under wraps."

"Exactly," she stated. "Which only made it worse. See, he had to spread this multibillion dollar loss over a few divisions, and blame it on strategic mistakes. His strategic mistakes."

"Ouch," Grimaldi said. "That had to leave a mark."

"A guy with his massive ego? It was like swimming in pig shit with your mouth open," Serrano said.

"Nice," Grimaldi said. He stuck out his tongue to underscore his distaste.

"He hated it. He kept getting paraded out on all the news shows, and interviewed about his huge mistake. A couple of weeks of that, and he was royally pissed."

"Still," Bolan said, "that alone isn't enough to make the guy a turncoat. Something else had to nudge him over the edge."

"Right," she replied. "Even for an egomaniac bastard like Bly, it was a stretch. Not that he was particularly patriotic, mind you. But he is insane about his image. Traitor wasn't exactly a tag he relished, either."

She brought a fist to her mouth and coughed hard.

"Anyway, he agreed to take one for the team. But he decided privately, of course, that he wanted to follow up with a killer year this year. The best way to get that, he knew, was to sell more contraband. So he sold some shoulder-fired rockets to Arthur Doyle."

"No harm in selling to the IRA, since they're under a cease-fire," Bolan offered. "Was that the thinking?"

Serrano shook her head vigorously. "Not exactly. Doyle told him they were intended for some right-wing paramilitary here in Bogotá. Since the Colombian government and the paramilitaries are buddies, Bly figured it was a good way to raise capital, and help the U.S. mission of supporting the local government."

"Sounds plausible," Bolan said. "Not that the paramilitaries are much of a prize, either."

"It gets worse," Serrano said.

"Why am I not surprised?" Bolan asked.

She gave him a weary smile. "Nice sandbox we've got down here, huh? With Marc Haley's help, Doyle handed the missiles off to Chiun for a tidy sum. He turned around and sold them to Hezbollah, Islamic Jihad and the Muslim Brotherhood in Syria."

"Nice," the Executioner said. "Some had to have ended up in Iraq or Afghanistan. They could be used against our soldiers."

She nodded slowly and licked her lips. "It's very possible," she said. "That's why I'm so damn sick about it. Thanks to Bly, Garrison either has or will have blood on its collective hands. He shamed an operation that was critical to American security. World security, for that matter."

"Wait a minute," Grimaldi interjected. "I thought Doyle and Haley worked with Bly. Why would they sell him out like that?"

"They got a better offer," Serrano said with a shrug. "At least that's the going theory. I mean, neither of these guys had an exclusive relationship with the United States. Haley sells information to anyone with the cash. From their standpoint, a rogue weapons smuggling operation probably made as much sense as any of the other crap they pull."

"Sure," Grimaldi said, nodding his understanding.

"The thing to understand, though, is that, yes, they set up and carried out the deal. But it was a means to a larger end."

"Explain," Bolan said.

"Chiun was the guy pulling the strings," she said. "From start to finish. He coaxed—" she gestured quotation marks around the word "—Haley and Doyle to set up the whole deal. My guess is he threatened to turn them into shark bait. So they kept records, notes, pictures, recordings of every transaction, including the plans for Firestorm. They handed them over to him."

"Blackmail."

"Precisely. And, to compound that, Chiun used some of his contacts to get photos of Bly during a three-day romp through Thailand."

Grimaldi slammed his right fist into his left palm. "Holy compromising positions."

The CIA agent looked at Bolan. "He always this way?"

Bolan nodded. "Yeah."

"No wonder you're so violent."

13

Bolan glanced through the crowd at the bustling fast-food joint. He was looking for his underworld contact, a guy who'd traveled halfway around the world to meet with him. He heard a shrill whistle, like someone summoning a taxi, to his left. He turned and saw Leo Turrin, standing next to a table. Bolan joined his friend. The stocky Fed gestured to a seat and took one himself.

Turrin raked his glance over the restaurant's interior. "Nice," he said. "I take a red-eye flight over here and this is where we eat. The wife and I were supposed to go to Cozumel for a week for our second honeymoon. She was packing suntan lotion when Hal called. Now she's pissed."

"Sorry," Bolan said. "I should've called somebody else."

"Then I'd be pissed," Turrin said. "So what do you have on Chiun?" Bolan gave him the details.

"I need to hit him," the big American said, "but he's got a small army working for him. If I tried to lop off the head, his people will come in from behind, swarm all over Jack and me."

"You want to dismantle his organization from the outside in," Turrin said.

"Yeah."

"What if it drives him to ground?"

Bolan shrugged. "If he goes to ground, that's fine," the soldier said. "I'm betting that if he does, he'll lead us to Firestorm."

"Possible," Turrin said.

"Probable," Bolan stated. "Serrano told me that Chiun and Bly consider the weapon their ace in the hole. As long as they have it, they have something worth selling, even if it's just pieces of technology. There's no shortage of countries willing to pay top dollar for that stuff. Hell, they'd pay hundreds of thousands of dollars just for the manuals. They're going to protect that thing with their lives."

"If they haven't already sold it," Turrin replied.

Bolan agreed.

"Which is where I come in, right?"

"Yeah, I wasn't sure what you're hearing." He paused. "What with you being retired and all."

"Retired? My ass! Every time I get more than ten miles from Washington, they call me back for something."

"It's hell being the best," Bolan said.

"That's what I tell my wife. Anyway, I still get out with the made men every now and again. After you called, I started working my sources, made a few calls. Nobody mentioned weapons, high-tech or otherwise. Lot of these guys, they don't get their hands dirty anymore. They think they've gone legit."

"Captains of industry."

"There's been some rumblings about the Garrison deal. The Italians up in Chicago bought a big stake in the company a couple of years ago. It's got its U.S. headquarters there, and Bly was happy to take their money.

"They didn't know his game, his covert-ops connections, I mean. And he knew they were mobbed up even though they'd cleaned up. So it's a bunch of Kabuki theater. And no one cares as long as the money flows, right?"

Turrin torched the end of a cigarette with a disposable lighter. "Can't smoke these things in American burger joints any more. What's the world coming to a guy can't light up after a meal?"

"Armageddon," Bolan said.

Turrin's lower lip jutted forward and he blew a column of smoke skyward. "Yeah, I'm on my soapbox. Anyway, the money guys, they see the stock trade. They ask questions. And they don't give a damn about insider trading. These guys have killed people. They aren't concerned about white-collar crime. The way they see it, they should be bigger than all the Justice Department lawyers put together. They see the stock going up. They hear that this company or that company is buying up the shares like they're going out of style. They make a few more calls." He snapped his fingers. "They figure that it must be a treasure, and it's getting stolen right out from under their noses."

"They think they're missing out on something," Bolan said.

Turrin lit his next cigarette with his last, stepped out the old one.

"These guys want to get everything they can as fast as they can. When they can. Screw everybody else. It's all jungle rules.

"Bottom line, if one crook sees another make money, he isn't going to sit back and clap. He's going to shank the bastard and take the money."

"Which means what for me?" Bolan asked.

Turrin groped around inside his jacket for a couple of seconds. When his hand came back out, he held a business card between his thumb and index finger. He slapped it on the table, its top facing away from him so Bolan could read it: Flint and Associates, Investment Bankers, Terry Flint.

Bolan memorized the address and other contact information. With his index finger, he pushed the card back across the table to Turrin, who nabbed it and returned it to his pocket.

"Explain," the soldier said.

"Terry Flint is a big deal in the investment world. The guys in the Treasury Department call him Magic, because he can make money disappear like it never existed. But he doesn't just hide it. He invests it, grows it. Does it for all kinds of trash—Russian mafia, Islamic terrorists, North Korea's government. You name it, he handles their money."

"Why hasn't he been shut down?" Bolan asked.

The corners of Turrin's mouth turned up in a weary smile.

"He grows people's money. He hides people's money, and he doesn't just do it for the bad guys. His client list includes guys like Chiun. But his other clients include members of the British Parliament, the U.S. Congress and the Chinese government. Whenever Justice or Treasury tries to push him, he runs behind some crooked politician's skirt, lets them put the kibosh on the investigation."

"So we know the moneyman," Bolan said. "What does that do for us?"

"Two things," Turrin said. "First, Bly has a relationship with Flint. Apparently he's been siphoning off money from Garrison for years, presumably without anyone's permission. This gives you someone with an inside track on both guys. He knows where the bodies are buried, so to speak."

Bolan nodded his understanding.

"Second," Turrin said, "Flint has another client. This one's out of Chicago. Vallachi. You familiar?"

Bolan nodded yes.

Turrin continued, "They have a history with Chiun. About ten years ago, he tried to grab a piece of Chicago. Vallachi got wind of this insanity and sent Chiun's guys back to him in trash bags. Chiun plays it cool, uncharacteristically so, if you ask me. Six months later, three of Vallachi's key men go to Hong Kong, along with the team of foot soldiers."

"Chiun's people nabbed them, killed them, all except one. They sent him back to America to pull off some back channel talks. The short version is that everyone decided to stay the hell out of everyone else's territory. That truce has stuck until recently."

Turrin cleared his throat.

"But," he continued, "that doesn't mean they like each other. Hell, they hate each other. You kill the largest people, and you've made an enemy for life. So, like I said, the talk runs hot and fast about this whole Garrison thing. Mind you, nobody understands the gravity of it. Not that I can tell, anyway. They don't know about Bly's government ties or about the Chinese government."

"They just know that Chiun's making big money, bigger than they are," Bolan interjected.

"And it chaps their asses like you wouldn't believe. Enough so that Chicago and New York and Philly have been wanting to have a powwow with Chiun. Or, more precisely, with Flint."

"They send anyone?"

"Yeah."

"Who?"

"You."

"Excuse me?" Bolan asked.

Turrin flashed the soldier his best sheepish grin.

"A buddy of mine down in Chicago was telling me about this whole thing. I kept him talking, and pretty soon he was telling me everything."

"The Turrin magic," Bolan said.

"I told him they ought to quit whining and go talk to Flint. You know, ask him, What the hell? We went back and forth like that for a while until finally he told me that he couldn't. Talking to Flint was above his pay grade. Guess no one there goes after Chiun without old man Vallachi's approval. He whined some more. I told him maybe he ought to play it cool. Or send someone else who can turn up the heat, if necessary."

"And you thought of me," Bolan said.

"Not you. Frankie Lambretta. He can kick Chiun in the balls a few times, disappear and no one is the wiser. By the time you finish with Chiun, he won't be in any condition to hit back at Chicago."

"We'll see."

"By the way, Hal sent some intel for you. Some more dirt they dug up on Chiun's organization." He patted his pockets until he stopped at the one on his shirt, and extracted a small memory stick, which he passed across the table. "Most of it is unclassified. A lot of it is open-source stuff. But there are a couple of affidavits from a couple of snitches. May give you a direction to go, if you run out of ideas."

"That should help," Bolan said.

"The big thing to remember is the sheer numbers," Turrin said. "Between Chiun and Bly there are probably 150-plus guys on the payroll. They do everything from protection, to smuggling to assassinations. That's a lot of people even for you and Jack."

"So what're you driving at?"

"You may need help."

"You feeling left out?"

"I'm in the neighborhood," Turrin said, grinning. "That's all I'm saying. Might as well put me to work."

A smile ghosted Bolan's lips. "I have just the thing."

14

The elevator, occupied by a single individual, slid to a stop at the penthouse. The rider, scarecrow-thin, barely paid attention, his mind already focused on work.

Terry Flint studied the stock quotes flashing across the screen of his handheld digital assistant. Calculations raced through his mind, erased and altered in the next moment as he filled out mental spreadsheets. Strategies fell into place. By the time the elevator door whispered open, he was ready to make trades that would net his clients millions.

He stepped from the elevator into the plush waiting room of Flint and Associates, noticed stray bits of lint on the carpet and made a mental note to dock the custodian's pay.

When he reached the office, he peered through the glass windows that looked into his executive assistant's space. His brow furrowed. Where the hell was his assistant? If she was late again…

Angry, he tightened his grip on the briefcase handle and stiff-armed the bronze pressure pad on the glass door, flung the door aside and burst into his office.

He tried to split his attention. After all, the calculations in his mind were the most critical thing to his clients. And the clients always came first. He knew that guiding principle was more than some PR bullshit written on the back of a brochure. When he lost his clients, they expressed their displeasure with a car bomb, or maybe a knife. He funneled money for mobsters, terrorists and the occasional African or Middle Eastern strongman dictator.

If he really screwed up, he wouldn't get fired. He'd be killed.

That explained the corrosive acid bubbling in his stomach and the heart-stopping pangs of fear that he experienced almost daily.

Seeing his office door hanging open, his rage intensified.

"Susan," he said as he moved through the door, "what the hell is going on here?"

A rumbling sound, instantly recognizable, sounded behind him, causing sweat to break out below his hairline. Someone cleared his throat. Flint whirled, unconsciously bringing his briefcase up in front of his torso protectively.

A guy dressed head to toe in black leaned against the wall, his arms folded over his chest. A toothpick jutted from between his teeth. Though the guy seemed focused on Flint, the investment banker also realized that he couldn't be sure, since mirrored sunglasses covered his eyes.

"Hello, Terry," the guy said.

"Who are you?"

"A friend."

Flint scoffed mentally at that. If he'd ever had any friends, he'd lost them decades ago. As far as he was concerned, two types of people populated his world—those whose money he wanted, and those who wanted his money.

But he knew better than to speak those doubts. Instead, he flashed the guy his best deal-closing grin. "A friend? I'm sorry. I don't recognize you."

"Good," the guy said.

Flint swept his gaze over the office. "Where's my assistant?"

"Sweet little piece of tail at the front desk? Gave her the day off."

Flint felt his face flush. "You what? And she listened to you? What the hell—"

"Shut up and sit down. And put that briefcase down. It won't stop a bullet. And that's where this conversation's going, if I don't hear what I came to hear."

BOLAN SAW FLINT'S FACE turn ashen as his words seemed to sink in. The guy seemed to study Bolan for a handful of seconds, apparently trying to discern the gravity of the threat. The Executioner kept his face inscrutable.

Bolan counted to five and said, "You going to stare at me all day, or you going to plant your ass in a seat?"

His words seemed to jolt Flint. He backpedaled to a wooden table surrounded by plush chairs, pulled one out and lowered himself slowly into it. "I could call security," Flint said.

"Your building," Bolan said with a shrug.

The soldier plucked the toothpick from his mouth, flung it to the floor and strode to the table. As he neared Flint, the investment banker shrank back into his seat, hunched his shoulders and balled himself up protectively. Perspiration beaded on his upper lip.

Flint flicked his gaze toward one of the air vents that Bolan knew contained a security camera.

The soldier snapped his fingers. The noise elicited a flinch from Flint, who whipped his gaze back to Bolan.

"Look at me, Terry. Forget the security cameras. My people took care of them. No one's going to disturb us. We gotta have a parley. And it needs to be private."

"Parley?"

"Talk, you moron. It means, talk."

The warrior slipped off his tailored suit jacket. The move revealed the Beretta holstered in his left armpit, and Flint squirmed a bit when he laid eyes on it. Bolan swore that, if possible, the guy would've rolled himself into a tiny ball and squeezed between the cushion and the chair.

The warrior draped his jacket carefully over the back of a chair. He straightened his black tie, wiped a piece of lint from his matching dress shirt.

Flint cleared his throat. "You have me at a bit of a disadvantage—"

"Shut up."

Bolan stared at the man, waited for him to make a move. Flint apparently realized that bluster bought him nothing, and decided to sweeten his approach.

He gave Bolan a smile. His lips parted and his impossibly big teeth came into view. They shone like he put bleach in his coffee. He gestured at a chair.

"Sorry, I overreacted," he said. "I wasn't expecting you, is all. Please, have a seat."

"I'll stand."

"Mr....? Really, there's no need for hostility here. If my clients are unhappy, then by all means, I want to make this right. You've come a long way. Let's sit down and discuss this, like businessmen."

"You tell me to sit again, and I'll take your teeth back to Chicago with me in a fucking cigar box."

Flint's smile faded and he paled a bit. He licked his lips and broke back into a warm grin.

"No sit? Why, that's just fine."

"I'm not here to talk. I'm here to tell. When it's time for you to talk, if that time *does* come, you'll know because I will tell you to talk. Then you damn well better do it. Until then, shut up."

Flint nodded.

"Chicago is pissed. Our investment people were going through the books, looking at our investments. Suddenly, they find something disturbing."

"Disturbing?" Flint asked. Immediately, he realized his error and clamped a hand over his mouth.

"Yeah, disturbing. We own a big stake in Garrison Industries. Yeah, that Garrison Industries. Eight percent, the money people said. That's big money. We find out you're the punk who's been buying it up. No big deal, right? Then we see it's not you that's getting the stock, it's that lowlife Chiun."

His mouth clamped shut, Flint nodded slowly.

"So, okay, that's your job. Except you're buying stock for our competitor," Bolan said, stressing the last word. "That, my friend, is bullshit."

"But if I buy it for them, the price goes up for everyone, including you," Flint protested. "That's a good thing."

"You're pathetic," Bolan said. He shook his head disgustedly. "You realize that? How pathetic you are? You don't buy that much stock without a reason. We both know that. So, give, what's the reason?"

For a second, Flint's lips moved independent of his vocal cords. Bolan grabbed the Beretta 93-R and Flint's eyes widened.

The soldier let the gun hang at his side, not directly threatening the other man.

"I can't really say," he replied. "I have strict confidentiality rules to follow." He spread his hands in a helpless gesture. "Surely you can understand my predicament."

Bolan squinted at him. "Are you nuts? Your predicament is that the Vallachi Family flew me overnight to this shit hole to grill you or kill you. Maybe both, the way I'm feeling."

"But I've made them so much money over the years," Flint protested.

Bolan snorted. "Money? Money's nice. Loyalty's better. We want the whole package. And we're not sure your head's on straight. We've had problems with Chiun before. That little bastard tried poaching on our territory in Chicago and Miami. The Vallachis, they got interests in both places. Chiun's people start shipping his bullshit counterfeit music and videos and software into our country. My boss hits the roof. Not only are those our cities, and we got to share them with the Colombians and the Cubans and the Russians, but now that little bastard sticks his nose in there, too. And we own stock in a couple of the software companies. Suddenly, he's fucking us coming and going. So you want to talk about making us money? To hell with that. You made us nothing if you're working with that bastard. That makes you disloyal and you're picking our pockets. So you better talk or I'm going to wallpaper this office with your skin."

He brought up the Beretta and aimed it at Flint. Sweat beaded the man's forehead. Bolan waited while the moneyman dragged his forearm over his head to dry it. In the meantime, Flint's other hand drifted up to the breast pocket of his shirt. He withdrew a gold-plated pen.

The soldier stepped forward. His arm whipped out and the Beretta struck Flint's jaw. A spray of blood exploded from his mouth and he yelped. Bolan pressed the gun to the other man's temple.

"Drop it," he growled.

The pen fell to the floor. Flint brought both his hands to his mouth protectively. Bolan bent at the knees, eyes fixed on the other man, and snatched the pen. He rose to his full height and took a couple of steps back. He turned the pen over in his fingers, studied it for a couple of seconds, then howled with laughter.

"A .22-caliber pen? You steal this from your old lady or something? You think this would've stopped me?"

"I didn't realize it was *that* pen," Flint said, his words slightly slurred from the bloodied mouth. "I would never do something so flagrantly obvious."

"So, if you were going to kill me, you'd be sneakier. That what you're saying?"

"No!" Flint said desperately.

The soldier shook his head in feigned disgust and holstered the Beretta. From a coat pocket, he produced a black silk handkerchief and tossed it at the moneyman. Deep furrows in his brow, Flint gave Bolan a guarded look. The soldier waited a few beats until Flint finally snatched the handkerchief and pressed it to his bloodied mouth. When he drew it away, one of the man's pearl-white teeth winked bright against the black background of the cloth.

"Now, talk," Bolan said.

Flint's left cheek bulged a bit and something rippled beneath the skin. The Executioner assumed that he was poking at the space formerly occupied by the tooth.

"Chiun's buying up shares of the company to gain a controlling interest in it. He's doing it through a series of front companies, but ultimately he's going to get enough of it to own it."

"When's ultimately?"

"He's almost there," Flint said, shrugging. "A couple more weeks. Maybe a month or two. But he's been leaning on people to sell their shares. Not directly, of course. But through intermediaries. Occasionally, he's had to play hardball with a couple of the board members."

"Define hardball," Bolan said.

"Threats. Against them. Against their families. He hasn't hurt anyone as far as I know. But the threat's out there. These people understand that he means business."

Bolan scowled. "Okay, so let's say this is true. It's a multibillion-dollar company. Where's our friend getting the cash to swing deals this big?"

Flint spit a gob of blood into the handkerchief and folded it neatly. He shrugged. "He has some backers."

"Be more specific."

"I'd rather—"

"Be more specific," Bolan demanded.

Flint sighed and his entire body seemed to sag, defeated.

"He has several investors in the Chinese community. And a few from North Korea, too."

"Investors? Like other gangs?"

Flint shook his head. "The government."

"Does it go all the way to the top?"

"No. It's very much an independent operation. Not sanctioned by the higher-level officials."

"You mean rogue."

"Yes, that's what I mean. It's a group from Chinese intelligence. They've decided that they don't like the policy and they plan to change it from the inside out."

"How so?"

"They want more technology. They see India getting more military sophistication, and they want it, too. This would give them the infrastructure they need to make it happen. Level the playing field, if you'll pardon the cliché. And it's already paying dividends."

"Yeah?"

"Yes. Or it soon will. They have some sort of lethal technology. I don't know what it is." He held up his hands defensively. "Really, I don't."

"Sure," Bolan said. His gut told him the guy was shooting straight with him. "Keep talking."

"From what I hear," Flint said, "this group has got a great deal of technology. They're paying for it with money gathered through illegal channels."

"Such as?"

"Moving drugs, selling small arms to other countries, the usual things."

"Well, here's the other part of the deal," Bolan said. He reached into his pocket and pulled out a plastic case and tossed it onto a coffee table. Flint looked at it, then shot Bolan a questioning look.

"What's this?" he asked.

"It's a CD," Bolan said. "We've hacked into Garrison's network, found all sorts of interesting stuff there. That's the other reason I'm here."

"I don't under—"

"We looked at Bly's records. Guess what? He's getting money from someone else, too. Looks like the Justice Department's been funneling cash to this jackass for months. At the same time, he's been getting his palm greased by this creep in China."

"You mean Chiun?"

Bolan massaged his temples and exhaled loudly, acting as though his head was about to explode. "We already knew about him. I mean someone else. Some guy named Deng. He's in Chinese intelligence."

Flint, who'd been rubbing his sore jaw, stopped. "That's not possible," he said.

"Why?" Bolan asked.

"Bly hates Deng," Flint said.

"Money talks."

"But Chiun funnels all the money from China to Bly after he's laundered it. Chiun was explicit. He's the conduit. He handles all the cash."

Bolan shook his head. "Take a look at the disk," he said. "It's all right there. Your boy, Bly, has a couple of accounts that are getting money from Deng. The trail's more complicated than that, that's the bottom line. They've got a little something going on and you have to wonder why that is. Why's Deng giving him money?"

"It doesn't make sense," Flint protested.

"So?"

"Why are you telling me this?"

"Couple of reasons. One, if my people could find it, that means someone else could find it, too. That means you people have exposed us to possible legal problems. That right there's enough to set us off. Two, we have an investment here. If it goes belly up because of all this cloak-and-dagger crap, it'll go very bad for you. We will hold you personally responsible for what happens."

"But—"

"Shut up. Three, I want you to deliver a message," Bolan said.

"Message?"

"Tell Chiun that he's going to be hearing from me. He won't know where or when. But he'll be hearing from me. And he won't like what he hears."

15

Chiun circled his opponent warily. The man, one of his foot soldiers, had his hands raised before him, fingers curled into fists. A sheen of sweat slicked the man's face and torso. A look into the man's eyes told Chiun he'd already won the fight. He saw the fear in the man's gaze.

Two more fighters climbed through the ropes that surrounded the boxing ring. Chiun shot the men a quick glance and felt his heart rate skyrocket. The surge of adrenaline made him slightly light-headed. Nothing he'd ever found made him feel as alive as did violence.

Chiun wore *gi* pants and a tank top. The thick fabric of the pants snapped sharply as he moved about the ring, feet in constant motion as he waited for the men to attack. The two men separated and advanced on him from his six-o'clock and nine-o'clock positions.

Unlike the first man, they kept their expressions stony. Before he could react to them, the first opponent darted at him. Chiun surged forward and came within striking distance of the man, who feinted left. His right hand shot out at Chiun's midsection. The gangster sidestepped the blow and hammered the man's face with a one-two combination. The man spun away. Rather than press his advantage, the triad boss waited while his opponent caught his footing. The man launched himself at Chiun, churning out a series of kicks that Chiun deflected easily with his shins and wrists. The gangster pressed forward. His fists stabbed out. The other man bobbed and weaved, trying to avoid the onslaught.

But Chiun's knuckles seemed to strike flesh every time, as though the man stood still. Finally, the man's body gave out under the punishment and he collapsed to the canvas.

Chiun's moves felt oily, smooth. His breathing came in long, rhythmic pulls. Each blow that hit flesh energized him. Movement registered in the corner of his left eye and prompted him to glance that way. A lean man with long arms and legs, a reach several inches better than Chiun's, barreled toward him.

The triad boss held his ground. His opponent snapped off a pair of kicks that blurred within inches of Chiun's face. Chiun batted one aside. The second struck him in the thigh, causing him to lose his footing. He stumbled back a couple of steps. His attacker saw an advantage and tried to exploit it by launching a series of punches at Chiun's face. However, he ducked at the waist and felt the rush of air from the blows as they passed harmlessly overheard. He surged at his opponent and pummeled his midsection with a punishing barrage of blows that caused the man to fold in on himself protectively. An elbow strike to the back of the head floored the man and left him unconscious.

A blurring figure hurtled toward Chiun, the last of his assailants. The man was less than six feet tall, but weighed well over 250 pounds, his body padded with layers of muscle. Before Chiun could react the man slammed into him, his arms encircling the gangster's waist, and they crashed to the ground.

Chiun found himself pinned beneath the other man. The triad leader's hand rammed forward, his fingers extended into a knife-hand strike that pushed into the man's solar plexus. His other hand stabbed out and hit the same spot. His opponent's hands dropped to shield his stomach and Chiun, feet flat on the canvas for leverage, bucked his hips upward to knock the man from him. As he scurried from beneath his bigger opponent, the man's hand lashed out and his fingers encircled Chiun's ankle. Without hesitation, he kicked the man in the head with his other foot. The blow knocked the man unconscious.

As he walked away from the downed men, Chiun noticed another had entered the room and stood several feet from the ring, watching the proceedings. Dressed in a charcoal gray business suit, his arms crossed over his chest, Colonel Chi Pu Deng glowered at the younger man. Chiun shot him a dismissive look and turned his back, his actions telegraphing the contempt he felt for the old man.

Outside the ring, he moved to a bench and sat down on it. Two young Chinese women, both taken from small farming villages, waited for him. He took a towel from one of them and sopped the sweat from his torso. A second handed him a fresh shirt, which he took without acknowledging her.

"This is how you spend your day?" Deng chided. "You dance around a boxing ring and spend money on whores and food and imported cigars?"

"Yes," Chiun said. He pulled the shirt over his head.

"It's disgusting," the other man replied. "Frivolous and disgusting."

"I'm sure you think that," Chiun said, "every time I send a woman over, at your request, to take care of your needs." He turned and saw the old man glowering at him.

"Be careful," the colonel warned.

"Shut up. I have no patience for your lectures, your faux morality. If you have a point to make, then make it. Otherwise, get the hell out of here."

Deng's face drew taut with anger. Chiun, his expression neutral, watched the colonel, waited for him to push the issue.

"I came here to learn of your progress," Deng said. "You must update me on the operation."

Chiun wheeled around. His eyes bored into Deng's. "Must?"

Deng didn't avert his gaze. But within a couple of seconds, the right corner of his lip twitched. Something flickered in his eyes, burned out almost as quickly. Was he scared? Angry? It didn't matter, Chiun thought.

"Must. Yes, that's what I said," Deng shouted.

"This is a partnership of convenience. I don't take orders."

"You work for us. For Chinese intelligence."

"When it suits me," the younger man said.

A storm of anger passed over Deng's face. "Insolent—"

Chiun's right hand flashed out, a blur. His palm struck the

other man's left cheek. The colonel's head jerked to the side. He stepped forward. His hands balled into fists.

An arrogant grin creased Chiun's features. With a dramatic sweep of his hand, he motioned at the space in front of him. "Please," he said.

Deng froze, his forehead creased with suspicion. He looked at the guards who lined the wall, all of them heavily armed. They watched the altercation with apparent interest, but remained rooted where they stood.

"You must think of your country," the colonel said. "We have paid for this whole operation."

"You did pay for it," Chiun said. "With a slush fund that you built up by selling shoulder-fired missiles and rockets to Hezbollah and the surplus to the Taliban. And you did all this without the government's approval, if memory serves. How might the State view such rogue transactions, my friend? My guess is poorly."

"You won't say a word," Deng said menacingly.

"Really? The reward for killing a traitor's quite handsome. A nice bit of money, and a chance to eliminate a man unable to understand his station in life."

"I'm not a traitor," Deng said.

Chiun shrugged. "So? What you or I think is immaterial. The State will take a dim view of your freelance activities."

"Don't dishonor me in such a manner again," the colonel said, though his voice was drained of its bluster. "We have other things to worry about without turning on each other. Are you certain Bly is still working with us?"

"He is."

"We can trust him?"

"We can trust him to do what he must. As long as he gets his money, he will hold up his end of the bargain," Chiun said.

Deng paced the floor. "Loyalty bought with money is not true loyalty."

"You know something that I don't?"

Deng shook his head. "Simply stating a fact. A man who betrays his country for money has no honor. A man without honor makes a bad partner."

Chiun lit up a cigarette and drew deep from it, enjoying the head rush from the nicotine. Tobacco was one of the few vices he allowed himself. With a lingering exhale, he drove twin plumes of smoke through his nose. He stared at Deng through the haze. "We've been through this before," he said. "He has too much to lose if he betrays us. One word from me, and his world crashes down around him."

"So you think."

Chiun felt his stomach churn with anger. "Explain," he snapped.

"Trust no one. That's all I'm saying. You've seen what these vehicles can do. You can turn a man into a charred husk in seconds. If we ever turned the device on American soldiers—"

"That's a big if."

"That *if* is why I'm paying you to do this. That's why I want this technology. We both realize that. I'm doing this for our country. The Americans come here, build factories, make jobs that lure our countrymen."

"Jobs that pay nothing," Chiun countered. He stubbed out the cigarette, left it in the ashtray. He made a sweeping gesture that took in most of the room around him. "Certainly not jobs that pay well enough to buy all this."

Deng stopped at the bar and poured himself two fingers of vodka. With a pair of tongs, he clawed two pieces of ice from a bucket and dropped them into his glass. He turned back toward Chiun, his expression hard.

"They don't need all this," he said, a trace of contempt creeping into his voice. "These are dirt farmers, poor for genera-tions. Now they have money. It may seem like nothing to us. But to them it's more than many of them accrued over generations. And they want more still. There's even rumors of unions." He drained his drink, then slammed the glass down on top of the bar.

"So?" Chiun asked.

"What of our country, then? The workers begin to make more money and then build more and more. How do you maintain order when people work for themselves and not for the State? I tell you—" he shook his finger vigorously as he spoke "—this will turn them against their homeland. And who invested the money? The West! They use our people to support their free market economy. Soon enough they will turn against their leaders. The Americans will subvert our whole country with its money. And our leaders, men with whom I've shed blood, are letting this happen. I want us to have an edge. I want us to take this technology and this company from them. Let them know fear. Let them know that we remain a force to be reckoned with."

He turned and made himself another drink, but he continued his lecture as he did.

"I will not let them destroy this. I will take Garrison's technology, all of it, and I will sell it to North Korea or Iran. Or maybe the Shiites in Iraq. Sell it to anybody with enough money to pay for it."

Other than making him more talkative, the alcohol seem to have little effect on the colonel, Chiun noticed. His glass full, he stalked about the room like a caged animal. On a roll, he continued ranting until Chiun ceased to listen to him. He had dealt with enough zealots in his time to recognize one, not that Deng made much effort to hide it.

Irritated, Chiun said, "So, you're doing this only for the country? Is that it? Your motives are altruistic, and the potential to make hundreds of millions of dollars doesn't drive you at all. I sit in awe of you."

The colonel wheeled toward him. His face was twisted with anger. "I waste my words with you."

"No," Chiun said, "you waste my time. Back to the topic at hand. Did you get me my factory?"

Deng stared silently at him, as though he'd just been slapped again.

Chiun tolerated the stupefied look as long as he could, then said, "Well?"

"Yes. I have gotten it."

"Good. Then we have nothing further to discuss. My people will show you out. I'm sure you have other details that need to be taken care of."

Deng's lips tightened and his eyes narrowed. Chiun grinned at him. He knew the old bastard took himself too seriously, and this was like running a knife blade through his ribs.

Deng set his drink on the bar and nodded once. "You just make sure you have Firestorm. Otherwise, we will have a much different conversation next time."

16

"We've hit pay dirt with this," Kurtzman said.

He scrolled through his computer screen, studying the contents of the flash drive that Serrano had secured for him.

Brognola stood behind him and tried to decipher the spreadsheets laid out across the screen. But Kurtzman, excited by the new influx of information, was scrolling through too quickly to follow. And from his angle, the big Fed found it even more difficult to read. He decided to bypass the eyestrain.

"Either tell me what you see, or slow down," Brognola groused.

"Sorry, Chief. Bank account numbers. Shipping manifests. Legal documents establishing Bly's various shell companies. Or at least what I assume are shells. I still need to sift some of this data, see which entity fits where in this whole mess."

Brognola nodded. He pondered what they had. "That's good. Very good. Start piecing together what you can. I want to know who's giving what to whom. Think you can pull together a chart so we can see how this is organized?"

"Done," Kurtzman said. "We can lay this out all the way down to Bly's milkman.

"Please don't," Brognola replied.

"Okay, we can set it so that the Treasury Department can seize every last dime that treasonous piece of shit has."

"That's better. Do the legwork. But sit tight on it until we decide how to use it."

Kurtzman, by now only half listening to his boss while he continued to pore over the data, broke away from the spreadsheets and other documents on his computer screen and stared at the big Fed.

"Why is that?"

"I want to monitor what they do," Brognola said. "Now that we know what they're up to, there's no rush to seize the money. Or stop any of their stock transactions, for that matter. They know Striker has the information. They'll be expecting us to make big moves, start snatching things up, closing things down. If we sit tight, watch, maybe they'll assume Striker didn't pass along the information. Or that we were too stupid to know what we had and exploit it."

Kurtzman nodded. "I see."

"Besides," Brognola continued, "the more aggressive we become, the deeper to ground they'll go. Striker's in the field, but he calls the shots. If he says grab stuff, great. Otherwise, we wait for actionable intelligence. But I don't want to spook them."

FLINT'S HANDS SHOOK AND caused him to fumble with the ring of keys. After several seconds, he found the right one and pinched it hard between his finger and thumb to make sure he didn't lose it again. He let the others bunch up at the bottom of the ring. He knelt next to his bureau. After two unsuccessful tries, he finally got the key into the hole turned it and pulled open the drawer. From inside, he withdrew a satellite phone, returned to his desk and set it on the blotter. Even as he powered it up, his mind raced as he rehearsed the conversation he would soon have with Chiun.

Yes, he had spoken with the mobster. No, he hadn't shared any sensitive information. Yes, the man had a message that he wanted delivered directly to Chiun.

After a couple of rings, Chiun answered.

"Speak."

"I had a visitor," Flint said.

"Yes?"

"He had a message."

"And it is?"

"They know what we're doing with Garrison."

Several seconds passed in silence.

"Did you hear—"

"I heard."

"He said the Families in New York and Chicago have seen what we're doing. He said that if they keep seeing it, you will, and I quote, 'think you've opened the gates of hell.'"

Chiun laughed. "How dramatic. Perhaps I should quit now."

"You think this is funny?"

"The notion that I'd quit because the American Mafia says so? Of course I think it's funny. What else did he say?"

Flint exhaled deeply, stealing a moment so he could search for the right words. "It appears," he said, "that Mr. Bly has been less than forthright with us."

"Explain."

"Apparently, someone other than you has been filling Bly's bank account. It looks as though our friend, the colonel, has been playing an end run around us. From what this man said, the colonel's been sending Bly money on the side."

"He can prove this?"

"He left documents."

"Send them to me," Chiun said.

CHIUN'S YOUNGER BROTHER, Lee, was very smart, a fact Chiun acknowledged only rarely, and then with a mixture of pride and envy. When Chiun had learned that Xhiung Cho had stabbed him in the back through theft and deception, he'd been awash in feelings of anger, betrayal and shame. Losing the money had been painful, of course. But having his fallibility—his gullibility—put on display for all to see had been nearly more than he could stand. It was a mistake his father never would have tolerated.

That was why he'd killed Cho's wife rather than the thief himself. Chiun wanted the other man to suffer. He wanted to leave others too scared to talk of it, let alone contemplate doing the same thing.

Chiun had vowed never to bring in an outsider to protect his most precious asset—his reputation. Lee, a child prodigy, had graduated with advanced degrees from Cambridge University at twenty. He had the skills of a forensic accountant and the computer savvy of a National Security Agency programmer.

All that was important, of course, but of equal importance, was his loyalty to his older sibling. Lee would cut off his own arm before he'd steal, which was the way Chiun wanted it.

The younger man was seated behind his desk, as he often was. Glasses with small, circular lenses sat perched on the bridge of his nose. The contents of his screen were reflected back in miniature on the lenses. Eyes focused intently on the job at hand, he didn't look up from his computer when his brother entered his office. Rather, he acknowledged him with a curt nod.

"Brother," Chiun said.

"Yes?"

"You can track Bly's accounts, correct?"

"You have his numbers?"

Chiun nodded.

"Set them there," the younger man said. He nodded at a clean spot on his desktop. "Give me an hour."

"YOU KNOW THIS TO be true?" Chiun asked an hour later.

"Absolutely," Lee replied. He nodded at the stack of printouts that rested on the table between them. "Go through them yourself if you like."

Chiun studied the top sheet, saw it was crammed with numbers and shook his head. "I'll take your word for it," he said.

Lee smiled. He laced his fingers together, then rested his hands on his ample stomach and stared over the rims of his glasses at his brother. Unlike some younger siblings, Lee never showed a desire to outdo his older brother. Lee understood that, while his older brother's power rested in his limbs and his heart, his power rested in his mind.

Chiun set his small cup of jasmine tea on the table.

"What can you tell me of this?" he asked.

"Your friend Bly is on the take," Lee replied.

"You're convinced of this?"

"You're not?"

Chiun dismissed the question with a wave. "I'm here to discuss what you think. Just who, specifically, is giving Bly the money?"

"Chinese intelligence."

"Excuse me?"

Lee crossed his arms over his chest and smiled at his sibling. "Your good friend, the colonel, has been sending Bly money. For the past six months, he's been sending it through an export company, one our government established several years ago in Brazil. From what I can determine our intelligence people established it to sell nuclear-weapons components to other countries."

Chiun's fingers curled into fists, one of which he began to tap on the arm of his chair. His jaw set, he nodded for Lee to continue.

"The company sells ring magnets and tubes for centrifuges to Pakistan, Iran and Venezuela just to name a few. It's made the government a nice chunk of money over the years. So how will you deal with this?"

"I've got a way," Chiun replied.

17

A gray Hummer slid to a stop in front of the small shop followed a few seconds later by another one, this one of limousine length and with tinted windows. Seated in a van parked a block away from the shop, the Executioner watched the arrival. Excitement fluttered in his stomach as the second car rolled to a stop and the driver killed the headlights. The doors of the first Hummer opened and, almost in unison, a crew of gunners disembarked. One man held in a pump shotgun in plain view. He moved quickly to the limousine, stood next to the driver's side and swept his gaze over the area. The rest of the crew, hands stuffed inside their jackets, presumably within reach of their hardware, scurried as a single unit to the larger vehicle and positioned themselves around it.

The rear doors of the limousine popped open and more hardmen exited, followed by Bolan's target.

Joe Fong grabbed a cigarette from his mouth and tossed it aside as he made his way to the sidewalk. Fong was a lieutenant in Chiun's gang of leg breakers and had risen far enough in the ranks to rate his own entourage of thugs. Bolan had Cho to thank for the information. During the past several hours, the former triad accountant had been laying out everything he knew about Chiun's organization to a pair of FBI agents. The agents had dutifully passed the information up the chain until it reached Brognola, who chucked it Bolan's way as soon as possible.

The soldier knew it was collection night for Chiun, work he left to his lieutenants.

With so many gangs operating in Ciudad del Este, the reasoning went, it sent out a message of strength to have the high-level gangsters collect protection money.

Fong strode purposefully toward a small storefront. A lighted sign that bore Chinese characters hung in the window. Bolan already had cleared that and a couple other businesses on Fong's hit list for the night.

As Fong and his crew disappeared inside, Bolan made his way between the van's front seats and into the rear of the vehicle. He grabbed a heavy duffel bag from the floor, slung it over his shoulder and slipped out a side door and onto the sidewalk.

The guard with the riot gun had stayed outside the store. Bolan edged along a row of storefronts, hung in every available shadow as he closed in on the lone gunner. When Bolan came within a short distance of the man, the thug whirled, the shotgun's muzzle hunting for a target.

The Executioner's Beretta chugged through a triple burst of 9 mm manglers that crashed through the man's nose and forehead. The guard stumbled back a couple of steps. His body sagged and he dropped to his knees. The shotgun slipped from dead fingers as he crashed face-first into the concrete.

The warrior legged it up the sidewalk. He halted next to the corpse, reached down and retrieved the shotgun. Emptying the weapon, he dropped the shells into his jacket pocket and thrust the gun beneath the nearest Hummer.

He planned to hit this crew hard and fast. If one of them ditched the scene, made a run for the vehicles, he didn't want the hardman to find a loaded weapon waiting in easy reach, if they didn't already have one.

Bolan backtracked several steps until he reached the limousine. He walked around the rear bumper and crouched behind the big vehicle. He attached a brick of C-4 plastique outfitted with a detonator to the car's underside. He was back on the sidewalk when the dead gunner's cell phone began to ring.

Bolan muttered a curse. Once they realize that their guy was down, he'd be up to his neck in thugs. The soldier fisted the second Beretta and started for the target site.

As if on cue, one of Fong's thugs exited the store and started down the sidewalk. He kept his pistol leveled in a two-handed grip and made his way toward his dead comrade. His eyes lighted on Bolan almost instantly. A tongue of flame lashed out from the muzzle of the man's pistol and a round whistled past Bolan's ear. The warrior wasted no time lining up a shot. Bursts from the twin Berettas ripped into the man's center mass, taking him down.

A second man popped around the store's door frame. He snagged a too-fast bead on Bolan, firing a small automatic. The rounds nipped at the tails of the warrior's coat but hit nothing vital. The soldier triggered both handguns. Three-round volleys bombarded the shooter's position. They didn't strike flesh but succeeded in driving the man to ground.

Bolan ducked into an alley for cover, but stayed on the move. More autofire rattled out in the street and he assumed the crewman had popped his head out for another go.

Bolan holstered one of the Berettas and from his pants pocket withdrew a small black detonator. With the ball of his thumb, he moved the toggle switch. Thunder clapped, accompanied by the groan of metal being lashed with flame and force. The explosion ignited a sudden burst of hellfire that shot skyward and filled his darkened space with a sudden flash of daylight.

Ahead, the alley opened into what appeared to be a small access road that ran parallel to the street he'd just left. A pair of shadows stretched over the broken pavement, growing larger as they closed in on his position.

The Executioner stopped at the mouth of the alley and from his duffel bag extracted a flash-bang grenade. With his teeth, he tugged the pin free and tossed the bomb around the corner.

Experience told Bolan that the sound of metal striking asphalt, particularly in an adrenaline-charged situation, would snag the attention of even seasoned fighters, for at least a moment. Someone with combat experience might assess the situation and try to react. Someone who spent their time muscling old men and women for their hard-earned cash likely would stand there, slack jawed, and take their punishment head-on.

The grenade emitted a sudden crack and an explosion of white light. As the last bits of sound died down, Bolan came around the corner low and found the muscle staggering about, armed but disoriented. The Berettas blazed to life once more, downing the three men.

Bolan reloaded and trudged ahead.

FONG FLINCHED AND GRITTED his teeth when the first explosions thundered outside the store. Take cover, his mind screamed.

He moved to the checkout counter, vaulted over it and hunkered down.

A moment later shock waves from the explosion, accompanied by shrapnel, shattered the big front windows, blowing in a hurricane of glass shards slicing through the air.

Multiple screams reached his ears. Whether they originated from one person or more, Fong couldn't tell. An unfamiliar sense of terror seized him, followed by a murderous rage. Who would do this to him? When the sound and fury of the initial explosion died away, he came to his feet and surveyed the room. He shook his head disgustedly.

Books, ripped and tattered, littered the floor. Stray pages wafted through the air, along with a thick haze of dust and smoke. The blast had spread glass all over the store's interior. From a short distance away, he spotted one of his men, laid out on his back, a dagger of glass protruded from one eye socket. A second man sat directly across from Fong, his back against a wall, his hands clutching something, his shirt dark with blood. He gasped for breath and gave Fong a pleading look.

His thoughts already shifting in another direction, Fong drew a bead on the wounded man. His pistol cracked. A hole opened in the man's forehead. Blood burst from the rear of his skull and splattered the wall.

Fong cared little about putting the dumb bastard out of his misery. Rather, he didn't want the guy making any noise that might draw attention to him, or drown out potential signs of danger.

Fong looked at his remaining men, all of whom were struggling back to their feet.

"You go that way," he said, nodding at the back door.

"What about the front?" one asked.

"Fuck the front," he said. "I'll handle that. You hit the back! Do it!"

They started for the rear of the store. Fong smiled inwardly and headed for the front door. Unless he guessed wrong, no one with stones enough to pull off this kind of attack would go through the front door. It'd be the expected route of entry and sure death for someone who tried to make their way through it. He was betting—betting his life, in fact—that whoever made all that noise out front likely would plan to sneak in through the back. Or, if it was multiple attackers, they might storm both entrances.

He crossed the room, ignoring the crunch of broken glass beneath his feet. As he moved, he fisted his phone, dialed Chiun and waited for an answer.

"Yes," Chiun answered.

"A problem," Fong said. He laid it out in as few words as possible.

Chiun said nothing and just listened. After several seconds of heavy silence, Chiun asked, "How many men do you have left?"

"Four, including myself."

By now Fong had positioned himself next to a window frame. Craning his neck, he stole a look out the window and took in the carnage outside. He spotted the dead gunner sprawled on the sidewalk and shrugged off the loss. When he spotted the limo, though, its steel body twisted, heaved onto one side, rage seared his insides. Flames continued to lick out from inside the vehicle, and fire pumped out thick columns of oily black smoke.

"Whoever it is, deal with them," Chiun said. "Now."

"I need more people," Fong replied.

His voice sounded tight, stressed, and his cheeks flushed with embarrassment.

"You'll get more people," Chiun snapped. "In the meantime, shut the fuck up and do your job. You catch these bastards, you kill them. No fucking excuses!"

Fong bit down on an angry reply. The phone went dead.

"Do my job," he muttered. "Right."

He shoved the phone inside his jacket. Though he heard

nothing, he suddenly felt the hairs on the back of his neck prickle.
He whirled, his handgun held high.

Nothing.

Just a storeroom.

The gang lieutenant took a step forward. Blood thundered in
his ears, and his heart slammed hard in his rib cage.

As he took a step through the doorway. Something registered
in his peripheral vision. Before he could react, though, something
hit his jaw hard, spinning his head left. His body followed his
head, twisted at the waist, and another blow struck his kidneys.
He gasped and went to his knees.

Overcome with pain and shock, his mind reeled, but he was
vaguely aware of a figure towering over him. A moment later,
his pistol was snatched from his hand, followed by his backup
piece getting snagged from an ankle holster. As he gasped for air,
a black hood was placed over his head and his wrists bound
behind him.

The man grabbed Fong's collar and jerked him to his feet
like a mother cat picking up a kitten. He felt himself being
flung around as though he weighed nothing. When he gained
his footing, he was shoved forward. He took a couple of
unsteady steps.

"The bus is leaving," the man said.

TWENTY MINUTES LATER, Bolan exited the car, slamming the door
shut behind him. He jerked open the passenger door, grabbed a
handful of Fong's jacket and yanked him from the front seat.

"Go," Bolan growled.

The gangster obeyed.

Bolan walked him to a corrugated-steel warehouse. He slid
the door open, pushed Fong inside, followed and shut door
behind them. The perimeter of the building's interior was dark.
Only a small yellow circle of light cast by single naked bulb that
hung from the ceiling slashed through the oppressive darkness.

When they reached the circle, Bolan ordered Fong to stop.
With a light kick to the back of his knee, Bolan knocked the
gangster into a kneeling position, let him stew in the silence for

a few seconds. Fong's breath came fast and loud. The fabric of the hood puckered and loosened against his face in time with the breathing of the terrified man.

"Relax," Bolan growled. "It's not your time."

It took several seconds for the Executioner's words to sink in. Finally, after about a minute, the man's breathing slowed and became quieter.

"If it was up to me," Bolan continued, "I'd kill you just as soon as look at you. But that's not why I'm here. I'm here to send Chiun a message. I want you to pass something along. You hear?"

Fong nodded.

"You tell him Bly's been playing both sides of the street with this little venture of his. Last we knew in Chicago, that little shit was helping us buy up Garrison. We've been working with him, working with our people in the Federal Trade Commission, pulling every string imaginable to put this deal together. Then we find out that double-crossing sack of crap's helping you guys, too. It's time you SOBs wised up on this play and backed away."

Grimaldi, who'd been watching the whole exchange from the sidelines, stepped out of the blackness. He handed an aluminum suitcase to Bolan, then disappeared. Bolan set the case next to Fong, who flinched at the sound. Bolan withdrew a set of keys from his pocket and tossed them to the concrete floor between Fong and the briefcase.

"Here's the deal," Bolan said. "I just set a briefcase filled with American dollars next to your sorry ass. I'm also leaving keys for a Mercedes. You take this case, and the two others like it, and drive the money to Chiun. Give him the cash and the car, with our compliments. Tell him to consider it repayment."

"Repayment?" Fong asked. "For what?"

"I'm about to do a shitload of damage to him. But I don't want to leave any hard feelings."

Bolan turned and exited the warehouse.

"EXPLAIN THIS TO ME AGAIN," Grimaldi said. "Why this is a good idea, I mean."

Bolan nodded. He stared through the windshield and watched

the road or occasionally stole a glance into the rearview mirror, as he collected his thoughts.

"I'm just giving them something to think about," Bolan said. "As it is, they could focus almost entirely on me hunting them or on smuggling Firestorm to China. But now they have another thing to worry about. That can only help me."

"Help you and your faithful sidekick," Grimaldi said with a grin.

"Goes without saying. But the way things are, I need them fighting with each other. The more internal strife I create, the easier it is for us to thin the herd."

Grimaldi nodded slowly. He was piloting a heavy duty black SUV that he had wrangled from the embassy.

"And the money and the car?"

"It's another thing for them to think about," Bolan said. "I want to piss them off, but I also want to influence their thinking. Or Chiun will take it as an insult. Like we can buy him off with a few million dollars and a car. He's going to blame Bly for bringing all this on them."

"Gosh, you're smart," Grimaldi said. "And sneaky."

"Watch and learn," Bolan said, nodding.

18

Fong entered the room, flanked on either side by a couple of Chiun's shooters. The triad leader sat at a table with his brother and a pretty young Asian woman in a navy blue business suit.

Chiun looked at his brother and the woman. "Get the fuck out of here," he said.

His brother mouthed a profane word at him, but stood, gathered his papers and waddled from the room. The woman stood, snapped her laptop closed and stored it in a black nylon tote bag before departing.

Chiun spun his chair so he could face Fong full on. Crossing his arms, he gave the man an appraising stare, noted his disheveled appearance, but said nothing.

Fong stood silently for several seconds, apparently waiting for Chiun to say something. Finally, he couldn't stand the silence anymore.

"He let me go," Fong said. "Can I get a fucking drink?"

Chiun pointed at the bar. Fong made his way over and started mixing himself a drink.

"Who let you go?" Chiun asked.

"The guy who hit my team," Fong said. "He killed everybody except me."

"Lucky for you."

Fong spun. Anger flashed in his eyes as he stared at his boss. But decked out in a torn, bloodstained suit, his skin smudged with dirt, he looked more silly than threatening. "What the fuck does that mean? You think I was working with this piece a shit? I lost my whole crew. I almost got killed myself. Now you want to say that I turned on you?"

"You're still here standing here, aren't you?" Chiun said coolly. "That alone raises all sorts of questions for me. That's what I'm saying. And the fact that he sent you here in a Mercedes stuffed with cash only makes it look worse."

"So it looks bad," Fong said with a shrug. "What do you want to do about it?"

"We'll see."

Fong picked up his drink and crossed the room. When he came within a few yards of Chiun. He stopped and took a long pull from the drink. He found a seat and dropped into it.

"You and I don't have a problem," Fong said. "At least not with each other."

"Explain."

"Bly is your problem. According to this guy, Bly has been running a scam."

Chiun straightened in his chair. "What kind of scam?"

ALI SALEM, DRESSED IN A designer suit, his eyes covered with expensive sunglasses, pushed his way through the bustling nightclub. His guards, two in front, two in back, formed a box around him. Beneath his suit jacket he carried a .40-caliber Glock pistol on his belt and two extra clips in his left front pants pocket. Passing the dance floor, Salem studied the tangle of bodies writhing, sweating, rubbing against one another. He spied a beautiful young black woman. Her straight brown hair hung well past her shoulders. He found himself momentarily mesmerized as he admired her taut curves while she danced. Perhaps after he'd concluded his business—

Suddenly, his team of guards began to tighten their formation around him. The change caused him to pay attention to the business at hand. The sudden tension reminded him again of the handcuffs that connected his left wrist to the black leather briefcase. He looked in the same direction as his guards and spotted the problem. From the one o'clock position, he saw two men, one in a suit, the other in khakis and a dark shirt. Both were cutting a direct line across the bar's seating area, neither making much of an effort to hide their approach. One of the guards cast a quick look over his shoulder at Salem, who nodded his understanding. One of the strangers carried his jacket folded over his forearm and in front of his stomach. His hands were hidden beneath the folds of the jacket, which made it impossible to tell whether he was carrying a weapon.

Sweat formed between Salem's palm and the leather handle of his briefcase. His lips felt dry, tight. His heart accelerated, hammered hard in his chest, as he waited to see how things played out. He'd been through such encounters dozens of times before, but never got used to the sudden terror that seized him.

Though Lebanese, Salem had spent most of his adult life as an operative for Iranian intelligence, much of it as a courier between his handlers and those who did business—most of it surreptitious—with the Iranians. This night the load was rough diamonds acquired by Hezbollah members in Sierra Leone. He was to trade the stones for cash, which he'd pass back to his brothers in Hezbollah.

He licked his lips to moisten them and brought his hand to belt level, putting it within easy reach of his pistol, should he require it.

When the men came within a couple of yards of him and his group, the pair broke off their approach, angled away. Talking animatedly, they reached a table occupied by two young women and took their places next to them.

In his line of work, Salem knew appearances could be deceiving, but instinct told him that the danger had passed.

He and his group climbed the stairs to the mezzanine level. They followed the mezzanine and headed toward a door guarded by a pair of Chiun's gunners. One of the triad thugs beckoned him, leading him to a retinal scanner. He looked into the device, waited a few heartbeats and heard the door latches open.

The guard nodded at the door. Salem stepped through, while his men waited outside. He looked around at the luxuriously furnished office. In addition to the woman he was to meet, two other gangsters were positioned around the room. A slim young man dressed in a conservative blue business suit sat at a desk, a laptop within reach.

The young woman, her dark hair tinted with blond streaks, took him by the elbow and led him to a chair.

"Here," she said.

Salem sat in the chair, set the briefcase on his knees and turned the side with the latches toward her. She knelt next to him, gave him a reassuring smile and began her work.

Her brows knitted with concentration, the woman used a red lacquered thumbnail to maneuver the tiles on the combination lock into position. The pair of combination wheels were wired to a brick of C-4. Not only did the young woman have to get the numbers correct, but she also had to select them in a predetermined order. Otherwise, the briefcase would explode and take everybody in the room with it.

The last carrier had been mugged, his team of guards killed and the case spirited away. Salem imagined the thief, filled with anticipation as he pried open the case, only to be killed in a massive fiery explosion.

The woman moved the last number into place. Salem held his breath while she opened the latches in unison and raised the briefcase lid. When it occurred without incident, he breathed a sigh of relief.

The woman took a small key from the pocket of her jeans and used it to unlock the handcuff bracelet that encircled his wrist. She handed it and the briefcase off to a man in an impeccable gray suit, who took the items and set them gingerly on a nearby chair. Using a set of wire cutters, he snipped the wires and nodded at everyone else. "Clear," he said.

From inside the case, he withdrew a black velvet bag sealed with a drawstring. He walked the bag over to a table and dumped its contents onto the tabletop. Satisfied with what he found, he turned to the man with a laptop and gave him a curt nod.

The third man returned the gesture and began a rapid-fire tapping on the keyboard. He moved two million dollars into Salem's account, and another twelve million into the accounts of a dozen front companies owned and controlled by Hezbollah.

Salem breathed a sigh of relief.

Then all hell broke loose.

BOLAN MOVED THROUGH THE CLUB, his expression grim as he considered his next move. He pushed past three women who had gathered next to a cigarette machine. They huddled close to one another, shouting so they could be heard over the loud music.

His cell phone vibrated in his pocket. He dug it out and brought it to his ear. He pushed the index finger of his free hand into his other ear so he could hear the caller.

"Go," he said.

"They went upstairs about ten minutes ago. If our intel's good, they should've made the exchange. Now we just make a grab and go," Grimaldi said.

"I counted five coming in," Bolan said.

"Five it is. Salem and his four gunners. And there's at least two more up on the mezzanine level. Those are Chiun's people. I snapped some pictures with my phone and sent them to you. Check them out."

"Fine," Bolan said. "Once I hit the stairs, you know what to do."

Bolan took a circuitous route toward the stairs. He scrolled through the pictures the pilot had sent him as he climbed. When he finished, he positioned the phone against his left ear and pantomimed a conversation with an imaginary caller. By the time he hit the last step, he had the Beretta in his right hand, pressed against his thigh to keep it out of sight.

Six guards stood at the other end of the hall. Bolan recognized two from the photos Grimaldi had sent him. The others were among those he'd seen with Salem. As he made his way down the corridor, a barrel-chested man with a shaved head rumbled toward him.

"I don't care what I said last night," Bolan shouted into his phone. "We're done. Quit calling me."

He glanced up and acted as though he saw the approaching guard for the first time. He caught the man's eye, gave him a can-you-believe-this-shit look and turned his attention back to the phone, while the guard stormed in his direction.

"Where am I? None of your business!" he shouted into the phone.

A shadow fell over Bolan. From the corner of his eye he caught a hand reaching out for him. In less than a second, the Beretta flashed and the warrior drilled a 3-round burst into his opponent's stomach. The guard had been moving ahead with such momentum that his body hurtled forward a couple more steps before it collapsed in on itself.

Even as the man crumpled to the floor, Bolan let the phone drop from his grip. He drew a bead on the knot of guards and tapped out three more volleys of 9 mm slugs. The quick onslaught mowed down two of the triad thugs almost immediately, while two of Salem's other thugs darted in different directions. By now, Bolan held the second Beretta in his grip. Both weapons chugged out 9 mm rounds, littering the floor with hot brass and cutting down the men before either squeezed off a shot.

Bolan's combat senses flashed red. He spun and caught a pair of Chiun's killers coming into view at the top of the stairs, weapons drawn. Almost in unison, their weapons began to churn out fire and fury, the rounds slicing through the air around the soldier. Bolan darted sideways, the Berettas ripping through what remained in their clips. He squeezed inside the doorway and took cover inside it, holstered one Beretta and reloaded the other. His spray-and-pray approach to shooting had forced the two men to dart in opposite directions. However, they continued to hammer his position with concentrated bursts of gunfire that ripped through the plaster and wood that provided his meager cover.

The sharp crackle of gunfire had risen above the din of the thundering dance music. It continued to play, but the frightened screams of patrons began to overwhelm it. Bolan knew it was only a matter of time before panicked throngs of people stampeded past one another, trying to escape the melee.

THE INSTANT GRIMALDI SAW the Chinese hardmen hit the stairs and close in on Bolan's flank, he went into action. Setting his drink on the table, he maneuvered between the throng of patrons, intent on getting to the stairway before the thugs reached his friend. With quick long strides, he quickly reached the stairs.

The pilot set foot on the first step. Gunfire rattled from above. Grimaldi's eyes flicked upstairs and he saw yellow muzzle-flashes strobe on the walls of the mezzanine.

He launched himself up the steps, took two at a time. Along the way, he fisted his Beretta 92-F.

Grimaldi hit the top of the stairs at a run. One of the two thugs he'd trailed up the steps sensed his approach and wheeled toward him. A micro-Uzi clutched in the man's right hand spat out a line of tracking fire at Grimaldi. The pilot's Beretta cracked twice, the bullets burrowing into his opponent's midsection. Shooter number two bolted right and spun toward Grimaldi. Three more shots hurtled from his weapon. Two dug into the gunner's throat while a third hammered into a wall.

Firing from a crouching position, another shooter dragged his submachine gun in a horizontal sweep. Tracking fire cut a sideways path toward Grimaldi. The pilot pivoted to line up a shot but knew he'd never make it.

The man's head exploded in a red mist. His gun went silent. His knees turned rubbery and he folded to the floor. The Executioner stood behind him, the Beretta still aimed where the man had stood, smoke curling from the pistol's muzzle.

Grimaldi got to his feet, raising the Beretta before him in a two-handed grip. He quickly bridged the distance between himself and Bolan. In the meantime, the Executioner slammed home another clip into his own weapon. He pointed at the door and, using hand signals, indicated that he'd go first. Grimaldi fell in behind the soldier.

BOLAN KNEW THE ENTRY would be hell.

They'd have to take down the door, rush through the room and kill any shooters without taking a bullet themselves. Nothing new. Cops and soldiers did these sorts of entries every day. But it was dangerous, especially without cameras and other equipment often used by entry teams.

Grimaldi drew down on the doorknob with his Beretta. He

loosed a half dozen or so shots that chewed through it, gave the door a hard kick and whirled out of the way. Guns immediately blasted from inside, bullets drilling through the doorway.

Bolan produced a flash-stun grenade from beneath his coat, pulled the pin and tossed the bomb inside. The device cut loose with a blinding white flash accompanied by a sharp blast. The gunfire stopped. Bolan guessed that the room's inhabitants were trying hard to get their bearings, though he couldn't be sure. Moving in a crouch, he rounded the door frame. The Berettas poised at shoulder level, he scanned the room, sizing up the situation.

Salem was on his feet, hands clamped over his ears. A young woman, a gun clutched in her right hand, stumbled around, her empty palm pressed over one ear. The gun in her hand exploded, dispatching several rounds in Bolan's direction. She fired blind, though, and the bullets zipped a foot or so overhead. The Executioner's Beretta coughed out a line of fire that sent her sprawling to the ground, her weapon sliding harmlessly across the floor.

Bolan crossed the room with long strides. He grabbed Salem, whirled him around and guided the man's hands to the tabletop. He offered no resistance as Bolan kicked his legs apart and patted him down for a weapon. The soldier took a .40-caliber handgun holstered under the man's jacket and stuffed it into the waistband of his pants.

Grimaldi had gathered up anyone else still drawing breath, forced them to lay facedown on the floor, their hands clasped behind their heads. Bolan covered them while the pilot patted them down. The big American took Salem by the elbow, led him around to the table and shoved him into a chair. The diamond courier shot Bolan a hard look, but made no moves against him.

"Who are you?" the Lebanese man asked.

"Lambretta," Bolan said.

"What?"

Bolan ignored him. He reached out and grabbed a cloth bag that sat on the corner of the desk. He tilted the bag and dumped a gray rock into his palm.

"Doesn't look like much now," Bolan said, "but I'm guessing

the cutters in Belgium can turn it into something nice. Maybe help make up for all the trouble your buddy Chiun's caused us."

"I don't know what you're talking about," Salem said.

Bolan shrugged. "I don't give a damn what you know." He took the bag and shoved it inside his jacket.

"Who's our computer genius here?" Bolan asked. He waited a couple of heartbeats. When the gangsters on the floor remained silent, he triggered the Beretta. It stitched out a line of Parabellum slugs that ripped through the carpet and floorboards a foot or so from their heads. The men, seemingly as one, flinched. One of them looked up and pointed at a skinny young man. "Him," he said. "Him."

Grimaldi grabbed the young man by the arm, brought him to his feet and led him to the computer. Bolan moved in next to him, drew a switchblade from his pants pocket and extended the blade. The young man's eyes grew big and he swallowed hard.

"Easy," Bolan said.

He moved behind the young man, pressed a flat palm against his back, between his shoulder blades, and pushed forward. He slipped the knife blade between the skin of the man's wrists and the plastic cuffs and pulled up hard on the blade. The cuffs fell away.

Bolan stabbed at the air in the direction of the computer.

"Hands on the keyboard," he said.

The young man complied.

Bolan extracted a square of paper from his pocket, unfolded it twice and dropped it on the table. "I know how you work the trade," Bolan said. "Salem brings the diamonds. You pay Hezbollah their cut. Salem takes his cut. And you do it all by electronic transfer."

The guy stared at Bolan but said nothing.

"What I want you to do," Bolan continued, "is to take the money you just moved and transfer it into this account. He tapped the piece of paper with the knife's blade.

The computer man stared at Bolan, his fingertips poised above the keyboard. He gave the soldier an imploring look.

Bolan shrugged. "That's right. I want you to steal money from Hezbollah and give it to me."

The young man drew back one of his hands from the keyboard. With his index finger, he pushed his glasses up the bridge of his nose. He licked his lips. "What?" he asked finally.

"Do it," the Executioner ordered. "And don't bother trying to take it back again. Once it goes into my account, it will automatically be disbursed to a dozen other accounts. You'll never find it."

"You can't do that," Salem sputtered.

Bolan didn't bother to look at the courier. "Thanks for the heads-up."

Slowly, the soldier pushed the knife blade forward until the tip touched the computer operator's temple, now shiny with a sheen of sweat.

"But you're right, Salem," Bolan said. "I can't do it. But our friend here can."

He edged the knife blade forward with just enough pressure to cause the computer guy's head to tilt away from it.

"So do it," Bolan said through clenched teeth.

Fingers blazed over the keyboard as the man punched in a rapid-fire series of commands. Bolan watched the screen intently, occasionally nodded his approval, as though he understood what the guy was doing. Finally, he saw the man type in the account number Bolan had given him and hit Enter. Text on the screen assured him that the transaction had been completed successfully.

He'd have Kurtzman double-check later, but he felt reasonably comfortable that they'd accomplished what they'd set out to do. After he shut down the computer, Bolan snapped the lid shut and snatched it from the young man. The way he saw it, the device likely was a treasure trove of intelligence that could be passed along to the Farm and any other users Brognola deemed appropriate, along with any mobile phones or other electronic devices Grimaldi had collected from the prisoners.

Bolan tied the computer operator's hands again, then led him to a spot on the floor next to his comrades. He then returned to Salem, grabbed hold of the man's jacket collar, hauled him to his feet and spun him so they faced each other.

Salem spit at Bolan and it landed on his cheek. "Pig," he said. "You're nothing more than a common thief."

Bolan drew his sleeve across his cheek to wipe it clean.

"Have fun when you get back home," Bolan said. "I'm sure your friends will want to hear all about how you lost their diamonds and their money. And how Chiun couldn't protect them either."

"Bastard!"

Bolan grabbed Salem's upper arm, wheeled him around and with a kick to the back of the knee, knocked him to the ground in a kneeling position. He handed the seized computer to Grimaldi. From his pocket, Bolan extracted a mobile telephone, one he'd purchased earlier from a street vendor. He tossed it onto Salem's back.

"Tell that son of a bitch I want to talk to him," Bolan said. "Number's already programmed in there. I'll be waiting for his call."

19

Bly paced the room and fumed. He didn't like to be kept waiting, particularly by a leg breaker like Chiun.

A woman giggled behind him. He halted, then turned. He eyed his entourage with unchecked disgust as they lounged around Chiun's study. They puffed on Cuban cigars and made small talk with three beautiful women—imported here no doubt by Chiun's snakeheads. Rage boiled up inside him as he watched the women distract his assistants. And, he had to admit they were a hell of a distraction. All three were petite. Their skin, darkened by Brazil's fierce sun, exposed by their bikinis and strapless dresses, made them tantalizing.

He knew he needed to keep his discipline. His indiscretions had pushed him into his current situation. He'd decided to suck it up and make the best of a bad situation, perhaps extract some payback later.

He studied the men, remained silent. Though their behavior caused his blood to boil, he wanted to observe their behavior, see what pushed their buttons. Dynamics changed, after all, and he might find it necessary to bend these men to his will. More to the point, bend them further to his will, in ways that money couldn't.

He'd lost his key partners and didn't know who to trust anymore. He regretting killing Marc Haley too soon. He'd have been useful now that things seemed to be spiraling out of control. The base had been hit and Serrano was gone. He didn't know when or where she'd surface, but it wouldn't be good news for him. He had to make a play—desperate as it was—before he lost everything.

His whole operation was collapsing around him, and Krotnic had never surfaced after the base was hit. All he could do was bluff and hope no one caught on before he could escape. As far as he knew, Chiun wasn't aware of the double cross being played on him. Bly knew he'd just have to keep it together awhile longer.

Finally, Chiun strode into the room, his face blank as he acknowledged Bly with a nod. Bly noted that the triad boss was accompanied by his three-person security team, but had otherwise come alone. A wave of suspicion crashed over Bly when he realized this.

"Where's the colonel?" Bly asked.

"He couldn't make it."

"Why?"

"He had other business." Chiun stopped a few feet from Bly, crossed his arms over his chest and stared at his visitor.

"What other business?" Bly asked.

"I don't keep his calendar. Maybe you should call him and ask. Maybe he'd fax his itinerary to Langley so you can approve it."

Bly felt heat rise up from his neck and shoulders. "If this is a trick—"

"What? What will you do?" Chiun asked, stepping forward. "Kill him? Kill me?"

"Perhaps."

A silence fell over the room.

Chiun cut the tension with a laugh. "Kill me? Please."

"Your confidence isn't an asset," Bly said. "The Balkans and Colombia are littered with the graves of men who thought they were smarter, tougher than me."

"Perhaps," Chiun replied. "But a man with your, um, predilections ought to realize that killing me would create more problems than it would ever solve."

Bly's cheeks emanated heat. When he spoke, his voice was barely audible to anyone in the room except for Chiun. "I want to know where that sneaky bastard is. You forget that thanks to you I'm left with little to fear at this point. Execution for treason would be a sweet relief."

He waited a few seconds while Chiun stared at him, apparently looking for signs of a bluff.

"He's in Beijing," Chiun said. "He was supposed to be here, but he got called back."

"Why?"

"I have no idea. That's the damned truth. Perhaps now we can switch the topic to something more productive."

"Fine."

Chiun snapped his fingers, pointing at the door without looking at his people. They moved to it, opened it and ushered the women out, followed by the bartender. They paused at the door and waited for Bly's men. The two remained in their seats, fully aware of the situation, but not moving.

"Go," Bly said.

Once the room emptied, Chiun moved behind the bar. Bly guessed that the man had done so to put something solid between them. The American knew all too well that in hand-to-hand combat, Chiun would kill him in a matter of moments. And Bly and the others had been scanned with handheld metal detectors and forced to surrender their weapons upon arrival. But that didn't mean that Bly couldn't have slipped something sewn into the lining of his jacket, a hard plastic knife or a vial of poison fatal when absorbed through the skin. Not that he had—he'd taken this whole thing too damn far to end it now. But Chiun didn't need to know that.

Chiun squirted some soda over ice and set it on the bar. "What's your damned problem?" he asked.

"The colonel," Bly said.

"Get over it. That silly old man matters not at all. He just supplies the money."

"Where is he?"

"Like I said, Beijing. That's all I know. If you're that hung up about it, call him and ask. When he's gone, I don't think about him."

"Bullshit."

Chiun filled a second glass with whisky over ice. He set it on the bar and pushed it toward Bly who picked it up, but waited for the ice to melt a bit.

"You'd do well to watch out for the colonel," Bly said. "He set me up. I'm sure he'd set you up, too."

"I appreciate your concern," Chiun said.

"Go to hell. I don't give a damn what happens to you, and you know it. I just don't want this whole effort destroyed because the colonel decides to stick it to us. I've put my reputation on the line. Hell, I've put my life on the line. I'm committing treason. If this goes south, I have nothing."

"You doubt we can finish this?"

Bly shook his head. "I have no doubt that *I* can finish it. Whether the colonel is up to the task is another matter entirely. He's a wild card. I hate wildcards."

"You leave him to me," Chiun said.

"Why should I?"

"Because I know what I'm doing."

Bly smiled inwardly. He knew he'd wounded the younger man's pride by telling him what to do. It was a small victory, sure, but one he'd savor.

"If I thought he was betraying us, he'd be dead," Chiun said. "Same goes for you. I haven't made it this far by being weak." Holding a cigar in one hand, he clipped the end from it and worked on lighting it.

"I'll check him out," Chiun said between puffs. "Don't look at me like that. I'll check on him, make sure he is all that he says he is."

"Fine."

Chiun snapped closed his stainless-steel lighter and set it on the bar. "What about the shipment?" he asked.

"On time. You?"

"Same. Boat puts in here tonight. You'll have your labor force within twenty-four hours. It will take weeks to train them, but they'll do whatever you ask. They're dirt farmers. They don't know any better. The simple fools are just happy to be out of China."

Bly greeted the news with a nod, and sipped from his drink. The two men lapsed into silence for several seconds. The American slid into a nearby chair and watched the other man as he circled the room. Chiun, the cigar clenched between his teeth, moved toward the sliding glass doors that led onto the deck. He stared at his reflection in the glass and smoothed down his hair with the palm of his hand. Vain bastard, Bly thought.

"Has the woman said anything yet?" Chiun asked.

"I haven't spoken with her personally, but my people say she's been quiet ever since she woke up," Bly said, his pulse racing.

"You should give her to me," Chiun said. "I'll make her talk."

"I don't need your help."

"What about the computer?" Chiun asked.

Bly shrugged and sighed. "Nothing. Maria Serrano is a CIA agent. A damn good one. She's been trained to endure harsh interrogation, torture, all of it. She has an iron will and a great deal of loyalty. We can't crack her open in one night."

"Can't or won't?"

"Back off," Bly said, hoping he sounded tough enough.

Chiun shot him a smug smile. "That's what I thought. She's an American spy, as are you. This worries me. Perhaps you're not as resolved to this as you should be. Maybe you're holding back a bit, reluctant to do what's necessary."

Bly gave him a blank look. "Nice try," he said. "But, please don't insult my intelligence with such ham-handed attempts at mind-fucking me. I can do whatever's necessary to make this happen. If I can't extract what I need, I'll find someone who will. And by that I mean an expert. Not some leg breakers in expensive suits."

Chiun flashed a smile, but Bly noticed that it didn't reach the man's eyes. "So, working with us, you are—what's the American term?—slumming."

"Just drop it," Bly replied. "Focus on delivering the cargo. Focus on Hong Kong. Shut up. Those are your priorities."

"I know my priorities."

"Good. Then perhaps you could make some progress on them."

"The longer she's alive, the more dangerous she is to us," Chiun said.

"The longer I have her," Bly said, "the more her capacity to harm us diminishes." He almost believed what he was saying was true. "Another two days and she'll be begging for us to kill her. We know how to break people. Trust me."

"If they know she's alive, they won't stop hunting for her. They'll be all over us, if they believe there's a chance of getting her back alive," Chiun said.

"There is no chance," Bly replied quietly, hoping to God that word of Serrano's escape didn't reach the mobster.

20

Bolan pumped the brakes of the Jeep Cherokee, bringing it to a stop at a traffic light.

It'd been thirty minutes since they'd ditched the club. Grimaldi sat in the passenger's seat. He puffed on a cigarette and bounced his left knee frenetically. Bolan, both hands locked on the steering wheel, waited for the light to turn green and launched the vehicle into a left turn. Once he hit a straightaway, he gunned the engine.

The phone rang and Bolan grabbed it.

"What?" he asked.

"What the fuck are you doing?" a man yelled on the other end. "You come down here and throw your weight around. You kill my people and steal my money. You want a war? I'll give you a war, you piece of shit."

Bolan killed the call. The phone rang twice more before he answered it.

"What the hell was that? You hang up on me? No one hangs up on me! What the hell are you doing to me?"

"Taking you to school," Bolan growled. "You need to learn a few things. Lesson one, watch who you screw. Same goes for Bly. That son of a bitch used us, used our money to build Garrison Industries into a big company, now he plans to dump it, hand it off to a dirt bag like you. That bastard used us as his personal bank. My people don't like it. We're going to show you how unhappy we are in ways you can't imagine. I offered you several million dollars to be a good boy and walk away. You didn't do it. Thought you were too big a man for that. Enjoy what's coming your way."

Bolan ended the call. The phone started ringing again. With his index finger, he hit the button for the electric window. The roar of wind pushing through the open window filled the car. The soldier took the phone and tossed it from the vehicle.

"God, you're nasty," Grimaldi said.

Bolan shrugged his shoulders. "Define nasty," he said.

"Maybe it's your thyroid," Grimaldi replied. "You getting enough iodine? Need a nap, maybe?"

Bolan grinned. "I'm good, thanks."

"I just know how fragile you are."

CHIUN UNCOILED FROM HIS SWIVEL chair and slammed the phone against the desktop several times, until the LCD screen cracked. He hurled the phone across the room and it struck a wall, bounced off it and dropped into a potted plant. Blood roared in his ears, and he felt a vein thudding in his temple.

He kicked the swivel chair, which glided several feet away until it struck an oak cabinet. He came around the desk, moved to the cabinet and grabbed a ring of keys from it. As he stalked past the guard, he drove a shoulder into the man's arm. The guard stepped back but kept his mouth shut and his expression stony.

That bastard, Lambretta, was tearing up everything, Chiun thought. He was taking things from Chiun, things he'd worked his whole life to get. Cash. Contacts. Businesses. This guy was robbing him blind—suicide by anyone's measure—and laughing at Chiun while he did it.

Chiun could almost stand losing the things. But he could tell the man wasn't afraid of him, and that was what really made him angry. He'd worked his whole life to make people fear him. Fear, he'd found, was a potent weapon. As a boy growing up in Hong Kong, his father gone, his mother working two jobs to support them, Chiun had taught himself what it meant to be a man. He'd shunned weakness and self-pity, considered them vices, ones he could ill afford. Rather, he'd spend his days walking the streets of Hong Kong, forcing himself to travel through the worst possible neighborhoods, hunting for a fight. Each time someone confronted him, he fought them. Sometimes he won, sometimes not. But he'd never backed down. When he'd gotten older, he'd become a legend on the streets, especially when he reached an age where victory no longer was enough, and he began killing his opponents to make a name for himself. Eventually, word got around and people began hiring him to eliminate people. With each new kill, his legend grew bigger, though never so big that he couldn't back it up with action.

He'd lived his life in a combat zone. One of his own making, sure. But one that rewarded him time and again as he sought more power and dominance.

He thought of Firestorm and realized that the money that selling it would generate was a secondary concern. So was providing China with a valuable weapon. He cared little for his country, but he knew having this machine would give him awesome power.

The thoughts exhilarated him, caused him to feel deliriously excited about what was to happen during the next twenty-four hours.

Then from the corner of his eye, he saw the discarded cell phone and he felt rage flare again. That son of a bitch! Who the hell did he think he was, coming to his town and trying to turn things upside down? He'd flay that bastard alive! And he might do the same thing to those fucks in Chicago who were trying to reach halfway around the world and steal his business.

He stalked onto his screened-in deck and watched the moon reflect white against the black current. Just off the shore, white-capped waves crashed, dissipated.

He watched his two guards—each dressed in black combat pants and armed with M-4 assault rifles—stand on the beach and watch the surrounding area for danger. He had an army of gunmen. But his core group was culled from the most elite soldiers from the Chinese army and intelligence services. Maybe two dozen of them were at his beck and call at any one time. None of them would hesitate to kill on command. And he only hoped he'd give the command soon to eliminate Lambretta.

DOYLE SAT IN HIS PRISON cell on his bed and wondered for the hundredth time how long he'd have to wait in this fucking hole.

He didn't expect a rescue per se. Objectively, he knew that Bly couldn't care less if Doyle spent the rest of his life in a prison cell. As far as the Ivy League prick was concerned, Doyle was just some uncouth punk with blood on his hands and contacts among the absolute filth of society. Doyle already knew that his boss was out for one person—himself—and, therefore, he wasn't surprised when the American abandoned him when he was in trouble. But he was surprised that Bly would leave him in American custody where he could spill his guts to anyone willing to listen.

And the longer he sat, the more willing to talk he became. The Americans had played it close to the vest as to what they knew and didn't know. They hadn't mentioned Firestorm to him, which led him to believe they knew nothing of it. They just wanted to find their agent, try to pull her fat from the fire, and be done with it. If they knew anything, he reasoned, they'd have said something. Doyle didn't know much about the weapon itself. He'd sold a lot of stuff in his time, but nothing of that sophistication. Assault rifles, grenades, rocket launchers, armored vehicles had all passed through his hands and over to some well-heeled despot or terrorist. He'd hate to screw up the operation, particularly since Bly had promised him a cut.

Another few hours in the tank, though, and he'd start to tell stories.

He guessed that he'd get a chance soon, and he hoped the woman who'd threatened his kids was the one who questioned him. Now that he'd had some time to think and to cool down, he decided that maybe she'd been yanking his chain. After all, she wouldn't really have his kids killed, would she? Still, he wasn't sure he'd leave that to chance. So he'd play the game with her.

With years of operating in the underworld, he knew plenty of people in the United States he could call. They'd be only too happy to cut down her family a couple of generations back, if he wanted them to. So, if she wanted to play rough with him, he'd show her who the hell was boss.

He ruminated over this for several minutes before someone appeared at the cell door and pulled him from his thoughts.

A Colombian police sergeant stood at the door. "Get up," he said. "You're leaving."

"How?" Doyle asked. "There haven't been any charges filed, which means that I haven't been arraigned. That means there's no bail for me to post. So how can I be getting out of here? You screwing with me, friend?"

The cop gave him a hard stare. "Stay or go. But decide now."

Doyle decided to go.

When he stepped outside the gate, he saw a black Mercedes parked outside the gate. Its engine purred and its headlights cast white shafts of light onto the ground. As he approached the fence, the headlights blinked. With no one else around, he decided they were trying to grab his attention.

His head felt foggy and he craved a cold beer. Several, in fact. And a damn cigarette. His hands shook and he shoved them into his pockets to hide them. He sucked in the smog-laden air as he closed in on the luxury sedan. When he reached the car, the rear door's latch clicked before he could grasp it. The door swung outward. He grabbed the frame and fanned it outward until it would move no farther. Bending slightly at the waist, he leaned inside for a look.

What he saw made his gut clench. An Asian man sat on a bench seat and stared back at him. The man had one arm in a cast. He wore his hair in a ponytail. Sunglasses covered his eyes and, with his drawn, angular face, they made him look like a black-eyed bug. He smiled at Doyle, then waved at the seat with his remaining arm.

"Please, Mr. Doyle," the man said.

Doyle hesitated and gave the car's interior a closer look. The back consisted of two bench seats, covered with tan leather, that faced each other. A smoked-glass shield separated the rear compartment from the driver's seat. Doyle saw a bulge under the man's jacket that indicated he was carrying a weapon.

"You're one of Chiun's flunkies," Doyle said.

The man gave him a curt nod. "We're associates."

"Well lah-tee-dah," Doyle said. "What the hell do you want?"

"Not to discuss my business in public, particularly in front of police headquarters. If you'd be so kind?"

Doyle glanced over his shoulder at the police station, then swiveled his head back and nodded his understanding. He climbed inside the car, dropped into one of the seats and pulled the door closed.

The man reached down to a refrigerator under the seat. He drew a beer from inside it and handed it to Doyle.

Doyle unscrewed the top and tossed the cap on the floor. Putting the bottle to his lips, he guzzled its contents greedily.

He emptied the bottle, made a satisfied sound and handed it back to his host. "Another," he said.

The man gave him another beer. As he grasped it, the engine revved and the car lurched forward. Doyle shot a concerned look at the man, who made a dismissive gesture.

"We're just going for a ride," the man said. "Don't worry. We're not out to harm you."

Doyle drank from the bottle, this time slowly. He believed that beer cleared his head, helped him think. But, until he figured out this bastard's game, he knew he'd better not indulge too heavily. "So," he said, "You the beer fairy or have you got a reason for tracking me down like this?"

"Mr. Chiun sent me," the man said. Doyle noted that the man's English was formal, but almost letter perfect. "He wants to ask a favor of you."

"What kind of favor?"

"Then you're interested?"

"Depends on the favor," Doyle said.

"Fair enough."

"You get me out of the tank?"

"We pulled some strings, yes."

Doyle held up the bottle and stared through the glass at the small pool of suds gathered in the bottom of it. He wondered whether the man wanted him to sell out Bly. If so, it wouldn't be a hard deal to close. If it hadn't been for Chiun, Doyle knew he'd still be marking time in a jail cell.

"I might do you a favor," Doyle said. "Lay it out for me."

The man did and the details caused the Irishman to smile.

CHO WATCHED THE IRISHMAN climb out of the car, slam the door and head down the street toward his house.

He opened the console next to him and picked up the receiver for his satellite phone and dialed the number the American had given him. Several clicks sounded on the line. He assumed that meant the call was being routed through a series of cutout numbers to make it harder to trace. Chiun had employed a similar system, though likely not to the technical sophistication of this one.

A gruff voice boomed in the earpiece. "Yeah?"

"I'm Cooper's friend."

"Yippee."

"How are my kids?" he asked.

"Fine. Jesus, they're kids. We aren't going to hurt them. Don't sweat it."

"Okay, then I'm not sweating it."

"Good," the voice said. "The verdict?"

"He agreed."

"All right. You give him this number to call?"

"You told me to."

"Doesn't mean you did it."

"I gave it to him," Cho said sullenly.

"Tell the driver to bring you home," the voice replied.

THE FALCON 2000 EXECUTIVE jet touched down at a private airport on the outskirts of Hong Kong. The wheels struck the tarmac and jolted the plane. Bly shifted uncomfortably in his seat. They'd encountered a violent storm during the trip, which forced everyone to remain belted in their seats. Bly had spent the trip in silence, either sleeping fitfully or working on his laptop, sending e-mails or checking Garrison's stock price.

The plane came to a halt. Bly unbuckled his seat belt. The executive snapped his laptop shut and slipped it inside a nylon shoulder bag. By the time the door had opened, he was packed and headed for the exit.

Two of his bodyguards stood in front of the door. One of them poked his head out, looked left, then right. He stepped back inside and waved the other guard through the door and he followed. By then, Chet James, Bly's security chief stood behind him, along with three more guards.

"Go ahead, sir," James said.

Bly nodded. He descended the steps slowly. He'd left his coat unbuttoned so he could easily reach the Glock handgun attached to his belt. He'd received a handful of e-mails from Chiun, each more cryptic than the last. He wasn't sure what sort of reception he could expect.

When they reached the arrivals, Bly found it bustling with people. The guards formed a square around him and began pushing through the crowd, their rough treatment occasionally eliciting a yell or a nasty gesture from some passerby.

By the time they'd reached the front doors, Bly saw a young Chinese man walking directly toward them. The man wore a navy blue pinstriped suit and a solid yellow tie. He stopped a few feet from Bly's entourage, clasped his hands in front of himself and smiled.

"Welcome to Hong Kong," the man said. "Chiun sent me."

"Where the hell is he?" Bly asked.

The man quickly swept his gaze over their surroundings. "He doesn't like such close quarters," the man said.

"I understand," Bly replied. It wasn't so much that he understood as he didn't care.

His group fell in step behind Chiun's man and followed him from the terminal to the parking garage. On the second floor, they located a limousine, its engine running, parked outside the elevator. Crew wagons stood at the front and rear bumpers of the limo. Their engines also hummed. Bly counted four more of Chiun's gunners poised around the vehicles. They openly stared at Bly and his group as they closed in on the line of vehicles.

As he sized up the situation, Bly felt his stomach roll. A film of sweat broke out on his palms. Fear constricted his chest muscles, making it hard to breathe. Instinct told him that something was wrong. Not just the show of strength warned him of possible danger. No, he expected that from a thug like Chiun. Maybe it was the dark looks Chiun's thugs shot at him and his men. He sensed danger.

Chiun's man walked quickly to the limo and opened the rear

doors. With a nod, he gestured for Bly to step inside. The American hesitated.

"Please," the man said.

Blood thundered in Bly's ears and a primal urge to run seized him. He ignored it and pressed ahead, pushing his way between his bodyguards. He climbed into the back, greeted Chiun with a nod and settled into a seat across from him. Chiun didn't respond.

The door slammed shut.

Bly kept his hand on his pistol. He shifted his thigh just a bit so he'd have a clear shot at the triad boss if things went south. If any of this registered with Chiun, it was impossible to tell. His expression remained stony.

"Why are we meeting here?" Bly asked. "In the middle of a parking garage. I want to see the damn factory."

"Tommy Vallachi," Chiun said. "Does that name mean anything to you?"

"Why?"

"That's not an answer."

"I know many people."

"Vallachi. Do you know him?"

Bly nodded slowly. "The Vallachis own a nice-sized chunk of Garrison, but less than five percent. They've owned it since the IPO a few years ago."

"So you do know them?"

"Like I said, I know a lot of people. A lot of people own pieces of the company. I don't police who owns what. And at the rate you've been buying it up, it doesn't matter how much the Vallachis own. You own more."

"Bullshit!" Chiun snapped through clenched teeth.

By now, Bly's fear had drained away, replaced by irritation. If it'd just been the two of them, he'd have been glad to pull the trigger and rid himself of this headache.

"You want to explain yourself?" Bly asked.

Chiun's jaw tightened and his lips drew into a thin line.

"Don't fuck with me," Chiun said. "Tell me what you promised these bastards, when you promised it, the whole thing. And tell me now."

"Like I told you, they bought stock several years ago," Bly replied. "They knew people we wanted to know. We struck a deal with them. I gave them stock through a third-party intermediary. They gave me information, occasionally provided an introduction."

"Did you promise them a cut?"

"Of what we're doing? Are you an idiot? I never even told them about any of this. Now, either explain yourself, or I'm walking out of here."

Chiun told him about the man from Chicago who'd burned up several of the gangster's business ventures.

"I know nothing about that," Bly stated flatly.

"What about Deng. He's been sending money to you. Or, more specifically, to an account in Zurich. We have proof of that," Chiun said.

His patience worn thin, Bly leaned forward and rested his elbows on his knees.

"I have no fucking idea what you're talking about," he said. "If this is another tale spun by your friend in Chicago, then it's bullshit. We could call the Vallachis, but then we'd have to explain everything to them, and possibly blow open this whole operation. And even then I can't guarantee that they'd confirm anything over the phone. So before I call them and make a complete ass out of myself, I want some proof from you to back up these allegations."

Chiun grabbed a handful of papers and handed them to Bly. The American leafed through them, recognized them as financial-transaction records of some sort, but otherwise they meant little to him.

"Here's your proof," Chiun said. "These records show that Deng has put millions of dollars into these accounts, accounts that can be traced back to you. And the deposits correspond with the dates of our meetings in Malaysia and Indonesia."

Bly felt his neck begin to burn. An electric charge raced through his arms, and he wanted to punch Chiun in the face.

"You mean the meetings where Deng blackmailed me into

working with you two? The ones where he flashed pictures of me in Thailand? Those meetings? And what do you think he was paying me for? I'd just as soon kill that little bastard as take a fucking dime from him. You know that as well as I do."

"What are you two cooking up? Is he a double agent? Is he helping you to set me up?" Chiun asked.

"I know nothing about these cash transfers," Bly stated. "Not one damn thing. Someone set all this up. They lured you in to one of the oldest counterintelligence scams in the book. And you fell for it. You're a fucking idiot."

Bly glared at the other man and let his words sink in.

21

Serrano leaned close to the bathroom mirror and studied the purple bruise under her right eye, a remnant from her captivity. Drawing back, she picked up a hairbrush that someone had bought for her and raised it over her head. The movement ignited a white-hot flash of pain that seared her ribs. She winced but kept her arm raised, forcing herself to ignore it.

When she finished with her hair, she set aside the brush, untied the sash that held her robe closed and drew the garment open. Another bruise, this one bluish and about the circumference of a grapefruit had formed beneath her right breast. A third started a few inches from her breast, but bled around the side of her torso. She touched it gingerly with two fingers, igniting more pain. She screwed her eyes shut and inhaled sharply as she rode out the hurt.

With her eyes closed, images roared through her mind: Bly standing over her, kicking her ribs, demanding answers. She still could smell the mildew that mixed with his rancid cologne, could feel herself hugging the cold concrete floor. The sensation of his boot thudding against her ribs, her kidneys, surged through her. She still could see his face, a stony mask, as he meted out punishment for a crime of his own determination.

Her eyes snapped open. Tears brimmed over and burned hot down her cheeks, blurring her vision. She wiped them away and stared down into the sink, unable to stand the sight of her tear-stained face. She drew her robe closed, gathered her things and returned to her room.

Seated on the edge of her bed, she wrapped a bandage tight around her rib cage. She slipped into new undergarments, jeans and a T-shirt that had been laid for her. The clean fabric felt good against her skin. Her first change of clothes in days, she thought.

Another torrent of memories slammed into her. She hugged herself, fingers digging into her triceps as she relived the mock execution. She could hear the small whimper she'd made when Bly had pulled the trigger. She'd felt so damned helpless. Now she just felt humiliated and consumed with self-hatred. She'd sworn a long time ago that she'd never allow herself to be helpless, but she'd been just that and she knew the bastard almost had broken her. Almost.

Lowering her arms, she forced herself to focus on the rage that roiled inside her. The emotion, she knew, would keep her alive, propel her forward.

He'd almost broken her, but he hadn't and she planned to make that a fatal mistake for him.

She slipped on her socks, shod her feet in canvas sneakers.

Rising from the bed, she crossed the room with fast, purposeful strides. When she reached the dresser, she grabbed the holstered pistol that lay upon it and clipped it to her jeans.

The SIG-Sauer's presence seemed to calm the butterflies that fluttered in her stomach. She took a couple of practice draws with the gun. The motion hurt her ribs, but not enough to slow her. She picked up a magazine from the dresser, slammed it into the pistol's handle, jacked a round into the chamber, decocked the weapon and set the safety. She slipped it into the holster.

She thought of the big man, Cooper. She never had met anyone quite like him before, she thought. She'd seen him kill a man, seen the carnage he'd wrought at Bly's compound. Yet if it fed his ego or troubled him deeply, he gave no outward signs. The pilot, she could tell, was brave. But he coped with humor and wolfish comments. Cooper, on the other hand, was an enigma. He seemed free of the remorse that haunted her and others she knew who'd killed. But he wasn't cold or without compassion.

A knock at the door drew her from her thoughts. Her hand was on the pistol's butt before she could think about it.

"Yes?"

"Cooper."

"Come in."

The door opened and he stuck his head inside her room.

"Let's go."

"Do you need directions?" Serrano asked.

"No," Bolan replied.

"Is that because you're a man or because you actually know where you're going?"

He allowed himself a smile. "Maybe both," he said. "We were already there once."

"What did you find?"

"That the CIA is very thorough."

"I guess that means my couch and chair have been ruined," she said.

"Most of your stuff's gone. Or torn up."

"For all the good it did them," she said.

"What do you mean?"

"If they searched the apartment, they came away empty-handed. I can guarantee that. Where's the last place you'd hide something?"

Bolan considered the question. "The first place someone would look."

"Like my apartment."

"Should I be going somewhere else?"

She shook her head no. Bolan navigated the vehicle through what had now become familiar territory. He'd learned a long time ago to find his way around strange areas, a skill he'd acquired during a career of deep-territory insertions. His mind automatically monitored his surroundings, cataloged streets, fallen trees, boulders, whatever landmarks might provide direction or cover if he found his back against the wall.

He guided the Jeep Cherokee into a gravel lot that sat behind Serrano's apartment building. He killed the engine and pocketed the keys. When they reached the front of the building, he felt a light touch on his arm. He looked at the woman, and she gestured with her head in the direction of a park situated across the street.

After they crossed the street, she led him onto a concrete trail that wound into the park.

Brow furrowed, Bolan studied his surroundings. The park was a strange oasis in the middle of a residential district. He judged the trees, based on their size, to be less than a decade old. Bolan noted a playground outfitted with brand-new equipment located in one corner of the grounds. Relief came over him when he realized that no children populated the grounds at the moment. He hadn't noticed anyone tailing them, but if someone was lying in wait for them, he didn't want any children caught in the cross fire.

Following Serrano's lead, he stepped off the path and angled toward a fountain that lay a short distance ahead.

"The park was built by a drug dealer," Serrano said. "Or he gave the right people enough money to build it. But it's no secret to anyone in the city who really paid the bill."

Bolan remained silent. He divided his attention between listening to the woman and watching for trouble.

"It was a transparent PR move," she continued. "But the dealer knows it works. They do this, maybe build a school or two, and people start to turn a blind eye to what they're doing. You can only terrorize people so long before they get pissed and fight back. But if you do nice things, they tend to grow numb to the bad things you do, turn a blind eye toward them."

They reached the fountain. Serrano sat on the edge of the pool that surrounded it. She removed her shoes and socks, and rolled up her pant legs to just below her knees. Stepping into the water, she traipsed over to the fountain, a concrete angel in midflight pouring water from a large vase.

She took a screwdriver from the back pocket of her jeans and set to work removing the screws that held a bronze plaque attached to the pedestal that held the statue aloft. When the plaque came free, she tossed it into the water. She reached into a small oval-shaped hole set into the concrete and pulled something from it. Her fingers dipped inside again and she withdrew some objects wrapped in plastic.

"A dead drop," she said. "One of them anyway."

"You mean for your team?" Bolan asked.

"No, for myself. If something ever happened to us, if we got compromised, this was my ace in the hole, so to speak." She held up a sealed plastic bag. Bolan saw that it contained cash and what looked like a passport.

She climbed out of the pool. Rivulets of water dripped from her bare feet and legs, splotching the concrete dark gray. The CIA agent extended her fist. Bolan took the hint and held out his palm. She dropped something in it. He looked and saw a plastic device that measured about three inches long. He immediately recognized it as a memory stick for a computer.

"I thought you stole a laptop," he said.

"I did," she replied. "I copied what I needed onto that stick and trashed the laptop. When everyone started disappearing, I imagined the worst. I brought this here and hid it in the dead drop. I knew that if someone had identified us—any of us—there'd been a leak. My identity was secret and so was the rest of the team's. If any of us got nailed, it was because someone had passed the information along to Bly. I wanted to make sure this information was in a place where Bly couldn't get it."

By now, she'd donned her socks and shoes. She rose from the edge of the pool, crossed her arms over her chest. She nodded at Bolan's fist.

"A lot of people died so we could get that little chunk of plastic," she said. "People who really gave a damn about their country."

Bolan nodded solemnly. "Understood," he said. "They didn't die in vain. Trust me."

22

Hong Kong

Donald Major climbed the steps to his apartment. The former Scotland Yard detective had to force himself to go slowly. Wired with energy and caffeine, the stick-thin detective was a model of frenetic activity. His mind usually raced several steps ahead of conversations, and he was given to sudden and rapid movements such as jumping out of his chair and pacing the room.

Many considered him prickly, impatient. He wasn't, but his brain moved so fast he found it excruciating to wait for others to spit out what they had to say.

Going up steps at a deliberately slow pace was like jogging barefoot over of broken glass. But the doorman, concern etched on his features, had taken him aside when he'd returned to the building.

"People were looking for you," the man warned. "They went to your apartment, but never came down."

"You told them which apartment was mine?"

The man shook his head emphatically.

"No." He turned slightly at the waist and motioned with an extended thumb at the desk clerk. "He did. They gave him cash."

"Asians?"

"The man's Caucasian. The woman looks Latino."

"Do I know them?"

"I've never seen them," the doorman said.

Major withdrew some money from his pocket. There goes

dinner out, he thought. The man snatched the money from his out-stretched hand, stuffed it into his pants pocket and walked away.

As he set foot on the first step of the last flight, Major drew the Glock 21 from his hip holster. His chest felt tight, a sensation he attributed to exertion. He usually took the elevator and he smoked three packs of cigarettes a day. A climb to the eighth floor wasn't something that came easily for him. But they might know that he usually took the elevator. If they were there to kill him, changing routines might just make the difference between life and death, he reasoned.

His mind reeled as he tried to figure out who might be there. He knew he had plenty of enemies. A person didn't spend twenty years chasing the Chinese mob through Hong Kong without pissing off a few people. Even after the British relinquished control of the city, he'd stayed on and continued his work, though now as a private detective. Occasionally, he came across a few nuggets of information he could sell to Interpol or the DEA or the Brits for a few bucks.

By the time he'd reached his floor, the sweat had collected in the small of his back, beneath his collar and in his armpits. Exiting the stairwell, he glided down the hallway. With each step, he quashed an urge to surge forward, kick in the door, confront the people looking for him. As he closed in on his apartment, he heard the murmur of a television from inside. They'd left the door cracked open.

What the hell was going on? he wondered.

If they were trying to surprise him, they were doing a damn bad job of it.

With the toe of his shoe, he edged open the door slowly. It yielded with little pressure. He ground his teeth together in anticipation of the squeak the hinges emitted. Usually, he appreciated the noisy door, considered it a security feature. Right now, though, he considered it a liability.

The door opened. His Glock held before him with both hands, he followed it inward. His eyes swept the room for targets. His chest muscles had tightened, and he found it even harder to breathe, a symptom not only of exertion but now of fear.

He found both the intruders seated in the living room. A big man with icy blue eyes sat on the couch, leaning forward, his elbows on his knees. The woman sat on an armchair. Both gave him benign smiles.

"Welcome home, Inspector," the man said. "Have a seat. I want to talk to you."

BOLAN WATCHED THE ENGLISHMAN'S face transition from caution to confusion to anger all in the span of a couple of heartbeats. Major looked at Bolan, then Serrano, then back at Bolan. He didn't lower his gun.

"We're not here to hurt you," Serrano said.

"I'll be the bloody judge of that," Major replied.

"Fair enough," she said.

Bolan had the leather wallet that held his fake Justice Department credentials fanned open on his right knee. Major's eyes lighted on them.

"Slide them over here," he said. "I like to know who I'm talking with. Same for you, young lady. If you have any identification, I'd like to see it."

Bolan followed the Briton's request. Serrano tossed fake State Department credentials in the man's direction.

Without taking his eyes from the two intruders, Major knelt, snatching up the IDs up with his free hand. He studied Serrano's first, then Bolan's. The detective gave Bolan a knowing look.

"Matt Cooper," he said. "Sounds like an extra in a Western. Or like a nomme de guerre. And you, miss, Gina Lopez. Of course that's your real name."

"Hal Brognola sent me," Bolan said.

"Ah," Major said. "Now we're getting somewhere. How's the old bastard doing?"

"He never sleeps," Bolan replied. "His stomach's killing him. But he says he's still taller than you."

Major allowed himself a brief smile. He did a quick walk-through of the apartment. When he returned, he backed toward an armchair and dropped into it. He set the gun on the chair's arm, hooking his trigger finger around the outside of the trigger guard. With a toss, he returned their IDs.

"So Mr. Cooper," he said, "what brings you here?"

"A triad."

"Big subject. Care to narrow it down?"

"Chiun."

"Ah, always an interesting topic. What's my friend got his damn nose into this time?"

"Weapons."

"Smuggling?"

"Making," Bolan said.

"I'll be damned. Seems awfully ambitious for that little psychopath. Must be awfully damn lucrative to make him step out of his comfort zone like that."

Bolan shrugged. "Maybe."

"Your question?"

"What've you heard?" Serrano asked.

Major shook his head. "Very little, I'm afraid. At least as far as anything that elaborate."

The woman pressed him. "Has he bought any property? Anything big enough to make weapons?"

"How big are the weapons?"

"Big," she replied.

"More specific, please."

"Sorry," she said. "It's classified."

Major heaved a big sigh. "Isn't it always? Hang on. Let me make some calls."

23

Beijing, China

Doyle hunched over a table at an outdoor café. Sunglasses hid his eyes and a baseball cap pulled tight over his head covered his head, which he'd shaved to his freckled skin. He studied the throngs of people who pushed past the fenced-in patio. The younger ones, he noticed, looked decidedly Western. They wore jeans and designer shirts, many of them made in their country, he guessed. They smoked cigarettes and spoke animatedly into mobile telephones. Several, he noticed, looked dour, careworn. Their eyes occasionally flicked to a pair of Chinese soldiers who stood alongside the curb, armed with AK-47s.

He smiled. Good, he thought, let somebody else worry. Once I make my score, living will be easy. I'll tell Bly to go to hell. Maybe I'll take a little time off. Hell, with the money that Chinese bastard has promised, maybe I'll start another club. Get back to a life of drinking and squeezing the flesh.

Checking his watch, he scowled and shot up from his chair. He was a minute off his timetable. Under most circumstances, it wouldn't be a big deal. But, with what he had planned sixty seconds meant the difference between success and failure, the latter of which didn't pay worth a damn.

He dropped some money on the table and exited the patio. He bulled his way into the heavy tide of people moving along the street, his bulk an effective tool for wedging his way in.

According to the intelligence provided to him by Chiun's

man, the colonel left the defense ministry each day at 5:00 p.m. A chauffeured state car deposited him at his home between 5:21 p.m. and 5:25 p.m., depending on the route he took. The driver wisely alternated routes daily to keep the colonel secure.

Deng, usually with at least one guard in tow, retired to his apartment where he'd eat dinner, work another few hours and end the night with a glass of brandy and the day's final cigarette. At least three times a week, sometimes more depending on his stress level, he had hookers brought in.

From what Doyle understood, the whores had been a blessing for Chiun's people. They'd been all too happy to provide detailed information on the old man in exchange for cash.

Doyle walked three blocks down from the target site. At that point, he veered left, stepped off the curb and squeezed between the bumpers of the countless cars stuck in gridlock. A quick check of his surroundings told him that Deng's soldiers still had their backs to him.

When he reached the other side of the street, Doyle stepped onto the curb and doubled back toward Deng's apartment building. The plan that Chiun's people had drafted would be easy to follow. Doyle had copies of the keys to the apartment. The maid, who was on Chiun's payroll, would lace the inside guard's meal with a tranquilizer so he'd pass out. Doyle would then slip in and kill the colonel and leave without further confrontation.

The Irishman spun his way through the revolving doors and into the building's lobby. He strode purposefully past the front desk and gave the man who stood behind it a slight nod. He moved down a wide corridor until it split into two more hallways. He veered left and continued walking until he reached a service elevator. He grabbed one of the rough-hewn wooden gates, pushed it open and stepped inside the car.

He rode the car to the eleventh floor. It shuddered to a stop and he exited, finding himself inside a room of bare concrete floors and unfinished walls with the wooden frames and insulation exposed. With long strides, he crossed the room, barely taking notice of a pull-down metal door installed in the far wall and the mop and bucket propped against another wall.

A small Chinese man dressed in a gray work shirt and matching pants, whirled at the sound Doyle made. When he spotted the hulking Irishman, his eyebrows angled downward in anger and he began to speak rapidly in a Chinese dialect Doyle didn't recognize.

His moves mechanical in their precision, Doyle raised the 9 mm Ruger he carried. The weapon spat a single round, the report muffled by a sound suppressor attached to the weapon.

The janitor crumpled to the ground and Doyle had to fight to stifle a giggle. He folded the man's slight form as tightly as he could, hefted him from the ground and stuffed his body into a rectangular trash bin on wheels that apparently was used for collecting garbage from the individual apartments. He ripped open a green plastic trash bag, dumped its contents on top of the body, then did likewise with a second bag. He arranged the crumpled papers and empty plastic containers until he was satisfied that the bin would pass casual inspection. He headed for the door.

With uncharacteristic gentleness, Doyle softly cracked the door open, peered into the hallway and saw it was empty. He exited the custodian's room and headed for Deng's apartment.

The exterior door was unguarded, and he moved quickly toward it.

When he reached it, Doyle readied his Ruger. He unlocked the door, pushed it open and went inside. A guard who'd been standing in the entryway whirled, his jaw dropping with surprise. The Ruger shot once. A small dark hole appeared on the man's forehead and the hollowpoint round exploded from the back of his skull. The guard fell to the floor in a heap.

Doyle stepped over the dead man and moved down the corridor.

He made his way through the apartment, gliding through the living room and down a hallway. The thick pile carpeting muted his footfalls as he hurried ahead, the Ruger held at the ready. Doyle sized up the corridor. He saw two doors on his left and one on his right. Light filtered into the hallway from the space between the floor and bottom edge of the door on his right.

As he closed in on the room, he smelled cigarette smoke and heard a decidedly feminine giggle.

He grinned. You old dog, you're going to die with your boots on.

Careful not to step in front of the door, where his feet would be visible, he pressed an ear to it and listened a few beats. A woman spoke rapidly in Chinese, then giggled again. Seconds later he heard a door close.

Gently, he tried the knob. The door was locked, so he threw a shoulder into the it. His substantial weight knocked it inward, and he bulled his way through. Doyle saw the colonel sitting on the side of the bed, smoking a cigarette. The man whirled to face him, his mouth opened with surprise. The cigarette fell to the floor.

Doyle drilled two rounds into the man's chest. The force of the bullets knocked the old man to the floor. A gasp sounded from behind, and Doyle spun. He saw a woman standing there, her hands pressed against her mouth, her eyes wide as she stared at the killer.

Doyle raised the gun and pointed it at her.

His finger tightened on the trigger.

Motion in the corner of his eye caught him by surprise. He turned to look and spotted a soldier, poised in the doorway, his weapon trained on Doyle's midsection.

Confusion and surprise caused his brain and his reflexes to freeze. The guards didn't change shifts for another hour, he thought. That's what they had told him. He swung the pistol around ready to squeeze off a shot. Before he could trigger his own weapon, the soldier cut loose with a long burst from his assault rifle. Pain suddenly cleaved through Doyle's body, stole his breath. He collapsed to the floor and the gun slipped from his grasp. He stared at the ceiling, wondering for a moment what the hell had happened before everything turned cold and dark.

24

Chiun's limo glided through the gates and into the factory compound. Seated in the back of the vehicle, he checked the load on his Heckler & Koch Mk-23 handgun and returned it to the armpit holster beneath his well-tailored suit jacket. He thought about the news he'd just received, and his lips tightened into a bloodless line. The heel of his right foot tapped against the floor at the pace of a jackhammer.

A half hour earlier, he'd received word that Deng was dead. Doyle had been the killer. The news stoked a fury inside him that he thought would immolate him on the spot. He couldn't care less about the old man, per se. Given enough time, he'd have put a bullet into the man's skull himself. He talked too much, thought too little. Their homeland was changing, but the colonel couldn't realize that. Eventually, he would've fucked something up, forced Chiun to take him out.

But Chiun needed the connection with the government, and the loss left him in a lurch.

Someone was making a fool of him. He was certain Bly had to have been behind Deng's murder. But nothing made sense. Everyone was double-crossing each other. Chiun vowed he would come out on top, and Bly would pay for his treachery.

The car slid to a stop. He popped open the door and uncoiled from the rear seat, not waiting for the guards to escort him out. He looked around the multibay loading area. The three Firestorm weapons stood alongside one wall. Four forklifts were lined up along another wall.

What was going on?

Before he could say anything, he noticed one of his people running toward him, his face a mask of worry. The two men made eye contact and the foot soldier opened his mouth to speak. With a wave of his hand, Chiun cut him off.

"Where are my trucks?"

The man stopped. A surprised look crossed his features. "Your trucks? You didn't hear?"

"Hear? What the hell you talking about?"

"They got blasted at the docks."

For a split second Chiun seemed to freeze, as though he'd gone into shock.

Almost as suddenly something snapped inside the triad leader. His jaws clenched, as he grabbed the pistol from beneath his coat. The worker's eyes widened and he started to raise his hands in protest. But before he completed the move, the pistol barked twice. The man crumpled to the ground. The shot continued to echo through the big bay, but Chiun barely noticed. Blood thundered in his ears. His adrenaline-charged heart pounded out a racing beat in his chest. He swept the gun over his people.

"What in the fuck is going on here?" he shouted. "Are you people trying to make me crazy? Trying to destroy me? What the hell is happening here?"

Each time the gun muzzle passed over someone, he held up his hands, palms forward, at waist level, gesturing surrender.

One man, a hulking thug named Phan stepped forward.

"No one's trying to mess with you," he said. "It's Bly. That son of a bitch is doing this. You know he is."

Chiun licked his lips, trying to gather his thoughts. Finally, he nodded.

"Yeah," he said. "It's Bly."

"He sent Doyle to kill the old man," Phan said.

"He hated the old man," Chiun replied.

"Yeah, but he didn't just send Doyle to do the job. He made it look like we—I mean, you—did it. We checked it out. Someone picked up Doyle at the prison. A Chinese man. He signed the paperwork to get Doyle out of prison. The desk people there saw him do it. Don't look at me like that. I know what the hell I'm talking about here," Phan explained.

"How the hell did Doyle even get out of jail?" Chiun asked, his voice calmer. "There's no way he ever should've gotten out of there, not unless he was being extradited to the United States."

"Yeah. But the okay to let him out came from someone high up in the government. You think Bly has the clout to make that happen? Bet your ass he does."

Chiun mulled what Phan was saying. Nausea overtook him and he swallowed hard. That bastard! Bly was making him look like an idiot! He wanted the Chinese to think he'd set up the assassination. Wanted him to take the fall for it. What else could it be?

25

"Striker, you there?"

"Go," Bolan replied. He wore a wireless earpiece and spoke into his throat mike.

"We just got word," Brognola said. "Doyle took out Deng. Then a guard killed Doyle."

"Cho did good work," Bolan replied.

"Deserves an acting award," the big Fed said. "We put him and his kids on an airplane a couple of hours ago. We're bringing him to Washington. From there, we turn them over to the marshall's office—right after we debrief him some more."

"Good," Bolan said. "I promised him I'd get them out safe. I'm glad it's working out that way."

"We've got other news, too. One of our assets at the Bogotá airport saw Bly and his crew hopping into a small jet. We tracked it. It made a couple of stops for fuel, but it landed in Hong Kong within the last couple of hours."

"Anyone see Bly get off the plane?"

"Unknown. I have a couple of agents at the airports in question. They're flashing his picture around to anyone willing to look. No takers as far as I know. I'll let you know if it changes."

"Do that," the Executioner replied.

BOLAN STOOD TO THE SIDE of the window. He gripped binoculars in his left hand. He peered at an angle through the window and down at the big factory sprawled below. The place had two massive single-story buildings, each at least thirty-feet high, a six-story office building and several other smaller structures.

He released the binoculars, felt the strap grow taut around his neck with their weight. Several men armed with assault rifles patrolled the grounds on foot, others with prowl cars and golf carts. A line of tanker trucks stood alongside one fence, while a single one was positioned next to the factory.

The sensation of someone staring at him overtook him. He glanced over at Serrano, who was crouched in the darkness, her body rendered nearly invisible by the skintight black combat suit she wore. Black combat cosmetics were streaked on her cheeks and forehead. But light filtering through the windows made her face visible, though muted.

"Well?" she asked.

"Compound matches the aerial photos," he said. "There are no surprises as far as that goes."

"This isn't a Garrison facility," she said.

Bolan shook his head. "Brits used to own it. They made cars here for a couple of decades before they closed it down about ten years ago."

"Looks pretty active now."

Bolan uncoiled from the floor and shot another glance out the window.

"Yeah," he said. "Major gave us good intel. He definitely knows his stuff."

A voice buzzed in the soldier's wireless earpiece.

"Striker?" It was Leo Turrin.

"Go."

"Looks like a convoy of heavies are coming your way," Turrin said.

"Who?"

"A couple of the license plates match cars in Chiun's fleet. But that's inconclusive since he may have sent them to hunt for Bly."

"Understood."

Grimaldi's voice broke into the conversation.

"That's Chiun's people," he said. "The AWACS planes are

picking up telephone traffic from inside the vehicle. According to them, whoever's talking's mighty pissed, too."

"About?" Bolan asked.

"Guess a team of Navy SEAL or something nabbed one of his boats. Lost lots of money on the deal."

"Sounds like a crime," Turrin said. "Maybe we should look into that."

A smile ghosted Bolan's lips. "At ease, you two. He's not beaten yet. You have a make on Bly yet?" Bolan asked.

"AWACS are scanning for his phone traffic. Wish we could have installed a GPS on his car."

"Get back to me when you hear more."

"If Bly comes this way, should we intercept?" Turrin asked.

"Negative. I want to see how this plays out."

"Clear."

Bolan saw headlights approaching below. He looked up the street to their source, and saw a line of cars slithering toward the gate.

"Looks like they're coming," he said.

Serrano nodded.

Bolan took up the binoculars again. He watched as the lead vehicle stopped at the gate and the vehicles behind it followed suit. A sentry stepped out of the small guard shack and walked to the driver's window. He bent slightly at the waist and spoke to someone inside the lead vehicle. Bolan focused on the guy's face as he spoke to one of the car's occupants. A moment later, the guard stood erect, backed up a couple of steps and spoke into a shoulder microphone clipped to his shirt.

The gates parted and the guard waved the vehicles through the opening. When the last car passed through, the guard motioned again with his hand and the gates slammed shut. Bolan watched the vehicles file through the property, a string of red taillights and gleaming metal. They passed the front end of the first factory building, came to a stop and began to unload.

"Bly's not with them," Serrano said.

"No," Bolan said.

She averted her gaze. One of her hands fussed with the flap of an ammo pouch fixed to her gear.

"He'll be along," Bolan said. "Is this going to be a problem?"

She gave him a hard look.

"There's no problem," she said. "I'm a pro."

"I don't question your skills, but you want him dead."

"You don't?"

"Not the way you do," Bolan said. "I want him dead because he's a traitor and a killer. I want him gone before he hurts anyone else. But there are probably hundreds of people in that category. And they make more everyday. So, no, killing him won't necessarily make me feel better or worse."

Her eyebrows arched slightly. "You think that makes you better than me somehow?"

"No," Bolan said.

"Then what's the problem?"

"I want to make sure your head's on straight."

"You son of a—"

"Answer the question," Bolan said quietly.

"Yes," she said through clenched teeth. "My head's on straight. I want to kill him, no doubt. But I'm not going to let my feelings interfere with my job. I'm a pro. I won't endanger the mission just to make sure we nail him."

"Good."

"You're a bastard."

"Yeah."

"THEY'RE COMING," Leo Turrin said.

"Roger," Bolan said.

He turned to Serrano, who'd spent the last few minutes quietly, lost in her own thoughts.

"They're coming," Bolan said. "Let's go."

By the time she'd gathered her weapons and equipment, Bolan already was at the door, his hand on the knob.

A brief elevator ride deposited them on the first floor. They made their way through a series of cubicles and desks. They reached the rear door. Bolan, with some coaching from Kurtzman, had bypassed the alarm on the door, allowing them to come and go as they pleased.

He stepped outside and felt the first drops from an impending storm strike his face.

He brought around the M-4 and thumbed an HE round into the grenade launcher while he sprinted down the length of the alley. He knew—thanks to surveillance by Grimaldi and Turrin—that Bly's caravan would be there in a few moments.

The front-gate sentry had disappeared inside the guard shack, presumably to find refuge from the rain. A pickup truck, headlights burning, idled about twenty yards from the shack. The raindrops pierced the headlights' glow, like a cascade of needles falling from the sky. Bolan counted two guards inside the vehicle.

The Executioner activated his throat mike.

"Jack?"

"Go, Striker."

"Sitrep."

"If we guessed their driving speed correctly," the pilot replied, "they should be coming our way in about two minutes."

"Leo?" Bolan said into the mike.

"Yeah, I've got a line of three cars coming my way. That corresponds with what the spotters at the hotel saw. Let me get a visual and I'll let you know where it stands."

The radio fell silent. Bolan waited.

"They're going to let Bly get here aren't they?"

Bolan turned to the woman behind him. "That's the plan," he said. "Whether it works that way is another matter."

She chewed her lower lip. "Sure," she said, nodding.

Bolan turned back toward the street and watched the hardsite. Turrin's voice broke the silence.

"Targets confirmed," he said.

"Do it," Bolan said.

GRIMALDI IMMEDIATELY RESPONDED to Bolan's command. He got to his feet, grabbed the handle of a black gun case that lay next to him and started for the door.

When he left the building, he sucked in big lungfuls of air. The abandoned structure that he'd been waiting in for the past hour reeked of urine and feces and rotten food. He'd smoked a couple of cigarettes to cover the stench, but to no avail. Even the smog-laden air of Hong Kong smelled like a country field compared to what he'd just left behind.

The pilot legged it to the edge of the alley, set the case on its side on the pavement. Kneeling beside it, he popped the locks, lifted the lid and studied the contents for a moment. Inside lay two LAW rockets. He grabbed the first, telescoped it open and raised it to his shoulder.

Headlights crested the hill. The rain had intensified. It gathered on his forehead, then rolled down into his eyes. He blinked the water away and began lining up a shot.

"I've got one vehicle," he said. "Repeat, one."

"Two single cars, each coming about a minute apart," Turrin said. "Then comes Bly's group. Copy?"

"Roger that," Grimaldi said.

A second car drove by, the tires kicking up a trail of rainwater as it passed.

Earlier, Grimaldi had broken a couple of exterior lights that illuminated the alley, plunging it into darkness. He adjusted the rocket on his slender shoulder, counting off the seconds until a full minute passed.

Nothing.

He counted down another thirty seconds, but still saw no one coming.

His brow furrowed.

"Leo," he called into his microphone.

"Yeah?" Turrin replied.

"I got nothing."

"What?"

"Zilch. Our target has disappeared."

"Maybe they stopped for something."

"Like what? They're less than a mile from their destination."

"Potty break?"

"Damn it, Leo."

"All right. I'll fall in behind them. See if they stopped along the road anywhere. Maybe they had engine trouble."

"Maybe," Grimaldi said without enthusiasm.

The way he saw it, if they'd had engine failure, they likely would've whisked Bly into one of the other cars and continued on. No security team worth its salt would want to leave him sitting in the open, stationary, with all that had happened during the last few days.

A couple of minutes later, Grimaldi heard the grinding of engines. He cast a glance to his right and saw a car come into view. The headlights of a second car were visible behind the first one. The driver of the lead vehicle gunned the engine. The crew wagon shot down the hill, gaining speed as it barreled ahead.

The pilot sighted down the LAW. He caught the big luxury vehicle in his sights.

With a gentle pull, he triggered the weapon. The rocket hissed from the tube, slashed through the air and drilled into the lead vehicle's engine block.

Thunder clapped; orange and yellow flames boiled up inside the vehicle. Windows exploded. The car launched into a sideways skid that carried it into a car parked alongside the road. A secondary explosion—caused by flames igniting the gas tank—tore through the car. The fire's glow illuminated Grimaldi, making him an easier target should another carload of Chiun's people happen by.

Grimaldi tossed the spent rocket tube and grabbed the MP-9 strapped over his shoulder. He darted sideways, putting some distance between himself and the launch site.

The second crew wagon released a full-throated growl as the driver kicked the engine into high gear. The vehicle shot past the pilot. Jagged yellow plumes of flame spit out from gunports in the car's doors. Grimaldi dropped into a crouch and cut loose with a burst from the Ruger. The wild spray of bullets from the speeding car blistered the air around him, chipping the brick of nearby buildings.

Then the car was gone. Grimaldi shot to his feet. He stared after it and watched the taillights wink out as it gained speed and disappeared.

He stared for a moment at the fire ripping unabated through the remains of the mangled crew wagon. The stench of burning rubber and plastic registered with him as black smoke poured thickly from the burning vehicle. The fire cast a glow on his face as he watched the car burn.

He activated the throat mike.

"Sarge," he said.

"Go," Bolan replied.

"Target's en route. One car's missing, though."

A pause.

"Leo," Bolan said. "Leo, check in."

Several seconds passed without a reply. Grimaldi was moving to pack up the LAW rocket and head for Turrin's position when the stocky Fed's strained voice sounded in Grimaldi's earpiece.

"Taking fire," Turrin said. "Got me pinned. Going EVA."

TURRIN GUIDED HIS SEDAN from the side street where he'd parked it and onto the main thoroughfare. He gunned the engine and headed in the same direction Bly's group had driven. His eyes swept over the streets as he searched out the third vehicle. Suddenly, a car rocketed from between two buildings. Its tires squealed as it fell in behind him.

The big car drew up on Turrin. Its grille and windshield filled his rearview mirror. The glare from the headlights flooded the vehicle's interior. Turrin stamped his foot on the accelerator, and his car hurtled through the intersection.

The other car stayed stuck on his trail.

A series of pops rose above the sound of the growling engines. Slugs lanced through the rear windshield, through the car. Some chewed into the seats or dashboard. Others whistled past Turrin's ears as he instinctively ducked in his seat. A couple of rounds hammered through the front windshield, leaving it lined with small fractures.

The stocky Fed glanced into the rearview mirror and saw the car racing up on his tail. Before he could react, the other vehicle hammered his. The force pitched him forward, though the seat belt prevented him from hitting his head on the steering wheel.

The crew wagon's grille pounded against his own car again, this time causing it to fishtail on the wet pavement. Turrin steered into the fishtail, bringing the car under control.

More gunfire erupted from the other vehicle. A few struck the car, sparked against the metal and ricocheted away. The blistering volley punched through Turrin's vehicle. He slammed his foot on the brake, bracing himself for the impact. Tires squealed behind him. The big car hammered into his, the impact jarring him. He clenched his jaw and gripped the steering wheel hard. Turrin's car veered right and vaulted a curb, crashing into a building.

Turrin's head felt like it'd been struck by a two-by-four. He tried to shake off the disoriented feeling. His hand scrambled for his Colt Airweight. With the other, he unclipped his seat belt. The car behind him had stopped. Car doors slammed. His hand darted out, and he wrapped his fingers around the door handle, yanking it toward him. In the same instant, gunshots rang out.

26

The final Lincoln Town Car raced up to the factory gates. The driver flashed his lights and honked his horn to get the guard's attention. The guard stepped from his shack, an AK-47 held at the ready. The driver shouted something at him. He paused for a second, and signaled to open the gates. Bolan watched the Lincoln pull through the gates and into the compound. The big car sped away from the entrance, drove a short distance, turned left and disappeared from sight.

The Executioner rose. He stepped from cover and triggered the grenade launcher.

The high explosive round sailed toward the guard shack. It pierced the window and exploded inside the small structure. Black-tinged flames boiled up from inside. Two figures, both engulfed in flames, sprinted from the building, arms waving wildly. Bolan took them out with quick mercy rounds. He sprinted across the street and ran until he spotted one of Chiun's cars. He reloaded the grenade launcher with a second HE round as he closed in on the factory. A quick glance over his shoulder told him that Serrano was just a step behind.

He triggered the grenade launcher again. The first explosion released a column of orange and yellow flame that shot skyward like an arrow loosed from a bow. A second explosion followed in quick succession as the flames reached the gas tank. The rear of the car flew up, then crashed back to earth.

One of Chiun's thugs broke out from behind the vehicle. He

loosed a blistering swarm of bullets that scythed through the air toward Bolan and Serrano.

Bolan triggered his assault rifle. Fire shot from the weapon's muzzle. A line of bullets missed the target by inches. Chiun's thug was spooked enough by his near-death experience to drop into a crouch and take cover behind the burning car.

A dozen of Chiun's men poured from the interior of a large factory building. Yellow muzzle-flashes strobed from various points throughout the compound as the panicked gunners unloaded their weapons at Bolan and Serrano.

The rain had intensified. It came down and slanted sheets, making it harder for Bolan to see anyone coming at him. Gunfire sounded to his right. He whipped his head in that direction and saw Serrano laying down a long burst with her MP-5. The bullets chewed into the belly of a shooter, who had tried to sneak up on them from behind.

The Executioner suddenly found himself bathed in light. Reflexively, he whirled toward the source, finding himself staring at headlights from an oncoming truck. He grabbed Serrano's wrist and jerked her toward him. They darted left, and the truck swerved to follow. Bolan released his grip on her. She dived forward and hit the ground. Bolan did likewise. When he struck the asphalt, he rolled and came up on one knee. The truck had launched into a wide J-turn that brought it face-to-face with him.

The engine revved and the vehicle rocketed toward him. Bolan aimed just above the headlights. The M-4 spit a fusillade of slugs at the oncoming vehicle. Brakes squealed and the vehicle swerved to escape the hellstorm of bullets pounding it. The truck sailed past the big American and crashed into a one-story building that stood roughly twenty yards away. Flames boiled up from the impact site and engulfed the truck's cab. The Executioner felt a wall of heat slam into him. He turned and continued his trek toward the main factory building. The grounds already smelled of burning rubber, and black columns of smoke pumped from the burning vehicles and choked the sky.

Chiun's people were starting to get better organized. Shooters crouched behind a line of fifty-five-gallon drums and unloaded their weapons at Bolan. The swarm of slugs chewed into the parking lot, kicking up small geysers of pavement. Even as they provided cover fire, two more shooters made a bold run at Bolan, their own weapons churning out deadly autofire.

The onslaught forced Bolan to run in a zigzag pattern to a parked car, where he took cover. He popped up from behind the vehicle and tapped out quick blasts from the M-4 that caught one of the approaching hardmen square in the chest. Seeing his comrade fall, a second man hesitated for a moment, apparently unsure whether to take cover or return fire. Bolan rewarded the indecision with a blast from the M-4. The bullets ripped into the man's midsection and caused him to jerk about spasmodically until the soldier let off the trigger. The thing dropped to the ground like a marionette with its strings cut.

The shooters behind the barrels responded with a torrent of gunfire that ripped into the car Bolan crouched behind. The windows disintegrated and the tires went flat under the withering hail of bullets. Bolan ducked behind the car and loaded another HE round into his grenade launcher. Moving in a crouch, he walked to the rear of the car and fired the weapon at a pill-shaped propane tank moored near the shooters.

A swirling storm of hellfire sprang up from the blast site. Tongues of flame lashed out and struck the shooters, setting them on fire. Seized by agonized panic, they broke from cover. The warrior dispatched them with mercy rounds to their burning midsections.

Bolan looked away from the carnage and reloaded his weapon.

By the time he reached the main factory, the site where he guessed he'd find Chiun, he'd taken down three more triad gunners.

The warrior slung the assault rifle and drew the Desert Eagle. He approached the door to the building. Taking the knob into his hand, he tried it. It didn't budge. He stepped back and squeezed the hand cannon's trigger twice. The bullets ripped through the lock and Bolan kicked the door free from the frame. He moved through the door and found himself inside a dimly lit, but empty room. He paused and keyed his throat mike.

"Maria?" he said.

"Yeah?" she replied.

"Give me a sitrep."

"I've probably knocked down a half dozen of Chiun's people," she replied. "I'm coming up on the big building now. Looks like someone blasted the lock from the door."

"That was me," Bolan said.

"Clear," she replied. "I'm coming in behind you."

RANK FUCKING AMATEUR. That's what Turrin pegged himself for.

Through the shattered windshield, he spotted two men silhouetted by headlights, lumbering toward his car.

He surged from the vehicle, raised his Colt revolver and squeezed off three shots at the approaching figures. The man to the left cried out. He bent, grabbing his belly, and dropped to the ground.

The second attacker seemed to have had more experience in a firefight. Muzzle flashes leaped from his Uzi. He swept the gun in a fiery arc, the onslaught tracking in on Turrin's position. The man held his ground, but dropped into a crouch.

Turrin swore under his breath. He dropped into a crouch, too, and emptied his gun at his opponent. The shots illuminated his face with flashes of orange. He saw the other man's head jerk back and his arm suddenly drop. However, in his death reflex, he continued to press the weapon's trigger. The spray of bullets ripped apart the earth, but did no other harm.

Hugging the side of his car, Turrin backed away from his front bumper. When he reached the rear end of the vehicle, he ducked behind the trunk. He snapped open the pistol's cylinder and emptied the spent brass onto the ground. Using a speed loader, he recharged the weapon and, with a flick of his wrist, slammed the cylinder shut.

At the same time, Bly's remaining thugs continued to pelt the car with autofire, but stayed put from behind the cover of their own car. Turrin guessed that they'd been startled to see two of their comrades fall so quickly.

Finally, Turrin saw a man's shadow fall across the wall behind him. It enlarged quickly, and the gunfire grew louder. The guy was making a kamikaze run. Bad move, Turrin thought.

Still in a crouch, Turrin moved to the other side of the vehicle.

He popped around the taillights and caught sight of the man sprinting his way. The Colt's front sight fell on the man and the stocky Fed squeezed off another two rounds. The bullets plowed into center mass, stopping the man dead.

Turrin thought longingly of the micro-Uzi stored in his car. He'd wanted to grab the weapon before going EVA, but had been unable to do so. The weapon had slid off the seat and out of reach, forcing him to abandon it.

So make it work, he told himself. You didn't survive this many years of deep cover with the Mafia, and this many near-death experiences at Bolan's side just to have some no-name street punk take you out.

Turrin reached up and closed a hand around the crucifix that hung from his neck.

He uncoiled from the ground and shot at the muzzle-flashes.

The shooting suddenly stopped. With the Colt leveled before him, Turrin cautiously approached the vehicle. He found the final punk sprawled out on the ground, a gun inches from his hand. Turrin kicked the gun away and gave the man a closer look. He saw that a portion of the man's head was missing. Guess that eliminates him as a threat, Turrin thought.

Returning to his car, he reloaded his pistol once more and waited for his ride to come.

"I ALMOST GOT KILLED out there. What the hell was that?" Bly yelled.

Chiun stood silent, fists clenched at his side. His eyes bored into the American's, and he didn't shrink from Bly, even though the American towered over him.

"Did you hear me? I said—"

Chiun's fist shot out. The knuckles struck just under Bly's chin. The executive's head snapped back and he grunted. He took a step back and rubbed his jaw. The Asian's hands hung back at his sides, as though they'd never moved. Bly's guards stepped forward almost in unison. But Chiun's men outnumbered them, and several had already had their guns in view before Chiun had thrown the first punch.

Bly gave the triad leader an appraising stare. The American's face revealed no fear, no confusion, just the same cold, calculating stare he always wore. "Bad move," he said.

"Arrogant prick," Chiun replied. "I could've killed you ten different ways, right here right now. And you want to threaten me?"

"And yet you didn't kill me."

"No need yet. I just wanted your attention."

"You have it."

"I want to know what your game is?"

"What game?"

"Deng is dead," Chiun said.

Bly paused for several heartbeats, apparently considering what he'd just heard. When he spoke, his voice remained flat. "I can't say I'm sorry to hear that. And I can't say I'm surprised either."

"No, you're not surprised. Why would you be? You fucking killed him!"

A smile ghosted Bly's lips. "Really? I wish I'd been there for it."

Chiun took a single step forward but made no threatening gestures. Still, Bly felt himself tense for a confrontation, his mind reeling at Chiun's words.

"You know you killed him. Don't play me for a fool on this. You sent Doyle over there. You got him out of jail, and you had him kill the colonel. Now we're going to have Chinese intelligence agents and soldiers crawling up our asses. They'll tear this entire operation apart and kill us in the process," Chiun shouted.

"Of course, you forgot to mention that it was your people who bailed Doyle out of jail," Bly said. "It was your people who bankrolled his fucking trip over here and provided the bad intelligence that got him killed."

Chiun shook his head disgustedly. "You are insane!"

"Am I?" Bly slowly reached into his jacket. The movement caused the tension to rise another notch and spurred a couple of Chiun's goons to step forward, guns raised. Their gun muzzles tracked Bly's every movement. The gangster waved them back.

Bly drew out a piece of paper folded into a small rectangle. He handed it over to Chiun, who eyed him suspiciously, but snatched it from his hand. Bly crossed his arms over his chest and watched while the other man slowly unfolded the document and stared at its contents for a few seconds.

"So?" Chiun asked finally.

"You recognize that man at the counter, don't you?"

"No."

"Bullshit," Bly replied. "He used to work for you. You cut his arm off for embezzling money from you and you killed his wife. His name is Cho."

Chiun shrugged. "So? Maybe I do recognize him. But a lot of people have worked for me. And more than a couple have spent time at the police station. This picture proves nothing."

"Look at the time stamp on the photo. It was taken at the same time as when Doyle was let out of jail. My contacts at the station sent it to me. I know a lot of people in the Colombian government, high-level ones who are only too happy to supply me with these bits of intelligence. And it's always accurate."

Chiun tossed the picture to the floor. "I don't believe it."

"Whether you believe it is immaterial. I just handed you proof. I know he is one of your people—"

"Ex-people."

"He paid big money to get the man who killed Deng sprung from jail. And then, while I'm driving here, someone tries to kill me. Can you explain that to me?"

"Are you saying I hired someone to kill Deng? To kill you? Why would I do that?" Chiun asked.

Bly heaved a sigh. "Money goes a lot further when you don't have to split it three ways. You've acquired a controlling interest in Garrison. You have several Firestorm prototypes. And, at the same time, I have proof that your organization was involved in Deng's murder. And someone almost killed me as I traveled here. Yet you continue to accuse me of undercutting our partnership. What's your angle?"

Bly steeled himself. He saw the smaller man tense as though he were about to attack. The executive's own hands curled into fists. He'd allowed one sucker punch, but he wouldn't take a second one.

Chiun started to reply. Suddenly muffled explosions sounded outside the building. He turned to one of his security people. "What the hell's going on out there?"

The man turned away and brought a phone to his ear. Seconds later, he began speaking with someone in hushed tones.

While he waited for an answer, Chiun turned back toward Bly. In the same motion, he drew his MP-23 and leveled it at the older man's chest. What he saw caused him to freeze. He stared directly into the muzzle of a handgun pointed at him by the executive.

"You'd better have a good explanation for this," Bly said, his voice quiet, but menacing. He stared at Chiun for several seconds, saw nothing in the other man's expression that indicated that the gangster had any answers, honest or otherwise.

An explosion detonated outside the building.

Chiun flicked his gaze at Bly's gun before he locked eyes with him again. "We deal with each other later," he said.

Bly nodded his agreement. Neither man lowered his weapon immediately, but instead backed several paces away from one another, each taking cover behind his foot soldiers.

27

Cooper had disappeared into the main building by the time Serrano reached it. She ejected the submachine gun's clip and inserted a fresh one. Slipping through a door, her weapon raised, she hunted for targets. That bastard Bly has to be here somewhere, she thought.

She trudged ahead through a pair of empty rooms that served as offices and came out in a long corridor. She followed it for a half-dozen paces, but came to a dead halt when she spotted a sentry approaching from down the hall. She hugged the wall until the last minute, trying to elude his stare. When he came within striking distance, she raised the MP-5 and loosed a brief burst of autofire. The rounds cut the man down.

She advanced past him, stepped over his body, barely giving the dead man a second thought. She was after much bigger prey, and she planned to get it.

BOLAN TRUDGED THROUGH the assembly area for the Firestorm weapons, the M-4 steady and sure in his hands. He found himself surrounded by huge machines—conveyors, presses, robotic welders. The heavy odor of machine oil tinged the air he breathed. However, the place was deathly still, as though it were completely empty. But Bolan knew better.

His combat senses were flaring. He felt a presence behind him. He whipped around, the M-4 looking to acquire a target, but found no one there. A flash of something black in his peripheral vision caused him to look up. He spotted a hardman armed with a submachine gun drawing down on him.

His opponent's weapon stuttered out an arc of gunfire that chewed into the ground, just a few inches from Bolan's feet. The Executioner sprinted away and he raised his own weapon. Jagged flashes strobed from the M-4's muzzle. The shots struck the guardrail and ricocheted.

His opponent had the superior firing position, Bolan knew, so he'd need to take him out with skill, firepower and audacity. Firing the rifle with one hand, he reached into his satchel and grabbed a fragmentation grenade. Yanking the pin free with his teeth, he tossed the bomb up onto the catwalk and ducked for cover behind a huge steel press. The explosion was sudden and startling. It swallowed the cacophony of gunfire that echoed throughout the building. An agonized scream sounded from above, followed a moment later by the sound of someone thudding against the floor. Bolan rose and spotted a ragged line of gunners sprinting toward their comrade. One of them saw Bolan, yelled and brought his weapon around. He was too late. The soldier's weapon spit a blistering swarm of autofire that cut his opponents down before they could advance farther.

Bolan continued to wend his way through the machinery.

Grimaldi's voice sounded in his earpiece.

"Sarge?"

"Go," Bolan replied.

"We're back in the compound. We're going to need to exfiltrate soon. I hear sirens coming and it's no surprise, considering all the noise we've made."

"Call our contact," Bolan said. "Have them ready to get us."

Bolan pressed on, aware that he needed to move quickly to end this.

BLY CROUCHED NEXT TO a large conveyor and scanned over top of it for any signs of trouble. The Glock felt steady and sure in his right hand. Gunfire crackled on the other side of the assembly area, and he wondered whether it was Chiun's people or the bastards who caused all this in the first place who were taking the bullets.

He ground his teeth together as he thought of all he was about to lose. He could not go back to his job or to national security work. He knew they'd seize his assets. He was, for all intents and purposes, broke and therefore of little use to a criminal organization. He was about to walk away from all this with nothing but the clothes on his back. And now that he was exposed as a traitor, there'd be no rest for him. He'd end up dead by an assassin's bullet—if he was lucky. Worse, he'd have to live each day as a failure.

He came up from the floor and, remaining in a crouch, edged alongside the big machines. If he died, so be it. But he wasn't about to sit on the floor like a crying child waiting for the reaper. He wasn't going to let these people take everything from him without a fight.

He saw a shadow move across the far wall. His heart began to race and he surged forward. If it was one of his people, fine. They could help him clear out the others. If it was the Americans or Chiun's people, then he'd cut them down before they got the chance to hurt him any further.

He heard the slightest scrape of a shoe sole against the floor. He looked up and saw Maria walking forward, her gun gripped with both hands. He drew down on her, planted the sight on her back.

Not like this, he thought. I don't want to shoot her in the back. That's too cowardly. The bitch ought to see it coming, ought to know I'm the one who pulled the trigger.

He opened his mouth to speak.

SERRANO CREPT THROUGH THE maze of equipment, her eyes and her pistol sweeping over the path before her. She knew Bly had to be here. She hadn't seen him among the dead, and she knew Cooper would've said something had he killed the guy. Sure, he could've ducked out and left Chiun holding the bag, but Serrano didn't see that happening. A guy with his massive ego wasn't going to let two people, especially one of them a woman, beat him.

Gunfire rattled a short distance from her. She wondered for a moment whether she should go in that direction, but decided that she'd continue forward and loop around the end of the building. That way she'd end up coming up behind whoever was shooting.

Someone cleared his throat from directly behind her. A cold wave of fear splashed over Serrano, and she halted.

"Turn around, please," a man said.

Serrano immediately recognized the voice. An urge to spin around and shoot, consequences be damned, welled from inside her. She squelched the desire and raised her hands and turned. She found herself face-to-face with the man she wanted to kill.

"The gun," he said. "Put it on the floor."

Serrano's mind raced through her options. She knew that if she surrendered her weapon, he'd kill her in a heartbeat. If she didn't, she might at best squeeze off one round before he shot her dead. She stared at him, saw the all-too-familiar stare. The cold smile mocked her.

"The gun," he repeated.

Blood thundered in her ears and his words seemed muffled, as though they were coming to her through a tunnel. Everything seemed to slow down around her. Bly's index finger tightened on the trigger. She folded at the knees. His pistol barked twice, but both rounds speared through the air where her head had been only an instant before.

Her weapon stuttered in her hand, spitting a line of bullets that chewed apart his midsection. In an instant, she saw his body, rent by gunfire, open up. Then he creased at the waist, folding like a jackknife, before his body tipped sideways and he hit the floor in a crumpled heap.

BOLAN REACHED THE LOADING bay and found two vehicles parked alongside the wall. He crawled beneath the first, extracted a thermite charge from a pouch attached to his web gear. He attached it to the gas tank, then repeated the same action with the second vehicle. He noticed that he smelled exhaust in the air, as though a car had just passed through. Working quickly, he attached the remaining thermite charges to the other cars and vacated the loading bay.

Where were Chiun and Bly? He began to retrace his steps. Just then a distant rumble snagged his attention. He turned and saw a truck lumberinig toward him. He brought around the M-4 and emptied the clip at the vehicle. Bullets struck the steel carapace, bounced off.

The big machine moved ponderously toward the soldier. He loaded another HE round into the launcher and fired it at the vehicle. As the projectile struck, Bolan sought cover among the labyrinth of machines that stood nearby. The explosion ripped through the air. Black-tinged flames swelled up, lashed out through the air before they drew back to the point of impact.

The warrior came up in a crouch and watched as the truck, shrouded with smoke, rolled steadily toward him.

CHIUN GUIDED THE VEHICLE toward the blacksuited soldier. He felt a thrill of excitement as he closed in on the bastard who'd done so much to dismantle what he'd built over the past several years.

He gave the big machine some gas and it lurched forward. Leaving one hand on the steering wheel, he flicked the switches that turned on the microwave emitter.

Flames leaped from the American's assault rifle. Bullets pelted the windshield, bounced from it.

Braking, Chiun cut the wheel left and gave the monster some gas. It lurched forward and fell in behind the American.

Chiun's grin widened. Run, he thought. It won't do you a bit of good.

THE BIG VEHICLE RUMBLED toward Bolan. The engine's growl echoed off the concrete walls. Fingertips curling around the edge of a bumper, Bolan ignored protests from his battered body and forced himself to his feet. He realized he never could outrun the vehicle in a straightaway, but he could outmaneuver it, particularly in these cramped quarters.

He launched out from between the cars. A sustained burst flamed from the M-4's barrel as he sprinted across the oil-splotched concrete. Slugs hammered against the truck's steel hide, sparked, careened away. He raised the weapon and loosed a punishing barrage that struck the reinforced glass windshield. He saw dozens of small fissures open across the glass, but it didn't break.

With the M-4 empty, the soldier sprinted left toward a pair of cars parked in the large bay. He figured that if he could squeeze between them and grab a second or two, he could use them for cover. Before he took a couple of steps, though, the soldier felt red-hot needles stab through his clothing and pierce his skin. For a moment, the pain caused him to hesitate and cost him a step. He swore under his breath and pushed himself forward, even though he felt as though his skin were on fire. The gun clicked dry. He ejected the old clip on the run and reloaded the weapon again.

The Executioner sprinted toward the Firestorm prototypes. By the time Chiun's vehicle reached him, Bolan had crawled across the floor and under a vehicle. He crawled out from beneath it and surged away. The building was in flames.

He stumbled forward and tried to gain some distance from Chiun. The warrior forced himself to run another couple of yards before his knees gave out beneath him. He collapsed to one knee, then both as the heat overtook him. He dropped to all fours.

Move! His mind screamed. Move or you're dead.

Bolan forced himself to crawl away from the machine. He wanted to gain enough distance that he could get away. He heard someone shout his name. He looked up and saw Grimaldi and Turrin surge into the room. Each grabbed an arm, hauled him to his feet. Once the three were out of range, Bolan reached into his web gear and grabbed the detonator. He thumbed the switch and the thermite bombs exploded, setting the vehicles on fire. Drums of solvents and other chemicals caught fire, too, and the room quickly filled with smoke. More explosions sounded from within the room, bright-orange flames dancing and pillars of black smoke beginning to billow out onto the factory floor.

"We need to get out of here," Bolan said. "Those fumes will kill us."

Where the hell was Serrano? Before he could give it much thought, he saw a figure appear a short distance away, a silhouette clouded by smoke. The Executioner raised the M-4 and aimed it at the approaching figure. A second or two later the figure became more defined and he could see feminine curves. Serrano stepped from the smoke. She brought her fist to her mouth and coughed hard. Bolan let the muzzle of the assault rifle drop.

"Bly?" he asked.

"Gone," she replied.

Bolan nodded. "Come on," he said. "It's done."

* * * * *

ROOM 59

*Welcome to Room 59, a top secret,
international intelligence agency sanctioned
to terminate global threats that governments can't touch.
Its high-level spymasters operate in a virtual environment
and are seasoned in the dangerous game
of espionage and counterterrorism.*

*A Room 59 mission puts everything on the line;
emotions run high, and so does the body count.*

Take a sneak preview of
THE POWERS THAT BE
by Cliff Ryder.

*Available January 8,
wherever books are sold.*

"Shot fired aft! Shot fired aft!" Jonas broadcast to all positions. "P-Six, report! P-Five, cover aft deck. Everyone else, remain at your positions."

Pistol in hand, he left the saloon and ran to the sundeck rail. Although the back of the yacht had been designed in a cutaway style, with every higher level set farther ahead than the one below it, the staggered tops effectively cut his vision. But if he couldn't see them, they couldn't see him either. He scooted down the ladder to the second level, leading with his gun the entire way. Pausing by the right spiral stairway, he tapped his receiver. Just as he was about to speak, he heard the distinctive *chuff* of a silenced weapon, followed by breaking glass. Immediately the loud, twin barks of a Glock answered.

"This is P-Five. Have encountered at least three hostiles on the aft deck, right side. Can't raise P-Six—" Two more shots sounded. "Hostiles may attempt to gain access through starboard side of ship, repeat, hostiles may attempt access through starboard side of ship—" The transmission was cut off again by the sustained burst of a silenced submachine gun stitching holes in the ship wall. "Request backup immediately," P-Five said.

Jonas was impressed by the calm tone of the speaker—it had to be the former Las Vegas cop, Martinson. He was about to see if he could move to assist when he spotted the muzzle of another subgun, perhaps an HK MP-5K, poke up through the open stairwell. It was immediately followed by the hands holding it, then the upper body of a black-clad infiltrator. Jonas ducked behind the solid stairway railing, biding his time. For a moment there was only silence, broken by the soft lap of the waves on the hull, and a faint whiff of gunpowder on the breeze.

Although Jonas hadn't been in a firefight in years, his combat reflexes took over, manipulating time so that every second seemed to slow, allowing him to see and react faster than normal. He heard the impact of the intruder's neoprene boot on the deck, and pushed himself out, falling on his back as he came around the curved railing. His target had been leading with the MP-5K held high, and before he could bring it down, Jonas lined up his low-light sights on the man's abdomen and squeezed the trigger twice. The 9 mm bullets punched in under the bottom edge of his vest, mangling his stomach and intestines, and dropping him with a strangled grunt to the deck. As soon as he hit, Jonas capped the man with a third shot to his face.

"This is Lead One. I have secured the second aft deck. P-Two and P-Three—"

He was cut off again as more shots sounded, this time from the front of the yacht. Jonas looked back. *A second team?*

And then he realized what the plan was, and how they had been suckered. "All positions, all positions, they mean to take the ship! Repeat, hostiles intend to take the ship! Lead Two, secure the bridge. P-Three, remain where you are, and target any hostiles crossing your area. Will clear from this end and meet you in the middle."

A chorus of affirmatives answered him, but Jonas was already moving. He stripped the dead man of his MP-5K and slipped three thirty-round magazines into his pockets. As he stood, a small tube came spinning up the stairway, leaving a small trail of smoke as it bounced onto the deck.

Dropping the submachine gun, Jonas hurled himself around the other side of the stairway railing, clapping his hands over his ears, squeezing his eyes shut and opening his mouth as he landed painfully on his right elbow. The flash-bang grenade went off with a deafening sound and a white burst of light that Jonas sensed even through his closed eyelids. He heard more pistol shots below, followed by the canvas-ripping sounds of the silenced MP-5Ks firing back. *That kid is going to get his ass shot off if I don't get down there,* he thought.

Jonas shook his head and pushed himself up, grabbing the submachine gun and checking its load. He knew the stairs had to be covered, so that way would be suicide. But there was a narrow space, perhaps a yard wide, between the back of the stairwell and the railing of the ship's main level. If he could get down there that way, he could possibly take them by surprise, and he'd also have the stairway as cover. It might be crazy, but it was the last thing they'd be expecting.

He crawled around the stairway again and grabbed the dead body, now smoking from the grenade. The man had two XM-84 flash-bangs on him.

Jonas grabbed one and set it for the shortest fuse time—one second. *It should go off right as it hits the deck,* he thought. He still heard the silenced guns firing below him, so somehow the two trainees had kept the second team from advancing. He crawled to the edge of the platform, checked that his drop zone was clear, then pulled the pin and let the grenade go, pulling back and assuming the *fire in the hole* position again.

The flash-bang detonated, letting loose its 120-decibel explosion and one-million-candlepower flash. As soon as the shock died away, Jonas rolled to the side of the boat just as a stream of bullets ripped through the floor where he had been. He jumped over the stairway, using one hand to keep in touch with his cover so he didn't jump too far out and miss the boat entirely. The moment he sailed into the air, he saw a huge problem—one of the assault team had had the same idea of using the stairway for cover, and had moved right under him.

Unable to stop, Jonas stuck his feet straight down and tried to aim for the man's head. The hijacker glanced up, so surprised by what he saw that for a moment he forgot he had a gun in his hand. He had just started to bring it up when Jonas's deck shoes crunched into his face. The force on the man's head pushed him to the deck as Jonas drove his entire body down on him. The mercenary collapsed to the floor, unmoving. Jonas didn't check him, but stepped on his gun hand, snapping his wrist as he steadied his own MP-5K, tracking anything moving on the aft deck.

The second team member rolled on the deck, clutching his bleeding ears, his tearing eyes screwed tightly shut. Jonas cleared the rest of the area, then came out and slapped the frame of his subgun against the man's skull, knocking him unconscious. He then cleared the rest of the area, stepping over Hartung's corpse as he did so. Only when he was sure there were no hostiles lying in wait did he activate his transceiver.

"P-Five, this is Lead. Lock word is tango. Have secured the aft deck. Report."

"This is P-Five, key word is salsa. I took a couple in the vest, maybe cracked a rib, but I'm all right. What should we do?"

"Take P-Six's area and defend it. Hole up in the rear saloon, and keep watch as best as you can. As soon as we've secured the ship, someone will come and relieve you."

"Got it. I'll be going forward by the left side, so please don't shoot me."

"If you're not wearing black, you'll be okay."

Jonas heard steps coming and raised the subgun, just in case a hostile was using the ex-cop as a hostage to get to him. When he saw the stocky Native American come around the corner, Glock first, Jonas held up his hand before the other man could draw a bead on him.

Martinson nodded, and Jonas pointed to the motionless man in front of him and the other guy bleeding in the corner of the deck. "Search these two and secure them, then hole up. I'm heading forward. Anyone comes back that doesn't give you the key word, kill them."

"Right. And sir—be careful."

"Always." Jonas left the soon-to-be-full operative to clear the deck and headed topside, figuring he'd take the high ground advantage. Scattered shots came from the bow, and he planned to get the drop on the other team—hell, it had worked once already. "P-One through P-Four, Lock word is tango. Report."

"P-One here, we've got two hostiles pinned at the bow, behind the watercraft. Attempts to dislodge have met with heavy resistance, including flash-bangs. P-Two is down with superficial injuries. We're under cover on the starboard side, trying to keep them in place."

"Affirmative. P-Three?"

"I'm moving up on the port side to cut off their escape route."

"P-Four? Come in, P-Four?" There was no answer. "P-Four, if you can't speak, key your phone." Nothing. *Shit.* "All right. P-One, hold tight, P-Three, advance to the corner and keep them busy. I'll be there in a second. Lead Two, if you are in position, key twice."

There was a pause, then Jonas heard two beeps. *Good.* Jonas climbed onto the roof of the yacht, crept past the radar and radio antennas, then crossed the roof of the bridge, walking lightly. As he came upon the forward observation room, he saw a black shadow crawling up onto the roof below him. Jonas hit the deck and drew a bead on the man. Before he could fire, however, three shots sounded from below him, slamming into the man's side. He jerked as the bullets hit him, then rolled off the observation roof.

That gave Jonas an idea. "P-Two and Three, fire in the hole." He set the timer on his last XM-84 and skittered it across the roof of the observation deck, the flash-bang disappearing from sight and exploding, lighting the night in a brilliant flash.

"Advance now!" Jonas jumped down to the observation roof and ran forward, training his pistol on the two prostrate, moaning men as the two trainees also came from both corners and covered them, kicking their weapons away. Jonas walked to the edge of the roof and let himself down, then checked the prone body lying underneath the shattered windows. He glanced up to see the two men, their wrists and ankles neatly zip-tied, back-to-back in the middle of the bow area.

"Lead Two, this is Lead. Bow is secure. Tally is six hostiles, two dead, four captured. Our side has one KIA, two WIA, one MIA."

"Acknowledged. Bridge is secure."

Jonas got the two trainees' attention. "P-One, make sure P-Two is stable, then head back and reinforce P-Five, and make sure you give him the key word. P-Three, you're with me."

Leading the way, Jonas and the trainee swept and cleared the entire ship, room by room. Along the way, they found the body of the young woman who had been at position four, taken out with a clean head shot. Jonas checked her vitals anyway, even though he knew it was a lost cause, then covered her face with a towel and kept moving. Only when he was satisfied that no one else was aboard did he contact everyone. "The ship is clear, repeat, the ship is clear. Karen, let's head in, we've got wounded to take care of."

"What happens afterward?" she asked on a separate channel.

"I'm going to visit Mr. Castilo and ask him a few questions."

"Do you want to interrogate any of the captives?"

Jonas considered that for only a moment. "Negative. All of them are either deaf from the flash-bangs or concussed or both, and besides, I doubt they know anything about what's really going down today anyway. No, I need to go to the source."

"I'll contact Primary and update—"

"I'm the agent in charge, I'll do it," Jonas said. He sent a call to headquarters on a second line. "No doubt Judy will flip over this. Do you still have a fix on that Stinger crate?"

"Yes, it's heading south-southwest, probably to Paradise," Karen replied.

"Naturally. See if you can get this behemoth to go any faster, will you? I just got a really bad feeling that this thing is going down faster than we thought." He gripped the handrail and waited for the connection, willing the yacht to speed them to their destination more quickly, all the while trying to reconcile the fact that his son was involved in a plot that could very well tear a country apart.

* * * * *